Texas Two Step

by

Jody Vitek

Published by
Satin Romance
An Imprint of Melange Books, LLC
White Bear Lake, MN 55110
www.satinromance.com

Texas Two Step ~ Copyright © 2014 by Jody Vitek

ISBN: 978-1-68046-014-8

Cover Art by Caroline Andrus

Special Thanks

This story would not be in existence if it weren't for my fans who asked what happened to Chloe and Chad. To Nancy Schumacher, for believing in me and igniting a bonfire. To my critique partners—without their tough love this book wouldn't be what it is. To my Turtle Lake girlfriends who brainstormed this story to kick me into gear. To my editor, Jane Carver, for making *Texas Two Step* ready for the published world. To my cover artist, Caroline Andrus, for putting up with me and creating beautiful artwork.

Chapter One

Chloe Atwood parked her Mustang convertible in the designated lot. Visits to The Arms of Safety Women's Shelter were a quarterly thing for her. With the upcoming fundraiser, the largest money maker for the shelter, her visits were now bi-weekly. The anonymity of the home's location was important. It wasn't something the shelter wanted known for the safety of the women and children. The area wasn't the best Dallas had to offer, but the neighborhood was safe and what the organization could afford with the non-profit budget.

The old brick building had a business appearance with apartments upstairs. Curtains covered the front windows. The only marking was the house number above the door. No one would guess this to be a shelter, she thought.

The small fenced-in yard was empty. The early August Texas heat and humidity was at its worst today. Temps were in the high nineties with no breeze for relief. She sat in her car with the air-conditioning gently blowing and looked at the time on her phone. Four o'clock. She'd be here for maybe ten minutes and be home by five-thirty depending on the traffic. That's if it was a good day with no accidents or unexpected road construction.

She hit speed dial and waited for her fiancé to answer.

"Atwood Foundation, Andrew Lockhart."

"Hi, Honey. Thank you again for the beautiful flowers." He'd sent her a dozen long-stemmed red roses that arrived at the office that morning.

"You make me happy, and you deserve them."

"They made my day." She smiled at the remembered rose scent that filled her office. "I was calling to let you know I'm at the shelter and then going home. I won't be here long, just dropping off Linda's tickets for the fundraiser."

"Why couldn't someone else from the office take care of that? You have people who work for you. Use them," he stated irritably.

"Andrew, she's a friend. I like to see her every once and awhile. It won't kill me to be here for a few minutes. Plus, it's good for the Director of Development to make an appearance once in a while. I'll call when I get home. I love you."

"Back at you. Bye."

Chloe slid her cell phone in her purse, picked up the envelope containing the tickets for Linda and stepped from the car. She moseyed to the front and up the brick steps, pulled the heavy metal door open and came to a sitting room. Thank God for air conditioning, she thought. Through another door, she entered the confines of the shelter. Stairs to the right led to the living quarters on the upper floors and to the left a small office for staff and volunteers. A large space beyond, littered with toys and games, was the designated play area for the children. In the far back of the first floor were the shared kitchen and dining room, along with bathrooms.

"Hi, Linda." Chloe raised her voice to be heard over the children playing and women talking in the kitchen.

She waved to Linda Morris, the center's director. Her dark hair with heavy streaks of grey was pulled into a low bun. Once a victim herself, Linda had recovered at the same shelter. Now she worked miracles with the women and their children.

"Chloe, what brings you here?" Linda approached her from the kitchen where several women prepared their dinner.

The smell of chicken wafted through the large area, followed by sizzles and pops as it fried in a pan. Chloe's stomach growled.

"I stopped by to deliver your tickets for Saturday evening's fundraiser. You'll be there, right?" Chloe handed over the envelope.

"Of course! My dress from last year is hanging in the closet. Hope the darn thing fits." Linda's hands ran over her tiny waist to rest on her hips.

"You haven't gained an ounce of weight since last year." Chloe shook her head with an indulgent smile. "I'm sure it will fit."

"I don't have anyone to bring. My daughters and sons are too busy with the grandkids and other activities. And one son still lives in Florida." Linda wrapped her arm around Chloe's waist.

"I know, but something could change." She bent her head to rest on the top of Linda's and squeezed her in an embrace. "I also stopped to let you know the Winlets lost a large donation from one of their lead sponsors. They wanted me to see if anyone had any connections that could possibly contribute an item for the auction or even multiple items to help make up the loss."

"I'll mention it to everyone working tonight and send an email. When does the committee need to know?" Together they navigated their way amid the children scattered about the play area.

"The sooner the better but even up to the day of the event will work."

In the small office area, Linda grasped a slip of paper and scribbled notes. "I know this is the Winlets' Fundraiser, but who should donors contact if they want to make a donation? The Winlets or the committee?" She sat on the desk chair.

"The committee. Do you have the contact information?" Chloe glanced around the tidy office. The flyer for the fundraiser was pinned on the information board. "Oh, you have it right here. Perfect." After a brief moment of silence, she asked, "How are things here at the shelter? I know funds are getting a little tight, but I'm working on several grants. I'm hoping to hear on one within the month."

"We're fine, Chloe. The women and children are so grateful for what the organization can offer them."

"You're so understanding and supportive. Take care, and I'll see you Saturday then." Chloe walked into the sitting room and pulled sunglasses from inside her purse.

As she stepped into the bright sunlight, a man wearing a Dallas Cowboys leather jacket neared. *A jacket in this heat?* And the piercings. She'd never understand people who put gauges in their ears to leave a gaping hole. When he approached the bottom step, she stepped down into the center of the stairs to block his entrance. He didn't belong there.

"Can I help you?" she asked politely, something instilled in her brain at a young age.

3

"Move, lady!" He spoke with defiance.

"I think you have the wrong building." Although her tone was authoritative, a sudden stab of anxiety hit her gut.

Fingers spread wide, his hands grabbed her shoulders. "I said move!" He shoved Chloe down onto the step as he sprinted into the building.

A sickening wave of terror welled up from her belly. Her breath quickened as she sat where he forced her on the step. Her eyes darted around for help, but she saw no one. She frantically stood and rushed back inside. She passed through the second door into the play area. Children were lying on the floor crying with their mother's trying to comfort them.

The guy's nostrils flared as he stalked toward Chloe. He pulled a small woman by the arm in a tight grasp.

"No, no. Please, Tony, don't do this!" The women wiggled in his hold.

"Bitch, I told ya you'd never get away from me. Quit your crying." He yanked her arm, and she cried out in pain.

Chloe stood paralyzed.

He put his hand in his coat pocket. "Lady, I told ya to move." He pulled a gun from the coat.

"Chloe, get out of his way!" Linda yelled from somewhere close by.

She couldn't move. Her pulse roared in her ears, and her breathing came quickly. Caught in a nightmare, Chloe was tackled to the floor as gun shots rang out twice. Her breath rushed out of her lungs.

"Now look what ya've gone and made me do, Bitch! I'm gonna give ya something to cry about later."

Something crashed against a wall. Chloe couldn't see anything lying on the floor.

"Move your fat ass!"

With another slamming noise, Chloe assumed it was the entrance doors to the shelter.

She blinked in surprised shock at the horror of what had just taken place. "Linda, you can get off me now. He's gone." Linda wasn't heavy, but the extra weight made it difficult to breathe.

No response.

With Linda on top of her, Chloe carefully rolled to her side, leaving Linda to sprawl on the floor on her back. Feeling something warm, Chloe sat up. *Blood.* A wave of acid welled up from her belly. There was a wet smear across the front of her white shirt. She hadn't been shot. *Linda!* Linda's left shoulder area was covered in blood.

"Call 911, and someone get me some towels," Chloe wailed with alarm.

A woman ran over, setting towels next to Linda's head. "The police are on their way. What can we do?" the woman asked shaken.

"Pray." It was a simple statement. Chloe gazed at her friend. "Linda, I'm going to put pressure on your shoulder. You've been shot." She grabbed a towel and gingerly lifted Linda's back left side to place a towel underneath. Another towel lay on the wound, and she applied pressure.

Linda's eyes opened to mere slits. "You're...crazy," she spoke slow and breathy.

"Don't talk." Chloe's throat constricted. She swallowed hard, fighting tears.

Linda's eyes closed. She held Linda's wrist and felt her heart rate slow.

She took a breath for strength. "Linda, stay with me. We need you." Now was not the time to break down. Her chin fell to her chest as she prayed for the ambulance to arrive soon.

Sirens screamed outside. Paramedics and police rushed inside. The piercing sound flowed through the open doorway. The twenty minutes it took them to arrive felt more like an hour.

A paramedic knelt beside Chloe. "Ma'am, we need you to move out of the way."

She did as asked, but didn't know where to go, stand or sit. The only words the medic spoke that stood out were *critical condition.* A group of uniformed officers and men in suits entered the area.

Chloe stared at a man in a suit as he frantically looked around and rushed to Linda. *His face is a little fuller. He has the same narrow nose. If his hair were sandy blond...*He turned, and familiar blue eyes roamed over her body in a non-sexual way.

It's not Chad.

5

His gaze remained on the bloodstain below her breasts until someone yelled out, "Rogers, this is out of your district. What are you doing here?"

"I heard the call and rushed here. My mom was shot." The Chad look-a-like stalked toward her.

This is one of Linda's sons?

"You." Chad's could-be-fraternal-twin pointed at her. "Come here."

Another man in a suit stopped the Chad double. "We got this. Go with your mom."

The paramedics adjusted the height of the stretcher, sending a clicking sound through the large area. Chloe jumped with each click.

"Ryan, we're leaving. Are you riding with us?" a medic called out.

"Yeah," Linda's son hollered, "Question her, Tony." His finger pointed at Chloe.

Ryan's height was close to Chad's, but his stance differed. Even after a year of not seeing Chad, Chloe remembered everything about him.

The ambulance whisked away, and the police separated everyone in the building. Chloe sat on the office chair, closed her eyes at the pounding in her head. She leaned forward, resting her head in her hands. Willing the pain to go away.

"Ma'am, I'm Detective Fuentes. Can I get you something to drink?"

"No," came muffled through her hands. "Wait." She lifted her head. "Yes, I'd like some water. I need some aspirin." Her leg jiggled nervously.

Detective Fuentes returned to the room with a glass of water, held a pink shirt and a brown paper bag. "I need the shirt you're wearing. It's evidence. I'll step out of the room. Put yours in the paper bag, please. One of the women offered the shirt."

"Thank you."

When he closed the office door behind him, she unbuttoned the shirt with shaky hands. As she reached the bloody buttons, the tears fell. Would Linda be okay? By the way her son pointed his finger at her she knew he blamed her in some way for the shooting. But why? The bag rattled as she placed the white blouse inside. The pink shirt was two sizes too big and swam on her small frame, falling off one shoulder. She didn't care. It was coverage.

There was a knock at the door.

"Come in." She sat on the chair with her hands on her lap.

The detective entered, rolled the top of the bag closed and exited the room. When he came back, he pulled a notebook from his shirt pocket before sitting on the vacant chair. "I need to ask you some questions about what happened. Would you like a female officer present?"

"No. It's fine. She needs to be with the other women." The women at the shelter were generally uncomfortable around men. Something she'd learned early on. "I just want to go home."

"So you don't reside here?"

"No." She shifted in the chair.

"Okay, first I need to get some basic information."

After Chloe gave him her name and address, she informed him about her job and how she came to be at the women's shelter this day. She swallowed some medication to rid herself of the worsening headache. She clenched her jaw which didn't help matters. As soon as she released the tension in her mouth, the headache tightened again.

"Can you tell me what happened?"

She closed her eyes and relayed the events leading up to the moment of the shooting to the detective.

"Can you describe the guy?"

"He wore a loose shirt and a Dallas Cowboys leather jacket. His hair was dark and cut really short. Almost shaved."

"Can you guess his age, height and weight?" Detective Fuentes continued scribbling in the notepad.

"I'm terrible with this. Maybe late twenties? He was short. A little guy but looked built. About five-seven? Maybe weighed one-seventy?" She couldn't keep her hands still in her lap and brought one up to play with her lower lip while the other lay across her stomach.

"Did you see any tattoos? Piercings?"

"He had piercings." She closed her eyes. "He had gauges. I can't remember anything else." Frustrated, she continued to shake her head even after answering his question.

"Do you know the woman who was forced to leave?"

"No. But she called him Tony." She shook her head worried. "Do you think you'll find this guy and the woman?"

"We'll do all we can." He put the pen in his shirt pocket. "I think we're done here. I have your information. If we have any further questions we'll be in touch. You've been a great help."

Chloe stood on shaky legs. "I need my purse. It's in the play area. At least that's where it was last."

"Come with me." The detective stood and waited for her to step from the room.

"Thank you, all of you, for your quick response today."

They maneuvered their way into the other room, and he picked up her purse. "Is this it?"

"Yes, thank you. Do you know where they took Linda?"

"Dallas Memorial."

"Thank you, again." The bloody scene pierced her vision. She barely managed to get outside without running.

* * * *

Chad Rogers earned his perspiration by cleaning stalls and moving hay bales, along with the other responsibilities of the horse ranch in the late summer heat of central Florida. The fans blowing in the arena stables provided welcome relief against his sweaty skin. Maggie Randall stood by a stall door, her pregnant belly protruding.

He strolled closer, overhearing a young client in the stall say, "My foot caught, and I tripped."

A few more steps and Chad stood next to Maggie. "Can I help with anything?" He made himself available to assist Maggie whenever a client or group arrived. She had been restricted from riding and lifting heavy objects. They were in this venture together.

The client, a young, attractive woman, turned but spun her focus to the horse.

Not quick enough. The golden-green skin coloring around her right eye couldn't be missed. He'd bet there would be bruises on her arms under the long sleeves of her shirt.

"No, I think we have it." Maggie smiled graciously. "Thanks, Chad."

"Radio if you need anything." He strolled out of the barn and leaned against the wall. Behind closed eyes, his mother's swollen, bloodied lip accompanied by a black eye and a broken, bloody nose flashed in front of him.

The client hadn't tripped. She was probably making excuses. Chad kept his eyes closed and inhaled, breathing deeply as his father stepped into the visions. A lump formed in his throat. He swallowed. His backside rode down the barn wall as his knees gave way. Squatting, his head fell forward.

'Angel' by Areosmith played on Chad's phone. His eyes sprung open. It was his oldest sister, Angela, the only sibling who knew his number. The small hairs on the back of his neck rose.

"Hey, Angel." *Angel*—a nickname for his older sister.

"Are you sitting?" Her voice was calm, which should've eased the worry, if a need to sit hadn't been advised.

"Yeah."

"Mom's in the hospital. She was shot."

"What the hell?" Sickness roiled in his stomach. "What happened?" His butt smacked the ground.

"She's going to be okay, Chad. She was at work, and somehow a guy found the location of the shelter. He had a gun and took his wife. The police are searching for him. Listen, Mom's okay."

"I'm leaving tonight. Where's she at?" Chad's palms grew clammy. He wiped his free hand on his thigh, switched the phone to the other ear and wiped the other hand.

"Dallas Memorial. They have the best doctors and surgeons for gunshot victims. Call when you get here. Where are you going to stay?"

"Don't know. I'll find something downtown and let you know." Chad hung up and pulled out his radio. "Trent? What's your location?"

"Barn one," Trent Randall replied.

"I'm on my way." Chad stood, leaning against the stable wall to steady his mind and body. He strode across the tree shrouded trail covered with wood chippings. A quarter mile to the main property and he entered the barn. "Trent?"

"Down here." Trent waved his hand. "What's up, partner?"

"I need to leave for Texas tonight. My mom's in the hospital. She was shot." The words spewed from his mouth.

Trent stopped grooming an Arabian mare and stepped to the side wall. "What the hell? Where?" The horse startled, slightly rearing his front legs at Trent's high pitched voice.

"At work." Chad paced the concrete aisle of the stable.

"Is she okay? What's the status?"

"My sister says Mom'll be okay. I don't know much more." He stopped pacing and stood in a daze.

Trent seized him by the shoulders. "What do you mean you don't know more?"

"It all just happened." He raised his voice. "My sister's at the hospital, and that's all she knew." Chad used the anger toward his father to halt crying in front of Trent.

"I'm sorry to have pushed, Chad. By all means, go. Take as long as needed. Maggie and I will arrive Wednesday morning for the engagement party on Friday night."

Chad nodded his head. How could he forget Chloe's engagement party? She'd invited her best friend, Maggie, but not him, her ex-lover. As much as he wanted to forget Chloe's engagement, he couldn't shake the idea of her being with another man.

"Before we take off, Maggie will make sure everything is covered for the riding business. Keep me posted. Do you need a ride to the airport?"

"I'd appreciate that. I've got to go make reservations. I'm sorry, Trent."

"What are you apologizing for? Go." Trent cocked his head at the door, and when Chad neared the exit, hollered, "Let me know what time we need to leave."

Chad tipped his head in acknowledgement and stepped into the sunlight. Straw hat pulled further down his forehead, he made his way to another wooded path and jogged the mile to his house.

Inside the modest rambler, he immediately sat in front of the laptop with his credit card. Reservations made for air, hotel and a car, he took a shower and allowed the emotions to take over. The water sprays washed the tears down the drain. Although his body was warm, a chill penetrated deep within. He stood under the heat of the water until it ran cool.

His mother was his foundation in life. Years ago, their first night at the shelter, she'd held him in her arms while speaking softly in his ear. "We're safe now. No more harm will come to us." She had been right— until today.

Chapter Two

The plane touched down in Texas, and Chad called his sister. "Is it too late to see Mom?"

"Yes. Get checked in at your hotel, and call me back. I'll fill you in then."

"She's okay, right?" His voice was edged with tension as were his neck, shoulders and back.

"Chad, call me when you're in your room. Not on the plane, in the airport or while driving. She's *o-kay*." Angel filled his mother's shoes by being there for him.

"I'll call in about an hour." Disconnecting, he waited in his seat to disembark from the plane. No need to battle the throngs of passengers crowding the aisle.

Once through the airport, he located his suitcase on the carousel and searched for the car rental station. The clerk at the rental desk informed him they couldn't accommodate what he reserved online. The closest vehicle to a truck they could offer was a minivan. After a tiring battle of words, he managed to snag a mustang. He disliked riding low to the ground, but he wouldn't be caught dead in a minivan.

Suitcase tossed in the trunk, he headed for downtown Dallas. His mom wasn't the only person downtown. Chloe Atwood lived in the city. *Damn.* Two years ago they were lovers and now, only distant friends. Shit, what kind of friend was he? He never called or visited. Then again, that's why their relationship lasted all of two months. He had his reasons though. He contemplated contacting her, but she'd found someone else. He was here for his mother, not Chloe.

Parking under the Pegasus hotel's canopy, he slid from the car seat and pulled his suitcase from the trunk. An older man approached in a suit, and Chad guessed he was the valet attendant.

"Good evening, Sir."

"Evening. I need to check in." Chad wasn't sure if the guy needed his room number or something.

"Your last name, Sir?"

"Rogers."

"Here's your claim ticket. Did you have more baggage?"

"This is it. Thank you." He tipped the valet a couple of ones and strolled through the front doors.

The hotel had an old feel with a modern appearance. Smooth curves and straight lines mingled, making up the building's structure. Colors of silver, white, black and gray accented with golds, reds, wood and metal. His time here didn't come cheap, but when it came to his mother, it didn't matter.

Room key in hand, he stepped into the elevator and ascended to the twentieth floor. Inside his room, tossing the suitcase on the bed, he pulled out his cell phone and called his sister. While waiting for Angel to pick up, he leaned back in the leather office chair. He spun around in the chair, stopping to rest his legs up on the bed.

"Hi, Chad," Angel's weary voice answered.

"Where was Mom shot?" Not able to sit, he paced the small room. "Did it do any permanent damage? Have they—"

"Chad! Stop! I'll tell you everything. She was shot in the chest. The bullet entered through the front left side, missing her lung and major arteries and veins. The bullet exited through the upper shoulder, breaking the left clavicle and narrowly missed the top of her lung. She lost a lot of blood. They've given her fluid volume replacement. They don't know about permanent damage, but it looked promising to the doctors. The tendons and muscles of her shoulder were torn by the bullet. Once she's healed and therapy begins, they'll know more.

"She's had a CT scan of her chest to assess any damage, and it was okay. There are a few other things hooked up to her beyond the usual monitors. One for pain medication and there's a drain in the wound site. She's in the trauma ICU for now. They'll probably move her in a day or so, where she'll stay for about another twenty-four hours. I'm leaving the hospital now. You should know, Ryan responded to the call. He was at her side in the ambulance. I'll see you tomorrow?"

"Yeah." Chad's mind spun with the information. His fingers ran through his hair. "What time do visiting hours begin?" The night sky glowed with city lights as he peered through the large hotel window. No stars were visible like back home in Florida. He ignored the last bit about his brother Ryan.

"Nine."

"I'll see you then. Angel...I love you."

"I love you, too." Sincerity filled her voice. "Ten years is too long to be gone. It'll be good to see you."

"You, too." Ashamed he had been away for so many years, he turned from the window with his gaze landing to the floor. His behavior replicated that of a scolded puppy.

"Get a good night's sleep, and I'll see you at the hospital." She disconnected.

He communicated with three of his siblings via email and texts only as needed. They rarely spoke. At this moment, the endearment needed to be spoken, and he smiled with the warmth of the words being shared with Angel.

As for Ryan, Chad never spoke to him and would never utter those three words to him. Chad prayed they wouldn't cross each other's paths at the hospital or while he was in town. The only good thing about Ryan, he was a cop and would search for the shooter. If Ryan were the one to find the guy, Chad prayed for the scum because Ryan would probably beat the shit out of him. Just like their old man had done to their mother.

* * * *

Chloe unlocked her apartment door and entered. The day's events had taken their toll on her mind and body. A hot bath called her name, but she and Andrew had dinner plans. The kitchen clock read six-forty. Would he understand if she cancelled their date? Only one way to find out.

"Hey, Darlin', I can't wait to see you," Andrew stated sweetly. "You're home later than you said."

"I just got home. Would you mind if I cancelled tonight?" She slipped off her heels, bringing relief to her feet.

"Everything okay?"

"I'm fine, but no, everything's not okay. Linda was shot at the shelter." She sat back against the cool leather sofa.

"See, the few minutes you *were* there, you could've been killed."

"Please lower your voice." Her eyelids closed as she rested her head on the back of the sofa. "I have a bad headache. My nerves are fried." The coolness on her neck delivered minor relief.

"No shit!" He lowered his tone. "Jesus, Chloe, you need to quit this job before you get killed."

"Andrew, I'm fine. I didn't get shot, but a dear friend of mine did. Can we please make plans for another night?" She extended her legs and flexed her toes, feet and ankles.

"Yes." He conceded with exasperation. "Where were you when she was shot?"

With an audible sigh she stated the truth. "I was the one he was aiming for—"

"Jesus Christ, Chloe! Stay away from that place. Do you understand?"

She winced at his yelling. "I don't normally go to the shelter. I can't make any promises."

"I'm coming over," he stressed. "I'll pick up your favorite, Kung Pao Chicken."

"I'd rather be alone. Do you mind?" She wiggled her leg with nervous energy.

"Yes, but I'll let this go…this time. I worry about you. You're sure you're okay?"

"I'm fine. I'm going to take a bath and then go to bed."

"Call if you change your mind. I could help wash your back."

"Good night, Andrew. Love you." As much as she wanted his comfort, he would try to lead them to bed for a round or two of sex. And she was *far* from being in the mood for sex.

"Sweet dreams, Darlin'." The line clicked dead.

The endearment of love wasn't returned because he was upset and disappointed. Her decision to be alone was the right decision. He wanted her in bed.

Across from her apartment, a brick building with windows stared at her through the wide expanse of framed glass making up her main living room wall. She pushed the button on the remote, and the blinds closed. Her parents didn't spare any expenses when it came to luxury. God forbid a person would have to get up and manually pull the blinds closed. Chloe had mixed emotions about living in their apartment and paying them rent. Residing here at their insistence was her concession to their concern for her safety. She did like the security the building offered. It also helped that their price was reasonable for her income.

Chloe shuffled to the master bathroom. While the hot water filled the bathtub, she selected a classical music channel on her phone. Music always soothed a bad headache. Sometimes she imaged herself performing a ballet to the music.

Her steps faltered at the mirrored reflection of her in the pink shirt. She removed it and noticed the dried blood smear remnants on her stomach. A sickening wave of guilt washed over her. She swallowed. Unbuttoning her black slacks, she didn't notice if there was blood on them. She'd take them to the dry cleaners.

Stepping into the large tub, she sank up to her neck in the hot water. Her skin quickly reddened, but the heat relaxed her tense shoulders and tight jaw. What a shitty way to start the week. Or anyone else's at the shelter. Tomorrow morning she'd go to the hospital and check on Linda. When her eyelids closed, Linda's son the detective and his similarity to Chad came to mind.

Chad never talked about his family, other than he was from Texas, but from where she didn't know. He'd mentioned siblings but said he never talked to them. As she reflected on this, maybe one of the reasons their relationship ended was due to his lack of openness and honesty.

The main reason for their failure…he wouldn't come to her. He wouldn't come to Texas. But why?

Chapter Three

Chad stopped short of the door to his mom's ICU room. Voices from the past floated from inside. Sweat beaded at his hairline. His stomach tightened.

I should leave and come back when he's gone.

Ryan's voice spoke in his head. *"Buck up, you pussy."*

Memories of the past.

And the voice was right. Not because it was Ryan's but because cowardness had kept him away long enough. Time to face his fears.

One step. Two step.

He gradually stood in the doorway to his mother's room.

The blinds were closed, with low lighting illuminating the room. Angel sat facing the door. Her long dark hair was now cut short. Amy, his other sister a year younger than Angel, sat with her back to the door. Her hair remained long. She had the two tone style with blonde on top and dark on the underside. A dark-haired man in a suit sat on the edge of the bed by his mom's feet. He assumed it was Ryan, having heard his voice drifting into the hall.

"Well, don't just stand there." Angel stood up. "Get in here, and give me hug."

The other two turned around to see who she was talking to. A grin grew on Amy's face and warmed his heart. Ryan tipped his head back with a half smirk in acknowledgement. Chad hugged Amy who stepped to him before joining Angel at the other side of the bed.

They embraced, and he whispered, "Angel, you look great."

"You, too."

Chad let go of his sister. "Ryan," he stated with the same head gesture of greeting. "Mom," he leaned down and kissed her forehead. "You need to retire. We knew the job had its hazards, but this is ridiculous."

"I'm not retiring." She breathed on her own, but winced when taking a breath. "The odds of this happening are little."

"Are they giving you pain meds, Mom?" He stood near the head of the bed.

"Chad, she's being taken care of. She has a drip." Angel gently touched his elbow, comforting him.

"I should probably get going." Ryan said as he stood. "Mom, I have to agree with Chad. Maybe you should retire."

"I'm not old enough, and I have bills to pay," Linda said in a whispery voice.

Ryan leaned carefully into their mother's side, delivering a gentle hug. He kissed her cheek. "I'll be back later tonight." He stepped to the open door nearly knocking down—

Chloe? What is she doing here? Chad's eyebrows shot up as his eyes widened. Blinking away the dryness, his face relaxed.

Chloe touched Ryan's forearm. "Did they get the guy? Have they found the woman?"

"Not yet. They know who the woman is. The guy has a rap sheet." He looked into the room. "Bye, Mom." That was probably all Ryan could reveal about the case.

Things got better when Ryan disappeared into the hall, and Chloe's brown eyes landed on him. Her mouth opened and closed like a ventriloquist's doll. No words were spoken.

As dumbfounded as she appeared, Chad approached with a hug. "It's good to see you. But why are you here?" *She's lost weight.*

"I work with Linda. What are you doing here?" Her eyebrows knitted together in confusion.

"You two know each other?" his mom asked with more gusto than he'd heard earlier.

They moved from the doorway into the room. "We met in college." Chad stood at the foot of the bed. "She's my mother, and Ryan is my brother. Mom changed her name when she divorced our father." He forced himself to identify his relationship with Ryan.

Chloe approached the bedside and gently hugged Linda. "I am *so* sorry. If I would've moved out of his way, you wouldn't have been shot. It's my fault."

"No, it's not. You didn't make me tackle you. I made that decision, and I'm glad I did. You're alive, and I'll be just fine."

"Wait," Chad exclaimed, grasping Chloe's forearm, spinning her to face him. "You were there?"

"Chad, don't yell. Chloe was trying to stop the guy from taking a woman out of the shelter."

"You stood there and didn't move after he pulled a gun and pointed it at you? Chloe, you put a lot of people in danger. My mom got shot because of you."

"Chad, enough," Linda said in a stern voice.

He stepped away from Chloe.

"Chloe." His mom gazed at her friend with gentle eyes and spoke softly. "It's not your fault. Don't *ever* think you did anything wrong." The kind eyes turned incriminating as they turned on Chad. He was in trouble and knew it.

"I told the cops everything I could remember about the guy." Chloe looked crestfallen.

Chad cringed. He'd foolishly said hurtful things, yet it troubled him to see his mother in the hospital bed.

"They'll catch him." His mother reached for her foam cup and sucked from the straw. "Let me introduce you to my two daughters. This is my oldest, Angela." She pointed with her right hand. "This is Amy. There's a year between them. Christopher's a lawyer and due in court this morning. Then there's Ryan whom you've already met. Chad is my youngest."

"Maybe I should come back at a different time." Chloe stepped back from the bed, one step closer to the door.

"Why?" Linda and his sisters asked.

"I feel like I'm intruding on family time." Chloe took another step away.

Another step toward leaving. He wanted her to leave, yet wanted her to stay. So much was left unsaid the last time they had talked over a year ago at Maggie and Trent's wedding. Not that he wanted to talk about things in front of the family or in a hospital.

"Nonsense. If you're a friend of Chad's, then you're as good as family. Sit," his mother ordered, taking a moment to catch her breath.

The diamond ring on Chloe's finger sparkled. The ring should've been from him and not someone else. But because he didn't buck up and make the effort to come to Texas to see her... Because he didn't make the effort to call more often... Because he let her go when she said it was over...she said yes to another man. A man who had plenty of money because that was a serious rock on her finger.

"Amy, come with me to get some coffee while these three talk." Angel waited by the door. "We'll be back."

"Chloe." His mother spoke. "I don't know if I'll be able to attend the fundraiser. Oh, that reminds me. You may want to send an email about the need for donations."

"That's the least of my worries. We'll let the Winlets and the committee handle finding a new contributor."

Chad sat on the chair Angel vacated, watching Chloe and his mother interacting. *Chloe, with Mom? What are the odds?* The two weeks they spent together in Florida and they never once put two and two together. "Why didn't we figure this out when you were in Florida?" he blurted.

"What are you talking about?" Chloe asked, turning her focus to him.

"Why didn't I know this when you came to Florida? You talked about your job, but I don't remember anything about a women's shelter."

"I changed jobs shortly after the wedding."

"Why?" Chad asked befuddled.

"Chad, we can talk later over drinks if you want. Your mother doesn't want to listen to you ask questions."

"Does tonight work? I have a car and can meet you. Or we can meet at my hotel, the Pegasus."

"Yeah, fine. Before I leave we can make plans."

Nervous excitement raced through him at the thought of having time alone with Chloe.

After a short while, Chloe stood to leave. Chad walked with her to elevator. "What time and where would you like to meet?"

"Let's meet at six-thirty at The Knoll. It'll be a short walk for both of us. It's on the corner of North Akard and Main."

"I'll see you then." Chad left her at the elevator as the doors opened. Entering his mom's room again, Chad asked, "What was Chloe talking about? The fundraiser and donation thing?"

"There's an important fundraiser event for the shelter on Saturday night, and one of the bigger contributors has backed out."

"That's not good." He held his mom's hand. "I want to donate something, but I need to check into it first. Who do I need to contact about my donation?"

"There's information on our website that should get you to the right people. Chad, thank you." Gleefulness filled her face, but quickly faded. "I was planning on attending, but now…who knows."

"I'll ask the doctor next time I see him what the odds are for you to go."

"Would you go with me? It's black tie so you'd need a tux." She gave him a smile of mute appeal.

"If you can go, I'd be honored to accompany you to the event." Chad bowed. They laughed together at his overdramatic princely speech.

His mother stopped chuckling. After a moment she said, "I'm okay. It hurts a little, but it feels good to laugh. Isn't Chloe wonderful?"

"Mom, she's the one I talked about." He glanced to the hallway, as though looking for his sisters to stroll through the door.

"The *one*?"

He nodded.

"Oh, honey, I'm so sorry."

"I'd rather not talk about her."

"Who's *her*?" Amy asked stepping into the room.

"No one. Since you guys are back, I'm going to grab some lunch and take care of a few things. I'll be back." He squeezed his mom's hand and left for the cafeteria.

He sat at a table and tapped on his phone's screen. While waiting for an answer, he took a bite of grilled chicken sandwich.

"Rolling Rock Ranch. Trent speaking."

"Hey," Chad swallowed, "I'm wondering if you'd be interested in helping me with something."

"What's up?"

"There's a fundraising event for the women's shelter my mom works for Saturday evening. One of the big donors backed out. I got to thinking and want to donate a week of riding. Lessons, if needed or wanted, with hotel for two?" The idea excited him. Maybe they could do this every year for the fundraiser.

"I want to be a part of this. Let's up the ante." Trent shared Chad's enthusiasm.

"What are you thinking?" Chad asked before shoving a French fry in his mouth.

"You cover the riding and lessons costs. I want to make it a week at a spa. I need to look into it first. As soon as I have the details, I'll shoot you an email."

"Sounds good. Thanks."

"Anything for a worthy cause. Listen, I've got to go."

Chad thought about Trent and Maggie. They'd been through so much yet managed to fall in love. He'd thrown away his opportunity when Chloe had been right in front of him. He'd thrown the chance away when she'd returned home. He'd thrown love away when she'd given him the chance.

* * * *

Chloe sat in her car as perspiration trickled along her hairline. Positioning the air-conditioning vents to blow at her face, she turned the dial to blast the cool air. *What the hell? I knew it!* Ryan's resemblance was too close to Chad's to not think they were related. She must've blanked out Ryan's last name the day of the shooting. Sure, Linda talked about her children but never mentioned anything about different last names. And she tended to talk more about her grandchildren than her adult children. Plus, their discussions usually focused on the shelter and its needs.

Chad looked great, as always. When he'd hugged her, she wanted to wrap herself around him. She couldn't. She was engaged to another man. A man she loved.

Damn it! Why did this have to happen? Why did he have to come back into her life? She closed her eyes and took several deep breaths. Her eyes shot open. *He's not in your life. He's your co-worker's son.* She chanted, *he's your co-worker's son,* multiple times.

At the office, she opened mail and checked her email. No letters for the grant requests. Any time in the next two weeks she should be hearing from her family's foundation. As a conflict of interest, her father wouldn't be eligible to vote, but that shouldn't hinder her chances of getting the grant for the shelter. She had researched the requests for proposal on the website, and the grant was perfect for the foundation.

Late in the day, as she wrapped up loose ends, someone knocked on the door. Standing in the doorway, a co-worker held a long narrow box.

"This just arrived for you." The receptionist set the box on Chloe's desk.

"Thank you."

Chloe opened the box to reveal one long stemmed red rose. It matched the roses in the vase Andrew sent yesterday. The card read, *'I will love you forever and always. Andrew'.* Randy Travis' song *'Forever and Ever, Amen'* came to mind. A tear moistened her cheek. She loved Andrew and how he expressed his love for her with flowers, small gifts, dinners and being at her side. She slid the card in-between the tines of the holder in the vase, behind the other card and slipped the rose into the arrangement. Andrew's timing was perfect, and he didn't even know it.

Chloe struggled to focus at work all day. After what happened yesterday at the shelter, her co-workers were shocked to see her. Her boss told her to take off as much time as needed, but she wanted to keep some normalcy in her life. Yet today, seeing Chad at the hospital stunned her. When she left the office earlier than usual, no one was surprised.

At home she took a warm bath to ease the nerves of being with Chad tonight. She questioned if meeting him in a relaxed environment was a mistake. If meeting him at all was a mistake. The answer came as a flutter in her stomach.

She picked a floral baby doll tank dress. Not wanting to expose bare legs to Chad, who loved her legs, she wore white leggings underneath. To cover her arms, she snatched a white cropped sweater, locked the apartment and left.

On the corner of North Akard and Main Street, she entered The Knoll restaurant. Chad sat on the leather bench near the hostess station. She waved. His genuine smile pulled her lips upward. A quick hello and an awkward hug told her something was different about him. Like he was unsure of how to act around her.

"You look good." He wore jeans and nice fitting black t-shirt with his Bay Apache Justin boots. *Damn.* She missed a man in jeans and boots.

"You, too. Let's get a table." He approached the hostess and returned. "About ten minutes. Do you want to go to the bar and get a drink?"

"Sure." At the bar she ordered a beer. No frilly formal girl drinks tonight like Andrew expected. With Chad, she could relax and enjoy a cold one.

"I'll have the same as the lady," Chad told the bartender, standing next to her while she sat on the only empty stool available. "This place is pretty nice."

She glanced around the bar area into the seating section. "It's no different than any other family restaurant." She smiled at his hearty laugh.

"Are you looking forward to seeing Maggie? I know she's excited about the trip." He leaned close, smelling of nothing but delicious soap. Andrew always wore cologne.

"I'm excited. Thursday we're going shopping for my wedding dress." She caught his obligatory smile. "I'm sorry. I didn't mean—"

"Don't apologize. I'm happy you've found someone." He appeared as if he wanted to say more, but took a swig of beer.

"How does Maggie look? She's shared some pics, but I want to hear about it."

"Being pregnant agrees with her. She shines like a light house beam. She and Trent are so happy. I'm glad we were able to bring them together."

"Me, too. They're staying with her folks tomorrow before coming downtown. Are you planning on seeing them?"

"No."

The restaurant's pager vibrated. "Our table's ready, my lady." Chad swept out his arm.

She shook her head at his silliness.

Seated at the table, he sat next to her as opposed to across the table.

"How's your mother?" She took a long sip of beer.

"I need to apologize first for what I said at the hospital. What happened to my mom is not your fault. I'm sorry." Embarrassed by his earlier behavior, he glanced at the table top.

"It's okay. I don't understand why I didn't move. I feel terrible."

"Well, you heard Mom, no blaming anyone. She's getting better. I think they're moving her tomorrow from ICU into a semi-private room in the standard ward."

"Let me know, please. You have my cell number, right?"

He nodded. "I will." He picked up his menu. "So, what do you recommend?"

"Their burgers are the best. The Barbeque Pit burger is the bomb. It has two slices of thick cut, smoked bacon, fried onions, smoked cheddar cheese and the rest of your normal toppings if you want, with a sweet barbeque sauce that has enough punch to have you wanting more."

"Damn, I'm sold. You have my mouth watering already." He licked his lips.

Chloe's heartbeat ticked a few extra beats remembering those soft lips on hers. Her tongue inadvertently moistened her lips. As she averted her eyes to peer at the menu, the waitress approached, and they ordered.

"So tell me about this business you and Maggie have at the Triple R."

"For right now Maggie's focus is on western riding and horsemanship, while I run the business side. I help her when needed, especially since the pregnancy. I want to expand into trail and reining in a year or so. Maggie talks about expanding her family."

Chloe laughed.

"It's good to hear you laugh. I've missed hearing it." His finger glided along her jaw.

"Chad..." She tipped her head to the side, away from his touch.

"I'm sorry."

Their conversation over dinner covered the Triple R's expansion and how Trent remained focused on the boarding and breeding side of the ranch.

Toward the end of their meal, he asked, "So, tell me what prompted the change in your job?"

"I came back from Florida after Trent and Maggie's wedding and decided I wanted a job that was more fulfilling than the hectic life I was living. The pay was great, but I was tired. And at our age, that's not good."

The waitress approached. "Can I get a box for the rest of your plate?"

"No, thank you, unless you want it?" Chloe looked to Chad, placing her napkin on the table.

"Thank you, but I don't think so."

"Can I interest you in dessert? Or will that be all this evening?"

"I'm full." She glanced at Chad.

"No dessert for us. Thanks."

"I'll bring your check shortly."

When the waitress stepped from the table, Chad asked, "I thought dessert was your favorite part of a meal?"

"It was."

"So you don't eat dessert anymore?"

"I have a wedding dress to fit into." Her eating habits weren't up for discussion. "Anyway, during my job search, I saw the opening for the Director of Development for the shelter. I applied, and the rest is history."

The waitress dropped off the check. Chad snatched the leather folder. "My treat. It was my suggestion."

"Liar. I said, let's go out."

"I got this." He placed cash within and set the folder in the middle of the table. "Are you ready to go?"

Chloe nodded, slid her chair back and stood.

"Chloe!"

She turned to find her good friend and Andrew's sister coming in their direction. *Shit!*

"Hi, I'm Stephanie. And you are?" She sidled up to Chad. Something twanged within Chloe.

"Steph, this is Chad." She gave the all-knowing look, as Steph knew about Chad. Chloe prayed the expression sent the message to stay away from him and not to mention this to Andrew.

"Nice to meet you, *Chad*." She sang his name.

Chloe's pang grew stronger. Chad's gaze roamed from Steph's face down to her curvy hips before focusing on the woman's face again.

"How long are you in town?" Steph wasn't backing down.

"My mom's in the hospital. I'm not sure how long I'll be staying."

"I hope she's okay?" Steph was killing Chloe with this exaggerated sweet act.

"She'll be fine. Thanks for asking." His focus remained on Steph's face while they conversed, which Chloe found oddly comforting.

At least he's not ogling her breasts. Something Steph had plenty of.

"Will you be attending the engagement party?" Steph slid her arm through his.

Chloe glared at Steph.

"No."

"Oh, darn. I was hoping we could dance and maybe get to know one another." Disappointment in Steph's voice and her salacious wink pushed Chloe's twinge to full-on possessiveness.

"It's time for us to go. Chad?" Chloe's hand grasped his muscular forearm.

"Yeah." His head swiveled to Chloe before glancing back to Steph. "Well, it was nice meeting you, Stephanie," Chad said as he removed her arm from his.

"I'll call you later," Chloe directed at Steph, who held up her drink and winked. *What the hell is that supposed to mean?* Jealousy ran rampant through her veins. Why? There was no reason for her to be jealous. Chad was free to be with whomever he wanted.

Street lights illuminated the sidewalk. The air was warm, and Chloe shrugged the sweater from her shoulders. Chad gently touched her shoulders. She jerked.

"I was only trying to help." His fingers lingered before gliding down her arm.

Her stomach fluttered. "I got a shiver." Her body shouldn't react this way to a man who wasn't her fiancé.

Chapter Four

Chad delivered a soft kiss to Chloe's shoulder as they stood on the sidewalk outside the restaurant. He was overstepping his boundary as a friend. But being so close to her was killing him. He refrained from placing kisses in other places, stepping to the side. "Can I walk you home?"

"Why did you do that?" her tone curious.

Not answering her question, they crossed the street.

"I don't know... It felt right." They waited for the light to change and crossed, meandering along Main Street. "So does Stephanie know about our history?"

Chloe's strides became longer and quicker. She could've damned well been running.

He never had a problem keeping up with her. Tonight was no different. "I'll take your silence as a *yes* then."

She stopped abruptly. He had taken two strides before his gait slowed. Passersby darted around them as he faced her.

"Yes, she knows about us. Yes, she knows about you." He opened his mouth, and she answered the unspoken question. "No, Andrew knows nothing about us." She continued down the sidewalk.

"Nothing?" He was baffled.

They stopped at the corner. They remained silent, oblivious to the clamor of people around them. Crossing South Field Street, they continued a short way along Main before stopping in front of a large building. An office building to him.

"He knows you exist. He knows you hurt me." She turned to the front doors.

"Chloe?" In a smooth fashion, his hands skimmed her waist to rest on her narrow hips. "I'm sorry. You have no idea—"

She spun around. "No idea?" Her voice dripped with spite. Her gaze was a different story.

Shit! He felt the pain and anger in her eyes.

"Chad, it's simple. You didn't love me." The fury was gone.

He slid a hand behind her head while his other glided around her waist, drawing her into him. Lips touched and parted as she returned his kiss. As quick as a heated passion raged through him, it was over. She shoved him away.

Chloe's gaze darted to the people around them as they silently stood there. She withdrew to the glass door. "Goodbye, Chad." She disappeared into the building.

Enough people eventually dodged past, staring at him, to take him from the mesmerized state. He pulled his vibrating phone from his pocket, turning in the direction of the hotel. "Hey, Trent, what's up?"

"I'm in a jam and can't come with Maggie. We thought since you were there, you could escort her to the engagement party Friday night."

"Are you shittin' me?" He halted, and a passerby cursed at him. "Seriously? Can't she go alone?"

"Yes, but I'd feel better knowing someone's there for her if something were to happen. Like going into labor. Please?"

Chad strolled again along the sidewalk. "Ah, I don't think this is a good idea."

"Why not?"

"I just left Chloe. I don't think she'd be happy to see me again. Especially at her engagement party." His pace quickened, and he turned the corner to his hotel.

"Shoot, she wouldn't mind. Plus, you won't be around her much. Come on. Free food and drinks. You can't pass it up. Please?"

"Fine. But only because it's Maggie."

"Thank you. Can you get a tux? I'll pay." There was no mistaking the relief in Trent's voice.

"I've got the tux, man. Listen, I've got to go." The line clicked, ending the call.

Chad entered the hotel, slid the phone into his pocket and waited for the elevator. Friday and Saturday would prove to be interesting. Chloe had no idea what was about to happen in her little world. Fate was throwing temptations at him. Had it been right to act on the first temptation? Yes.

* * * *

Chloe shouldn't have returned the kiss. She scolded herself and tossed her purse on the kitchen counter. Why did Steph have to be at the restaurant? She didn't worry about her telling Andrew anything, but Steph's flirtatious behavior with Chad sparked a jealousy match, lighting the flame.

She threw herself on the couch, stretching as her head rested on the cushioned arm. Closing her eyes, she willed her body to relax as her mind replayed to the point where Chad said, *you have no idea.* What more could there be other than he didn't love her?

She fell into a deep sleep and awoke startled on the couch. Dark in the apartment, she stumbled to her room, glancing at the clock reading three a.m. She flipped the alarm switch to wake her in three hours. As she collapsed on the bed, she covered herself with a throw blanket.

Loud classical music invaded her sleep. She rolled and hit the snooze to turn off the alarm noise. Blinking slowly several times, her eyes adjusted, and she scooted upright wearing last night's clothes. She slid the switch back, turning the alarm off and showered.

Chloe made a cup of coffee and left for the office. Today was her Friday since she had off the next two days. Of course, she would check phone messages and email. Parked in her work ramp, she reached for her coffee when her cell rang. "Maggie! Are you here?" She answered, recognizing the caller.

"I'm on my way to my parents as we speak."

"We have *a lot* to talk about." She slipped her purse and tote bag straps onto her shoulder.

"Like what?"

Grabbing her travel coffee mug, she exited and locked the car. "I work with Chad's mom."

"What?" Maggie exclaimed loudly.

Chloe drew the phone away from her ear as she headed for the building entrance. "I was there when she got shot."

"How didn't you know it was her all this time?"

"Their last names are different. Anyway—"

"Wait! Did you say you were *there*? When she got shot? Chloe, that could've been you."

"Actually, he fired at me, but when Linda pushed me to the floor, she got hit." She entered the building and took the stairs to the third floor.

"She saved your life," Maggie spoke humbly.

"Yes. I visited her the next day at the hospital. There he was. Quite the surprise, for both of us."

"I bet. What was it like when you saw Chad?"

Chloe's heartbeat did a little two-step. "Awkward."

"That's it? *Awkward*? You disappoint me."

"I'll go into more detail when we talk in person."

"Okay. So, how is his mom?"

"She's recovering. Chad said she may be moved from ICU today." Her stomach fluttered when talking about Chad. *What the hell?*

"That's good. What time is the dress appointment tomorrow?"

"We need to be there at three. I've made dinner reservations for us at Festivités."

"Are you kidding? I love you. They have the *best* French cuisine."

Chloe smiled, knowing she made Maggie's day. "You're my best friend. I had to make a reservation. How are you feeling?"

"Good. When I talked to my mom while making plans for this trip, she told me about all the stuff she's purchased. She's spoiling me and the baby."

"The baby?" Chloe was confused since the baby hadn't been born.

"She's bought all kinds of toys and clothing. *And* she's planning on us going shopping today for more. I'm going to have to pack another suitcase and pay the ridiculous fees to get it home."

Chloe strolled through the open office door with the phone at her ear. She stopped in the waiting area. "Pack the items in a box or two and ship it. Don't pay to fly it home."

"You're a genius. I'll plan on being at your place by one tomorrow. That will give me time to unpack and us a chance to catch up."

"I can't wait. I'd better go. I'm at the office."

"No problem. See you tomorrow."

As her matron of honor and best friend, having Maggie in town to help pick her wedding gown meant the world. And to have her here near the beginning of her ninth month of pregnancy meant even more. Although she had told Maggie there was no need to make the trip, Maggie had insisted the doctor was fine with her traveling.

Her phone rang.

"Ms. Atwood?" a professional male voice asked.

"Yes?" Chloe stopped at the receptionist desk.

"This is Detective Fuentes."

Worry flooded her. "Is everything okay?"

"Yes, fine. I'm calling because we believe we have the man in custody who shot Ms. Morris. Can I send an officer to your office? We'd like to see if you recognize the guy in any of the photos."

"Don't I need to come to the station?" This earned a chuckle.

Her shoulders relaxed. A tension she was unaware of but that had obviously been there eased.

"No. We'll show you a group of computer generated photos. If you see him, you simply point him out."

"What time?"

"What would work best for you?"

"Any. I just arrived at work."

"Expect an officer in about twenty minutes. Thank you for your assistance, Ms. Atwood."

"Have a good day." Their call ended, she informed the receptionist about an officer coming to visit.

Chloe cleared off the papers on her desk, knowing the officer would need a place to lay the pictures. Thirty minutes later two officers stood in her office.

"I'm Officer Espinoza," a full figured female held out her hand. After shaking hands, she hooked a thumb saying, "This is my partner, Officer Hartman." A tall man, Officer Hartman sported a beer belly.

Chloe wondered if he had the stamina to chase down a suspect. They shook hands. "Would you like to sit?"

She shook her head. "This should only take a moment of your time." Espinoza opened a folder. "I'm going to give you a sheet of paper with several pictures on it. You tell me if you see the man you saw late Monday afternoon at The Arms of Safety."

Chloe swallowed. "Okay" flowed from her mouth, and her head bobbed like a child agreeing to an adult's instructions. Her pulse skittered as Espinoza handed her the paper. The paper shook as she held it. She set it on her desk.

"No need to be nervous." Espinoza touched Chloe's hand.

"Take your time. Carefully look at each photo," Officer Hartman stated.

Chloe glanced from the paper to the officers. Officer Hartman nodded his head.

Several men were quickly dismissed, but three others she studied carefully. One more eliminated, down to two men. She closed her eyes, going back to Monday and opened them. After a minute of focusing on the two photos, she pointed to a picture. "This is him. I can tell by the eyes and piercings."

The guy in the photo gave the impression of having been roughed up. He had a bloody lip, and his cheek appeared to have been scrapped, as if he'd been slammed into a cement walkway. She didn't say anything. In her opinion, he deserved what he got.

"Are you a hundred percent certain?" Officer Espinoza asked, bending to see the picture.

"Yes. No doubt."

"Please show Officer Hartman the picture of the man you are identifying." Officer Espinoza stepped from the desk, and Hartman approached.

"This is the man at the shelter on Monday." Chloe's finger tapped on the picture of the guy.

"Thank you for your time, Ms. Atwood." Espinoza placed the sheet of paper in the folder and jotted notes inside. "If we have any further questions, we'll be in touch."

"Can you tell me," Chloe swallowed, not knowing if she should ask, but had to. "Is the woman he took away okay?"

"She's fine, but that's all we're able to say."

Chloe escorted the officers to the reception area where they shook hands and said goodbye. Once back in her office, she fell onto her chair, shaking out the tension in her arms and shoulders. It was over. No more bad guy stuff. On to happy things, like making wedding plans.

* * * *

Relocated from trauma ICU to a private room in the medical ward, Chad's mom took an afternoon nap. While she slept, Chad finalized the donation package he, Trent and Maggie would make to the Winlets fundraiser on Saturday evening. The doctor informed him his mom would be released Saturday morning. She could attend the event, as long as she had a chaperone and transportation.

"What are you working on?"

Chad looked up from his computer. "Hey, Angel. I didn't hear you come in. I'm just checking emails. Taking care of business. Listen, what are you doing Saturday?" He kept his voice low to insure their mother got her sleep.

"I'm busy with the kids. Mom asked me, and I already told her." She sat next to him.

"Would you have *any* time to help her get ready? She won't be able to do much because of her arm."

"I could help early in the day with her hair, but not with getting dressed. I'll see what I can do. You know she won't be able to drive?"

"Oh, yeah." He thought for a moment before a broad smile filled his face. "I'll take care of it."

"What are you up to?"

"I'm going to have her ride in style. Nothing that would make her feel uncomfortable though." He tapped on the keyboard of his laptop and bookmarked a page. He'd make the call later for the car service.

"Ryan called. They got the guy. Your friend ID'd him." Angel winked, and his eyebrows drew together, wondering what she was talking about. "What's her name? Chloe? You two have a story to tell."

"Chloe?"

"So, what's the story?" She nudged his shoulder.

"We're college friends. They've arrested the guy?" A little too excited about the news, his voice spiked. He turned quickly, checking to make sure he didn't wake their mother.

"You're not getting off easy, baby brother. We'll go back to the conversation about Chloe. They arrested him, she made the ID, and now he's been officially charged with attempted murder. But Ryan doesn't think it'll stick. He thinks he'll end up with second degree assault. Either way, he'll serve time. Plus, he has other charges surrounding the incident. Ryan couldn't talk about it though." She leaned close. "Now, tell me what the real story is with you and Chloe."

"There's no story. She's engaged." He pretended to be browsing email messages.

"But you have feelings for her?" Angel pushed down the top of his laptop. "Talk to me, Chad."

"Two years ago she came to Florida. For two weeks our friendship became more. She returned home here, and for a short time things were going well. We talked on the phone, texted and sometimes video called each other. When she wanted me to visit, I made every excuse possible to avoid coming back here."

"Why?"

"You know why." With a stern expression, he said, "Don't push me."

"Okay, keep going. So you didn't visit her. Or your family. What happened?"

"All conversation slowly came to an end. Maggie told me Chloe was seeing another guy." He closed the laptop. Nothing would get done with his sister around, asking questions. Questions he didn't want to answer. "I've tried dating, but it's tough."

"How have you *tried*? Have *you* dated anyone else?" Angel remained against his arm.

"I went on a couple of dates with girls the guys on the ranch would set me up with. But they just weren't...what I was looking for."

"Because they weren't Chloe. Right?"

The questions were darts being thrown, hitting the bull's-eye. He hung his head. "Yes."

"Love is tough. It never gets any easier when you find that special person. But when you do find the right girl, Chad, you'll do whatever is necessary." Angel rested her hand on his forearm. "Even if it means going places that make you uncomfortable or facing your fears."

"How do you always know what's going on? And how did you become so wise?"

"I got married and had kids of my own. No more questions about Chloe. But I believe you have a lot of thinking to do." She sat upright, signaling the end of their private conversation. "Do you want to go get something to eat? I'll stay here with Mom. I already ate lunch."

"Yeah." Chad slid his laptop into the neoprene case, set it on the window sill and left for the hospital cafeteria.

Angel could read him like an open book. She knew exactly what to say and when to say it. He sent a simple text to Chloe with his mom's new room number. Angel was right. He had some thinking to do.

The cafeteria tray contained a bland looking burger with some toppings, a plate of fries and a bowl of cut-up fruit. As he paid, his cell vibrated in his pocket, jolting him and the tray of food. He set the tray on the nearest table. "Hey, Maggie," he answered cheerfully.

"How's your mom?" she asked with genuine concern.

"She'll be released Saturday morning. They've arrested the guy who shot her."

"I heard. I didn't know Chloe worked with her, Chad. If I had known I would've told you." Guilt filled her voice.

"How would you've known? She changed her last name after the divorce. We were both shocked at first, but it's all good. So, what's the plan for Friday night?" He bit into the burger.

"Guests can start arriving at seven, so I was thinking of leaving at six-thirty. Since I know where we're going, I thought I'd drive. Where are you staying?"

"At the Pegasus downtown on Commerce Street."

"That's not far from where I'll be staying. I know right where you are."

"I could meet you at her place to save time."

Maggie coughed. "You know where Chloe lives?" she asked surprised.

"I know the building." Not wanting to explain any further, he prayed Maggie wouldn't question him.

"Okay. Be at Chloe's by six-thirty. She's in apartment 901."

"I'll see you Friday."

"Hey, Chad?"

"Yeah?"

"Thanks for doing this. I know it's the last thing you wanted to do, but I really appreciate it."

"I'd do anything for you and Trent. See you Friday."

Chapter Five

Chloe left the office and sat in traffic thinking about the warm bath waiting for her at home. Chad had sent her a message with Linda's new room number. She contemplated whether or not to stop for a visit. The soak in a tub won. The risk of seeing Chad again also affected her decision.

The police visit to the office set off alarms inside her head. She considered the safety of the women in the shelter. Changes were needed. Make the house safer, not only for the women, but the employees, too. After the police left, she searched available funds or services the shelter might qualify for to make the changes. Several available, she bookmarked them in a Favorites folder on her computer.

Pulling into her assigned parking stall, she exited the car and pressed LOCK on the fob. She cringed at the site of Andrew's black Mercedes parked in her second spot. *I'm avoiding my fiancé.*

"Damnit! Why did Chad have to come back?" She shook her head at her own stupidity. He wasn't back for her. He was back because of an unfortunate incident with his mother.

She drew her cell phone from her purse while strutting to the elevator and dialed Linda's hospital room.

"Hello." Chad was cordial.

I can't avoid him. "Can I speak to your mother, please?" With nervous energy, Chloe paced in front of the elevator doors, waiting for it to arrive.

"Chloe—"

"Your mom, please." Anger fuelled firmer footsteps. Her high heels clicked on the concrete.

As the phone was passed, she heard mumbling between Chad and his mother.

"Hi, Chloe. Is everything okay?" There was urgency in Linda's voice.

"Fine. I wanted to see how you were doing. Chad told me they moved you today. That's good news. I'm sorry I couldn't stop by."

"No worries as I know you're busy. Plus, I have my family here to keep me company."

"You have a great family. It was nice to meet them." Love and caring warmth oozed from Chad's family, something Andrew's family lacked. Sure, Andrew, his parents and siblings expressed their love for one another, but it was *anything* but warm. *Cordial, formal* and *cold* were words that came to mind.

"Chad told me he's escorting Maggie— I guess that's not something you need to know." Chad must've said something to Linda for her to cut off the sentence.

"What?" Chloe exclaimed.

"Nothing, dear."

"Can I please talk to Chad, Linda? I'll talk to you later. Take care."

"I didn't—" Chad stated on the line.

"Didn't want me to know, right?" Chloe's volume level hit the roof. "What the hell are you up to? You can't come. I didn't invite you for a reason." The echo of her words bounced off the concrete walls.

"Trent couldn't make it."

"I don't care. *You. Can't. Come.*" Not able to deal with the situation at the moment, she ended the call. Her fiancé was waiting for her. In her apartment. *Damn it!*

She stomped into the elevator, pushing the button for the ninth floor with more force than needed. Her chest heaved with anger. Quickly, she pushed the button for the lobby floor. In a matter of minutes the doors opened. She exited and marched to the reception area. Phone in hand, she located the number and waited for an answer while taking calming breaths.

"Chloe, hi." Maggie answered.

"What is going on?" Chloe paced on the area rug in front of a couch to keep her steps quiet.

"Hi to you, too. I don't know what you're talking about?"

"Chad. Why? Why is he coming with you to the engagement party?" She plopped onto the leather couch.

"Because I would like to have someone there if something were to happen. I am in my last month, you know."

Chloe's leg bounced with nervous energy. "I know, but your parents will be there. Couldn't they help if you needed it?"

"I guess. I never thought of that. But—"

"But nothing, Maggie." *To hell with sitting.* She resumed pacing the area. "Call Chad and tell him you don't need him to go."

"Chloe, relax. *What* is going on? Why can't Chad be there? He's your friend."

"I don't want him there. That's all. Plain and simple."

"Are you running a race? You're panting. Sit down." Maggie's voice was calm but forceful. "Are you sitting?"

"Yes," she huffed, as she dropped to the couch.

"Stop wiggling, and sit still."

"I'm sorry. I don't mean to be angry with you, but this whole situation has me worked up. You're going to be a great mother. You can already sense things." The pair chuckled, but it didn't last long.

"I sense something's going on between you and Chad. Otherwise, you wouldn't be so upset about him coming to your engagement party."

"Nothing's going on. I just don't want him there. Please rethink this, remembering my wish. I need to go. Andrew's waiting for me. I'll see you tomorrow."

"Okay. But I'm not done discussing this."

Chloe clicked END. *I just hung up on my best friend.* The tips of her fingers typed a quick apology text to Maggie. She glanced to the glass entry doors, a reminder of the kiss last night with Chad. *That* was why he couldn't come to the party. Feelings for him still lingered. She wasn't over him.

* * * *

"Mom, why did you do that? Why did you feel compelled to tell Chloe I was going to her engagement party?" Chad sat in the hospital room with his head in his hands.

"I'm sorry, honey. I didn't know it was a secret."

"Don't worry about it." He faced her. "For one, I wasn't invited. Another, I knew it would bother her."

"Why would it bother her? You're friends."

"Mom, you know about our past relationship. It can make things awkward."

"Only if you let it. I'd go with you, but I'll still be tied up here." She lifted the arm with IVs, wiggling it around. They laughed.

"Thanks, but it's not who I'm going with that makes it awkward. It's our history."

His mom yawned. "What did Chloe say to you?"

"She doesn't want me there. Asked me, no, *told me*, to tell Maggie I can't go. Then she hung up."

"You need to go for Maggie. Chloe will be fine. Now leave. I want to rest."

"I love you." He bent over and hugged her, mindful of the injury.

"I love you." She lowered the top of the bed down. "I'll see you tomorrow."

Grabbing his laptop case, he ambled to the door. "Tomorrow."

It was quiet in the hall and on the elevator ride. The entry area was another story. People strolled around, stood in the pharmacy line and waited to be admitted. Not wanting to eat hotel room service, he wandered down the sidewalk through the streets of downtown Dallas. The Knoll restaurant shined like a beacon. He approached the hostess.

"How many in your party, Sir?"

"It's just me. Can I get a meal at the bar?"

"Yes."

"Thank you. I'll order there then." Chad stepped into the bar filled with business men and women. In the far corner he spotted a high table. As he dragged a stool to sit down, a dark haired waitress drew near.

"Hi! I'm Morgan." She set a cardboard coaster imprinted with a beer advertisement on the table. "What can I get you to drink tonight?"

"A shot of tequila and a bottle of Corona."

"Are you waiting on others to join you?" Her bubbly attitude helped to lighten his mood.

"Nope. Just me. Thanks."

"Did you want a menu?"

"No need. I'll have the Barbeque Pit Burger, please."

"How'd you like that cooked?"

Raw, to fit my mood. "Medium." For safety sake. Then again, if he got sick that'd get him out of going to the party.

"I'll be back with your drinks." Morgan left the table

He scoped out the patrons while checking the TVs around the large area. Various sports channels played, discussing preseason football. From the colleges to the pro teams. He bounced from watching the TVs to who came and went from the area.

"Here you go. Drinks are on the brunette at the bar." Morgan turned to give him a view of the bar.

Chloe's friend from last night. *Stephanie.* She waved and sauntered toward him.

"I'll be back shortly with your burger."

"Thanks, Morgan." He smiled, warmed by Stephanie's presence. *Company. Female company.*

"In need of some company tonight?" She pulled a tall bar chair close to his and sat. "Rough day?" She nodded at his shot of tequila.

"No, just...life." He tossed the light golden liquid down his throat and sucked the lime wedge. "So, you're Chloe's friend *and* her fiancé's sister?"

"Yep. We've been friends since birth. Our parents have been friends since their college days."

"Wow. Keeping the families together, aren't they?"

"What do you mean?" Her brown eyes concentrated on him. She tipped her head to the side. Auburn hair cascaded over her shoulders.

"Chloe and...Andrew." He purposefully stumbled on his name. "By marrying each other they're keeping the two families together. Cozy, don't you think?" The last part came out more spiteful than he meant. But who cared. He took a long pull from the bottle of Corona.

She leaned into him. "I don't think it's as cozy as *we* could be." A long red painted fingernail trailed slowly down his chest. "Let Chloe have my brother. You can have me. Even if it is for only a couple of days."

The crotch of his jeans tightened. His body was trying to do the thinking for him. The last time he'd had sex was over a year ago. He had an itch that'd love to be scratched by the female persuasion. "I'm sorry, but as enticing as that sounds, I can't." He removed her hand and took another swig of his beer.

"Why not? You don't have a girlfriend. So?"

He looked into dark smoldering eyes. "How do you know I don't have a girlfriend?"

"Chloe told me. So if you don't have a girlfriend, why not have some fun?" Her full lips pouted.

So, Chloe had kept tabs on him all this time. "I can't." He shifted as his jeans loosened. Did she still have feelings for him? She had returned the kiss last night, but was also the one who pushed away, putting space between them.

"Hello? What are you so deep in thought about?" Stephanie's hand waved in front of his face.

"Sorry. Thinking about something."

"More like someone, someone named Chloe. I saw the way you were with her last night. Let me help you take your mind off her." She snuggled closer to him.

His waitress approached. "Stephanie, can I bring you a drink?" Morgan set the plate in front of him. "Here's your burger."

"I'm good, thanks." Stephanie's eyes remained deadlocked on Chad's.

"Can I bring you anything else?"

"Can I get this to go?" He pointed to his plate. "And the check, please?" Temptress Stephanie worked an evil magic on him.

"Sure." Morgan snatched the plate, leaving him alone with Stephanie.

He took a gulp from the bottle.

"Did you want to go to my place or yours?" A red nail leisurely maneuvered down his arm as her large breasts rubbed against him.

"What do you think you saw last night?" Another long pull of the Corona and he drained the bottle.

She licked her full lips. "You, kissing her shoulder. In the most seductive way that got me hot and bothered," she whispered in his ear, "Like I am right now." She nipped his earlobe.

The jeans tightened again in the crotch. "It was a friendly kiss on the shoulder. Nothing more." His voice cracked.

Morgan stepped to the table. "Here you go."

"Just a minute." Chad opened the check to see the total. From his wallet, he handed her thirty dollars. "Thanks, Morgan. No change."

"Thank you. Stephanie, did you need to settle your bill?" Morgan looked at the brunette practically sitting on his lap.

He pulled out a twenty. "Does this cover it?"

"Yeah, I'll get your change."

"Your tip. Thanks for the great service."

"Okay, thanks." Morgan maneuvered away wearing a gleeful smile.

Chad snagged the foam box and growled, "Let's go. Now." Taking her hand in his, he hurried her out of the restaurant and to the hotel.

Alone in the elevator, he backed Stephanie against the wall. Without a care, he took possession of her mouth. Tongues collided, and her hands roamed his back, drawing him closer into a lean body. The door dinged open, and they stumbled out. Her hands slid around his waist, down his hips to his inner thighs. He fumbled with the key card.

Once the door closed, he yanked her into his arms. They kissed their way deeper into the room. Closer to the bed. Hands glided over bodies. Lips exchanged kisses. His eyes shot open at the realization that what he was doing was wrong. This was Chloe's friend and...damn, her fiancé's sister. Wrong on every level.

He pushed away from Stephanie. "You need to leave." He moved so the bed separated them. "I'm sorry, but I can't."

"What?" she exclaimed. "You entice me. Bring me back to your room. Now you want me to leave?" She slinked toward him. "You want me." The voice of a seductress. "I could feel it. Let go, and give it to me. Give me what I want."

"You don't know me. Please, leave." He strode into the bathroom, locking the door. Ashamed at his behavior. But how do you explain your love for another woman? A woman who happens to be their friend and brother's fiancé?

Chapter Six

Chloe stepped from the elevator and strolled down the hall to her corner apartment. Pausing at her front door, she slowly inhaled and exhaled. Andrew waited inside. The aroma of Chinese food wafted through the air as soon as she cracked open the door.

"I was beginning to wonder if you were coming home," Andrew called.

Further into the apartment she found him in the living room. He sat on the couch, his shoes off, feet on the coffee table and a plate balanced on his lap. "I ordered your favorite. It was getting cold, so I started eating. Sorry, Darlin'."

"That's okay. It smells good, and I'm beat." She slipped off her shoes and wiggled her toes. Her bag and purse dropped to the floor without a care. In the kitchen, she took a plate from the cupboard. "It's been an exhausting day."

"Well, I can help with that. Come on in here." He rose, answering his ringing cell phone. An index finger in the air, he glanced at her for the first time. He disappeared into her second bedroom slash office, closing the door most of the way.

Through the crack of the doorway, his voice carried. "...voting is Friday...go elsewhere...discouraging...in the mail." Since he worked at the foundation, she wondered if he left the room to talk about the grant she had applied for. She tamped her curiosity, knowing *not* to ask or talk business with him. Kung Pao Chicken scooped on her plate, Chloe sat at the dining room table.

"Sorry about the call." Andrew entered the living room. He snatched his plate from the coffee table and joined her in the dining room. "What

46

happened at work today that has you so tired?" he asked in a condescending tone.

"The cops came to the office today with some pictures. I ID'd the guy who—you know." She waved her hand in the air as though she could dismiss the shooting from her memory.

"I want you to give your two week notice." There was no joking behind his statement. His face was stone sober. He rested his hand on hers, and his facial features softened. "I can take care of you."

"Andrew, not tonight or any other night, are we discussing this. You know how I feel about my job, let alone working."

His mouth crimped in annoyance as he removed his hand. They both took a bite of food. The TV voices floated through the room, filling the void.

"Your job has turned dangerous. It could've been you in the hospital. Or worse."

"My job isn't dangerous, and I will *not* quit." Chloe chewed with more force than needed. The tension wore on her. "Let's talk about something else." She needed a glass of wine.

"I may not be able to escort you to the fundraiser Saturday," he said as she entered the kitchen.

"When will you know?" She grasped a wine glass and filled it three quarters full of merlot.

"Not until late in the afternoon. But I might be able to make it at the last minute."

She took a long, slow sip with eyelids closed. *Typical of him. Not showing his support.* "That's fine. I'll be busy socializing with attendees." She sat back at the table to finish eating.

"That's what I thought. You won't even notice I'm not by your side." He lacked thoughtfulness, pushing her life to the side. "Why don't we stop talking and start by taking a bath together." A suggestive smile grew across his face.

"Andrew, I'm not in the mood."

"I can change that." He reached under the table, sliding a hand on her thigh.

"No, you can't." She jerked her leg, making his hand fall. She shoved a bite into her mouth. Her appetite lost, she took her plate to the kitchen. "I'd like you to be here to comfort me tonight. That's it." The plate sealed with plastic wrap, she placed it in the refrigerator.

"Come on, Chloe. We haven't had sex in a week. Normally we romp three to four times in the week. What's going on with you?" He joined her in the kitchen with his empty plate. "Are you seeing someone else?" He seized her arm.

She inhaled sharply, surprised by his action.

He yanked her to face him. "Is that why you were home late?" He released her arm.

"No! I'm not seeing anyone." Her voice cracked, and she softened the tone.

He rested his hands on her hips. "You make me happy." His hands slipped to her backside, grabbing her butt. "I worry you'll meet someone."

Not that she was *seeing* Chad on the side, but when she did, he stirred up old feeling. His kiss left her wanting more of him. But their time was up and over long ago.

"I was late because I was talking to Maggie." Chloe broke from his hold and went to retrieve her glass of wine. His mood flipped as quickly as a coin toss at a Cowboys game. "We're going dress shopping tomorrow."

"For your wedding dress?" he asked with a genuine smile.

She rocked on her heels. "Yup."

"Maybe you shouldn't have eaten the Kung Pao. No more Oriental for you." He feigned a laugh. "You need to fit in your dress."

You ass.

"I didn't eat much." She knew better than to eat her favorite meal, much less with Andrew around. "I'll eat lite tomorrow. Okay?" Two months ago he developed an interest in her weight. She'd catch him looking at thinner women. He'd make comments about women letting themselves get too big.

He slid his arms around her waist, bending to kiss her. "Okay. I like my women small. You know that." He kissed her again, but with more force than before.

When he yanked her blouse from the hem of her skirt, she pushed him away. "Stop! I said not tonight." Sex was a routine activity for them.

48

But since the shooting and Chad's arrival, it was the last thing on her mind.

"I had to try. Maybe you should skip a meal tomorrow." He sauntered to the living room, plopping himself on the couch. "Hey, Darlin', do you mind if I watch a movie?"

She cut a path through the living room. With a glower, she stood in the bedroom doorway and said sourly, "I *was* hoping we could watch one after my bath."

"I'm talking about something to aid in my release since you won't play with me."

"Porno? Are you kidding me? Jesus, you're gross."

"You're such a prude. If you'd come over here, then I wouldn't have to get a movie."

Her eyes narrowed in contempt as her voice carried an edge of indignation. "Maybe you should go home. This week has been a little nerve racking, and you've been *anything* but sensitive to my needs."

"That hurts my feelings. I brought dinner because I was thinking of you."

"Yeah, then you make a snide comment about my weight. Nice, Andrew. Nice." She spun around. From over her shoulder she stated, "I'm going to take a long relaxing bath. You decide what to do. Leave or change your attitude."

Her clothes off, she sunk into hot water filled with bubbles. Her eyelids closed. Relaxation didn't come easily. *Does Andrew truly love me for who I am?* The comments about her weight raised the question. If she dropped any more weight, she worried how it would affect her health.

A cell phone rang. Andrew's, but she couldn't hear what he was saying over the music.

The front door closed. Andrew left. Left without saying *goodbye* or *I love you*.

With a deep inhale, she sunk a little lower into the water and exhaled.

Did we rush into this engagement? Things were changing in their relationship. Her jobs had never been an issue. The shooting gave him an excuse. Something bigger was behind his motive to get her to quit working.

What if Chad asked her—*Stupid question.* He wouldn't ask anything, because he couldn't, no, *wouldn't*, visit her. Because he didn't care. There was a lack of effort on his part. She had travelled to Florida to see him. He never reciprocated. They both called, which in time turned into emails that had grown infrequent. She had told him a long distance relationship wouldn't work.

The kiss dug up the buried feelings from years past. *Damn it! He has me questioning my engagement. Not to mention my commitment to Andrew and our relationship.*

Chloe ducked below the water's surface.

* * * *

Chad's hotel door opened and closed. Stephanie had left. Would she or wouldn't she say anything to Chloe about this evening. A large part of him prayed she'd remain quiet. The smaller part hoped she'd say something, anything, to set off a spark of jealousy in Chloe. He hoped their shared kiss from last night expressed his feelings. If the kiss didn't do the job, he wondered what it would take.

He turned on the shower then faced the mirror. A coward looked back at him. *Do you love her?* Is that what this was—Love? *Are you willing to give up everything to be a part of her life, in Texas?* She wouldn't be willing to join him in Florida. They'd been through this before, and neither of them was willing. So what changed between them that would make either of them move?

Nothing.

In the shower, water cascaded over his head. Putting his hands on the wall, he leaned forward as hot water spilled across his back. Time to face his demons. He'd start with his brother Ryan.

* * * *

Chloe and Maggie sat on a couch, surrounded by wedding gowns and bridesmaid dresses, waiting for the bridal shop consultant. The store was so brightly lit, Chloe thought about wearing sunglasses. Two other brides also waited to meet their consultants. Other women perused racks of dresses.

Last night Chad consumed Chloe's dreams. She had awakened frustrated and confused. But today she would focus on the task at hand, wedding gown shopping with her best friend.

A woman dressed in black approached. "Hi! Chloe?"

Chloe nodded, a little spaced out, thinking about last night.

They shook hands. "Yes. This is my friend, Maggie."

"Nice to meet you." She shook Maggie's hand. "I'm Angie. I'll be helping you find the perfect dress. Have you tried any gowns on before today?"

"No. This is my first time."

"Can you tell me what you are looking for in a wedding dress, Chloe?"

"The little looking I've done, I'm thinking satin or silk fabric. My fiancé prefers I wear something that shows my figure. So maybe something fitted. I'm open to anything though."

"What size dress would you say you wear?"

She reversed her crossed legs. In the last two weeks, she'd lost a few more pounds. "I think a six."

"Okay, what about color? Do you want white, cream, blush or maybe something with an accent color?" Angie scribbled on a piece of paper.

"It has to be white based, but I'll try something with color."

"Do you know what color your bridesmaids are wearing?"

"We've discussed a December wedding. I'm thinking of crimson red." She smiled. Red was her favorite color.

More notes were written down. "What about the top of the dress? Do you want straps, sleeves, or strapless?"

"So many questions. I never thought of any of this." They all laughed. "No sleeves. I'm thinking strapless but I'll try straps."

"What about embellishments or beadwork?"

"Yes, but nothing excessive. I don't want to be weighed down or be glittery like a disco ball." Chloe giggled.

"Do you have a designer preference?"

"None."

"Okay, the final question. What's your budget?"

"I would have to say the max would be five thousand, but I'm willing to go higher for the right dress."

"That's a great budget and will make it easy for me to find something. Let's get started. Chloe and I will be back shortly with the first dress, Maggie."

In an ample sized fitting room, Chloe sat alone wearing a robe, waiting for the consultant to return. Although excited to be trying on dresses, something was amiss. Ever since Chad's arrival, she questioned herself and her engagement to Andrew. Andrew should be at the fundraiser. After all, he expected her to be on his arm for every one of *his* events.

A knock at the door and Angie entered with an armload of gowns. Chloe forced a smile.

"I have eight dresses for you to start with. If you don't like the way they look, you don't have to try them on. Are you ready?" With Chloe's nod Angie continued. "This is an Ines Di Santo A-line."

"I like how it looks on the hanger." Chloe untied the robe, sliding it off her shoulders. To be standing in front of a stranger in nothing but her lace panties and bra felt a little odd. On second thought, she concluded this woman had seen it all. She carefully stepped into the center of the gown. Angie zipped the back. Angie used clips to pull the dress tight to fit Chloe's slender figure.

"How do you like the first one?"

"It's beautiful. I love the top with just enough beading, but I'm not sure about the full skirt. Let me see what Maggie thinks." She wondered what Andrew, often critical of her style choices, would think. He preferred tighter fitting clothes.

"Ooh," Maggie said as Chloe approached. "I like the simplicity of the dress. The beading at your waist is beautiful. The beaded offset styled shoulders is feminine and elegant. But I don't think Andrew would care for the full skirt."

"I agree. Keep it as a contender?" she asked while swishing the skirt around.

"For now, yes. Let's see the others." Maggie laughed. "We're just starting."

Back in the fitting room, out of dress one and into the next.

"This is another Ines Di Santo. It's a trumpet style, fitting to mid-thigh and giving you a fuller skirt at the bottom. A change in fabric, as this one is covered with lace," Angie described assisting Chloe with the gown.

The dress was boring. Lace covered the entire dress. Not a fan herself, she showed Maggie who didn't care for the simple garment. So back to the fitting room.

The third dress, a Douglas Hannant, a strong contender for Chloe. The dress was gorgeous and made her feel beautiful.

Maggie's hands covered her mouth as she sat on the edge of the couch. "Oh, I like this one, Chloe. It's stunning."

"I like it too. But I'm not sure about the silver grey flowers."

"Turn for me," Maggie asked. "I like the way the fabric flows on the bottom of this trumpet style. Andrew would approve of the fitted body. The flare at the bottom gives you the skirted feel."

The dress was easy to move in, which surprised her since it was fitted over the hips. Maggie was right about Andrew appreciating the fit of the gown.

"I like this one more than the first. Next one."

Chloe stepped off the pedestal and went back for dress four.

"This is a Jenny Packham. This is a simple yet glamorous design of the traditional style wedding gown." Angie held the dress for her to step into.

"It's okay but not as wowing as the last one."

Maggie shook her head as Chloe approached. She turned, returning to the fitting room.

"This is a sheath with detailing on the bodice."

Chloe stood in front of the mirror. "I don't think so. This resembles something I would wear in the bedroom on my honeymoon." The lightweight fabric in the cool room exposed the perkiness of her nipples. Not to mention the deep v-cut in the front. There was no hiding the valley of cleavage she was blessed with. Or maybe it was a curse.

Angie laughed, helping her out of the dress and into another. "This is another Jenny Packham. This has a high neckline with beading throughout the dress. There's beading around the waist giving the appearance of a belt."

"It's so lightweight." Chloe stated as the dress easily slid over her hips. "I like this. It has the right amount of beadwork. Very elegant. I feel as though I'm going to walk the red carpet." Chloe exited the fitting room.

Perched on the edge of the couch, Maggie exclaimed, "This is gorgeous," and raised her hands resting on her baby belly.

"Do you like this one more than the other ones?" Andrew would approve. But would he accept the high neckline.

"This one is a definite contender. Do you have more to try on?"

"Yes, we'll be back." Chloe stepped off the pedestal, returning to her room

The last two dresses in the room she turned down without trying on.

"Would you like me to look through our collection and pull a few more?" Angie asked, assisting her out of the gown.

"Could you please find a few more? Maybe something with color."

"Okay. Can I take some of these out of the room?"

"I'd like to keep the Ines gown and the Douglas trumpet." Chloe smiled at the contender choices.

"I'll be back."

Chloe waited while Angie looked for new options.

When she entered the room, Angie had five dresses. One was a full deep red color.

"I want to try the red one first." Her excitement contained on the outside, anything but on the inside.

"This is a Romana Keveza." She zipped the back.

Chloe turned, viewing the dress in the mirror. "Oh...my...God. This is stunning." Her eyes moistened. "I didn't think I'd like anything but a white gown, but this...this is breathtaking. The style and the color make a statement."

Exiting the fitting room, she couldn't help but touch the mild ruching at the top, down the waist, gathering on the left hip, where it draped. Subtle and elegant.

Maggie sat perched on the couch. "Chloe, that is...stunning."

"What do you think of the color?"

"I love the color,but is that what you want? How would Andrew feel about you wearing something other than white?"

"I don't know. I like it. It's different, and it feels great on."

"Okay, keep it as a contender. Let's see another."

Chloe quickly dismissed another Romona Keveza. The style of the dress was right, but she didn't care for the all over lace. She put on a tulle skirted a-line gown with a sweetheart beaded embroidery top.

"Oh, Chloe, it's beautiful. What do you think?" Maggie asked.

"I like it. I'm keeping it as a candidate. I'll be back."

"We have one more to try on," Angie stated, escorting Chloe from the stage. "The last gown is a Rivini silk chiffon sheath."

In the room, Chloe carefully stepped out of the skirt with Angie's help, careful not to step on the tulle. The Rivini slid over her thin frame. "As flimsy as this feels, making me think of the bedroom, it's much more than that. I love the low cut back. The top is elegant. And this curved drop waist is amazing."

"The bodice is hand embroidered organza with pearls and crystals. The skirt is fluid, forming a sweep train."

They entered the waiting area where Maggie drank from a water bottle. "Wow."

"I think this may be the one. But I don't know. I really liked the red one, too."

"Can I see you walk in it?" Maggie asked, sitting on the edge of the couch.

Chloe strolled away, when she turned around, Maggie was crying.

"Really?" Her vision blurred with unshed tears. "You think this is the one?"

"It's beautiful, Chloe. Your mom and bridesmaids need to see this one, the trumpet one with the heavy silvery grey floral top that cascaded down the front and maybe the red one. Those are my top four choices." Maggie genuinely smiled, wiping the tears away.

"I guess we're done," Chloe said, inching her way back to the fitting room.

"It sounds as though you won't be ordering the dress today. Would you like me to write the dress information down for you?" Angie asked while hanging the dress on the hanger.

"No, I'm sorry, I won't be ordering today. But I would appreciate the information, and I appreciate your help."

"It was my pleasure. We have plenty of brides who come in, try on dresses and don't order one. Especially when it's their first time looking and trying on dresses. I would suggest looking through bridal magazines to get more ideas of what you may want. Or unless you're happy with the dresses from today, then bring those whom you want opinions from in to see the dresses on you."

"Thank you." Angie left Chloe to change.

Shortly Chloe rejoined Maggie in the show room. "Are you ready for dinner?"

There was plenty of time for purchasing a dress, with no wedding date set. But one thing was certain: she would not buy a dress to meet Andrew's approval. It was *her* wedding day. No one was going to tell her what dress to buy. Not her mother. Not her friends. And definitely *not* her fiancé.

* * * *

Festivités wasn't at its full capacity with their early dinnertime, but that would change as the hour wore on.

"How did you get a table on short notice?" Maggie asked after they were seated.

"I made reservations as soon as I knew you were coming. I knew you'd enjoy this."

"Thank you. It's a pleasant surprise."

"Is Chad still planning on attending the party with you?" Chloe played with her salad fork and avoided direct eye contact with Maggie.

"As far as I know. I haven't told him otherwise. You should know that Chad resisted when Trent first asked him."

"I don't care. It doesn't change the fact that he's going to be at my engagement party."

"It makes me more comfortable knowing he'll be there."

"I had dinner with him the other night. He walked me home and kissed me." She paused before adding, "And I kissed him back." Chloe fidgeted with the menu on the table in front of her.

"What?" Maggie's voice raised then she whispered as patrons turned. "You two kissed? And?"

"And nothing. I pushed him away and went inside. I'm engaged to marry another man." She placed the cloth napkin on her lap.

"Do you still have feelings for him, Chloe?" Maggie inquired.

"If I do, I need to push them away. Things didn't work out when we *were* a couple."

"That didn't answer my question. Look at me."

Chloe glanced at Maggie then away again, about to admit feelings for a man other than her fiancé. "Yes. Yes, I still have feelings for Chad."

"Does he know?" Maggie's tone softened from the inquisitive to the concerned friend.

"No. Because nothing's going to come of it. Maggie, he never initiated any sort of visits after I left. Sure, we talked on the phone, but that became sparse after a year."

Their waiter approached. Chloe was thankful for the interruption. Their lunch orders taken, they were alone again. A chance to change the subject. "Is Trent getting more excited or nervous as time nears for the baby's arrival?"

"Ecstatic. He struggles at each doctor's visit whether to learn the sex. We both made the decision not to be told, but it kills him each and every time we go shopping. He wants to buy gender specific items and gets frustrated not knowing. It's quite funny."

"I can only imagine."

"Have you and Andrew talked about starting a family?"

So much for the subject change. "No. It won't be anytime soon though." She glanced from Maggie to her water glass. "I'm not ready."

"Do you want to have kids? The way you said it and looked away leads me to think you don't want them."

"I do want to have kids. Just not right now." After returning from White Sand Key several years ago, she'd dreamed of having children with Chad. She couldn't imagine having children with Andrew. "Let's talk about those dresses today."

Their conversation during lunch remained on the topic of wedding gowns and the baby.

Waiting for the bill, Chloe said, "It was nice, just the two of us today. I didn't want a whole gaggle of women there giving me their opinions. I only need one…yours."

"Not even Stephanie or your mom?"

"*Definitely*, not my mother. Our opinions of what my dress should look like are galaxies apart. Steph can come with me at a later time. I wanted time with you. I miss you—more now that you're having a baby. I'm going to be there for you after the baby's born. I plan on taking two weeks off."

"I know, just plan on coming after my parents. We don't lack space, but you know how my mother's going to be. You'll never be able to get close to the baby when she's around." The women laughed.

The waiter placed their bill on the table.

"I've got this." Chloe snatched the black leather folder. "My treat." With her free hand she covered Maggie's hand and squeezed.

"When you come to visit, I'll treat to lunch. Although I'm sure the bill won't come to near the same amount."

"Doesn't matter." Her phone binged, signaling a text. A message from Andrew. *'Ride home was a HARD one. Missed you and the 'girls' in bed.'* With a shake of her head, she slid the credit card in the holder and set it to the side.

"Why are you shaking your head?"

"A text from Andrew. He can be so disgusting sometimes. All he thinks about is sex, I swear."

"Are things good between you two? You know, in bed."

"Yeah, it's good." A lie. Usually it was about his gratification. "He wants it *all the time*. When I turn him away he gets mad. He'll say that I don't find him sexually attractive. Last night he asked if I was seeing someone else because I got home late."

"How does he get mad?"

"Maybe mad isn't the right word. Frustrated is maybe better."

"I understand frustrated." Maggie's eyes rolled. "We're both frustrated in our house. I'm worried I won't be able to walk when the doctor gives the all clear after the baby's born."

They both roared in laughter. Chloe signed the receipt that came during their conversation. Placing her card back into her wallet, she said, "This was good. Do you want to do some shopping?"

"Let's go. I need to work off some of this lunch. Not to mention move a little."

"You have an excuse for weight gain. I don't." If she gained a pound, Andrew would be sure to notice and say something, like last night. Tonight's meal would be apple slices with a wedge of light cheese and water.

Chapter Seven

Chad entered his mother's hospital room Thursday afternoon after eating lunch at the cafeteria. His brother Ryan sat bedside where their mom slept. He kept his voice low and asked, "I'm glad you're here. Can we talk in the hall?" His jaw clenched tight.

"Yeah," his brother spoke easily.

His mouth relaxed for a moment, then tensed again. Whether good or bad, he had to confront Ryan to move forward.

One step. Two step.

The two men entered the hall. Chad motioned to a sitting area. "How 'bout we sit down." The navy vinyl furniture was arranged in several small groups consisting of two chairs and a sofa. When Ryan sat on the sofa, Chad sat on a chair across from him as he didn't want to be sitting next to his brother.

"What's up?" Ryan spoke in a relaxed and casual tone.

This was something Chad seldom heard in their childhood from Ryan. There was never a friendly, casual moment with Ryan. Chad had walked on eggshells throughout his childhood.

"I need to get beyond our differences—" Chad's leg bounced with nervous energy as his stomach clenched.

"Our differences?" There was the brother he remembered. Butting in and raising his defenses.

"Let me finish."

Ryan crossed his arms across his chest. When he slouched on the sofa, the 'I'm-not-listening-to-my-little-brother' attitude was apparent.

Chad sat on the edge of his chair, leaned forward, lacing the fingers of his hands together. His elbows on his knees, he breathed deeply and exhaled. "I need to understand what happened between us growing up. Since the day I can remember you have always been out to get me." He wanted answers to the questions he had carried around for years. "You blamed me for things I had nothing to do with. You teased me. You beat me up. You—"

"I'm sorry. I was a five year old kid when you were born. I was hurt."

Chad peered at his brother who mirrored his position. Ryan didn't make eye contact.

"Things were going good until you came along. I resented you because Mom no longer gave into my needs. It was you. Always you. Dad never meant to hurt Mom."

"Are you going to make excuses for him?" He sat upright. Angry at Ryan for defending the man they called dad.

Ryan's blue eyes locked dead-on with his. "No. He's a different man from back then."

"Explain to me what went wrong. What happened that made Larry, *dad*, snap?"

"After I graduated college, Dad told me that he and Mom had trouble brewing prior to Mom getting pregnant with you. When she did get pregnant, that's when everything went to hell." Ryan's gaze fell to the floor. "There's more to this. I think you should talk to her."

"Why? Why don't *you* tell me? We're talking now. Tell me what you know." Both of his legs bobbed. His stomach knotted. What was the unknown?

"I watched Dad with her and how he hated you. Yes, he hated you but wishes he had handled things differently. I do, too. I have no excuse. I learned from Dad, a bad example."

"I can never forgive him."

"Can you ever forgive me?"

Chad regarded his brother. "This is a start. A good start. But tell me what you're not saying." He had a right to know what the hell his brother wasn't telling him.

"I'm sorry, Chad, but there are things I'm not at liberty to share." Ryan glanced at his watch. "When they release Mom, ask her about your father. I need to leave. Duty calls." Ryan stood from the couch.

Chad rose so Ryan couldn't look down on him. He wanted to be on equal ground. "What the hell? That's it?" His voice raised an octave, cracking. Looking around, he lowered his voice. "We make some progress in our relationship, and you're leaving me to talk to Mom?"

"Chad, I'm glad we took a step toward being better brothers than we ever have been, but it's not my place to tell you more." He shuffled from the small furniture grouping. "Don't talk to Mom about this until she's out of the hospital. Tell her I'm sorry I missed her and will call later." With that, he walked through the corridor toward the elevators.

Chad fell onto the sofa and rested against the back. What the hell was Ryan keeping from him that he couldn't say about their father? He wouldn't ask his mom until she was home. Until then, it was going to drive him crazy.

He returned to his mother's room. The nurse stood by the bed checking the wound site, changing the bandage. "Sorry I wasn't here when you woke up." He took his spot on the chair by the window. "Ryan and I were talking. He's sorry he missed you and will call later."

"You two talked?" His mom's eyes widened.

"Yes, we needed to resolve our issues."

"And did you?"

"We had an interesting conversation, but yes, we're on the right path."

"I'm all done." The nurse stepped from the bed, depositing the old dressing into a red bin. "You can lay back and relax," she said before exiting the room.

"Interesting conversation? What did you two talk about?" The all-knowing eyebrow shot up as she asked the questions.

"Our past. We can talk about this another time. I want to talk to you about Saturday night. I've arranged for a car service to pick you up and bring you home after the party. Angel's going to take you home from the hospital. She'll do your hair and make-up. Your neighbor, who was more than happy to help, will be over to help you get dress."

"A car service? Chad, you shouldn't have."

"You can't drive, and no one else is around to help you as I'll be getting ready myself. Plus, you deserve it. Enjoy the relaxing time in the car because you know once you arrive, you'll be bombarded by people."

"Thank you. You're always looking out for me."

"Always."

But who's looking out for me?

* * * *

Chad rode the elevator to Chloe's apartment on the ninth floor. Although she wasn't there, he couldn't relax. Shaking his hands and arms to release the angst, he knocked at the door. A few more shakes and the door opened.

"Come in, Chad." Maggie closed the door. "I'll be ready to go in a second."

"Wow, you look beautiful." She wore a blue gown that flowed over her round belly. "How you feeling?"

"Good. I'll be back in a minute. Make yourself comfortable." She left him standing by the open kitchen.

A corner apartment had to cost a fortune. The view wasn't the greatest, but the all glass wall didn't hurt. *Plush.*

"Her parents didn't spare any expenses on this place. They went all out for Chloe."

Entranced by the luxurious apartment, he spun around, startled by Maggie's voice.

"She told me you two had dinner together."

"Yup."

"And?" Maggie's hands rested low on her belly.

"We went out. We talked. Had a nice time catching up. Are you ready?" He gestured toward the exit, changing the topic. Chloe was engaged. There was nothing further to discuss with Maggie.

"Uh, yeah. Let me grab my purse and keys."

He waited by the door and opened it for her. "You lead the way."

"I'm parked in the garage." As they waited for the elevator, she said, "I talked to Trent, and he told me about the auction. It should be a strong item for bidding."

"Did you say anything to Chloe?" Chad asked nervously as they stepped into the elevator. Chloe had no idea he would be attending the event with his mother. If she knew about the bidding item, she'd know he knew about the event.

"No. I take it you don't want her knowing?"

"I prefer she doesn't."

"I won't say anything."

The rest of the ride to the garage remained quiet. Maggie started the rental, a little sports car, and exited the garage. As she maneuvered out of downtown Dallas, she asked, "You want to tell me about the kiss?"

"I kissed her. What else is there to say?" The city scenery passed by the window as he contemplated how much to reveal to Maggie.

"She kissed you back. How did that make you feel?"

"Good. Bad. Listen, Maggie, she's getting married to another man and—" He turned to face her.

"And if you have strong enough feelings for Chloe, then you need to do something."

"Is there something you know that you're not telling me?"

"I know her fiancé, Andrew. He's a *good* family friend. He cares for her, but yesterday when we went dress shopping for her wedding gown, Chloe didn't seem herself. I think your presence has her second guessing this marriage." Maggie's eyes glanced away from the road for a second.

In that moment, he saw she spoke the truth. He didn't know how to respond. Silence filled the car for some distance.

"Why didn't you come home to Texas...to see your family or Chloe? What happened here, Chad?" Maggie broke the quietness.

"Since when did you become a psychologist?"

"I'm just a caring friend. Let's blame it on this mommy-to-be thing." She chuckled.

"My father and the younger of my two brothers have kept me away. I talked to Ryan, my brother, yesterday. We had a rough childhood. Let's just say he wasn't a kind brother. But I made a step in the right direction." The city landscape had changed to green-filled scenery with fields separating the houses. Quiet for a moment, he continued. "My father...my father was worse than my brother. He was a monster. My mother was badly abused. I watched, defenseless against him. Me? I was verbally abused. I guess you could say marked, too."

"Chad, I'm so sorry." She touched his knee for a second before returning her hand to the steering wheel. "I didn't—"

"Don't apologize, please." Although his voice was saddened, a relief of sorts came over him. "As difficult as this is to talk about, you're the first one I've ever told."

"I'm—"

"My relationship with Chloe didn't end because I didn't come back here. It ended because my feelings were too strong. I was afraid."

"Afraid of what?"

"I'm afraid I'll turn out like him." His voice softened with sadness.

"Like your father?"

"Yes. When I talked to Ryan, he hinted that there's more to this than I know. I'm going to talk to my mom once she's released from the hospital."

"Which is when?"

"Saturday."

"Chad, you and your father are two different people. I don't know him, but I know you. You wouldn't harm a thing." She pulled into a long crescent driveway where a short brick staircase led to the front entrance. "Except maybe barn flies. I hate those things and kill them when I can." She chuckled, waiting to get closer to the valet. "We're here. Remember, you are *not* your father." Her hand rested on his knee. "Think about what you really want. *Who* you want in your life."

They exited from the car, and he waited for Maggie to join him at the bottom of the stairs. He took her arm while taking a deep breath.

One step. Two step.

* * * *

In four-inch heels, Chloe towered over her mother who listened to one of her friend's complaining about their help. Is this what her life would become by marrying Andrew—talking about the help and hosting parties? With a Bel Air smile plastered on her face, she silently pleaded for an escape. She scanned the family dining room where the furniture had been removed to host tonight's engagement party guests. As her eyes continued to roam the rooms, Andrew's long silhouette in the study caught her attention.

Handsome. Endearing. Funny. Edgy. Mysterious.

The last thought of her fiancé caught her off guard. She'd known Andrew all her life and never once did *mysterious* cross her mind. The low lighting in her father's study and Andrew in a tuxedo enhanced his James Bond man of mystery appearance.

"If you will excuse me," Chloe spoke in a respectful manner. The beaded Jovani gown trailed behind, with the slightest hint of a train. The modest sweetheart neckline with on-the-edge-of-the-shoulder straps exposed her collarbone and arms to the cool air of the house. If she could step outside, she'd warm instantly with the low eighty-degree Texas summer evening.

As she neared the study's entry, Steph approached. "You look amazing tonight. The beadwork is stunning. I love the slight floral pattern. The way it curves from the waist around down the front to the other side, is so figure flattering."

"Thank you. You look beautiful, too."

Steph said something, but Andrew's voice stole her attention.

"Winlet is holding their annual black tie fundraiser for the women's shelter Friday. Chloe's trying to get me to attend."

"As important as it is for you to attend," her father spoke. "Try and find an excuse to miss the event. We need to discourage that girl as much as possible. Her marriage to you will be the best—"

"Chloe?" Steph touched her forearm. "Are you okay?"

She gazed out the dining room window. A pregnant blonde wearing a blue empire waist gown stepped onto the drive. "Maggie," she quietly exclaimed. "I'm fine. Sorry, excuse me," and hurried to the main entrance to greet her.

Chloe had anxiously waited all day to see her. As she stepped through the doorway, her forward progress halted. Frozen on the cement landing, she blinked and regained her forward momentum.

Clean-shaven and in a tuxedo, Chad escorted Maggie up the stairs.

Her pulse quickened. Anxiety stabbed at her gut. She swallowed hard. *Andrew.* Keeping the two men away from each other would prove to be a challenge.

Chad was out of his element. He would be eaten alive by the guests. By her parents. Although an educated Texan who spoke well, he was different from her parents and her social circle. He was a laid back, casually dressed, beer drinking, rodeo attendee, rancher. He wasn't a tuxedo, hors d'oeuvre, seven course meal, polo match enthusiast, socialite.

But damn, he managed to appear comfortable in the penguin suit. Her pulse quickened. The suit fit well, with plenty of room for the rock-hard muscles she remembered. She swallowed the lump that formed in her throat.

Chad's blue eyes pierced her soul with sadness, while his face was bright with happiness. Her own happiness at Maggie's arrival dissipated as her heart stammered for a man she once loved.

But she had never confessed that love.

Chad and Maggie reached the top of the stairs. He took Chloe's hand, leaned into her and, on his toes because of her high heels, kissed her cheek. "It's good to see you again. You're breathtaking."

Chloe's heart rate accelerated. She blinked several times as he stepped sideways allowing her to welcome Maggie. "You look amazing." She embraced Maggie and whispered, "He *had* to come."

"It'll be fine."

"Come in. I'll introduce you to Andrew, my fiancé." Chloe turned from Chad. She swore his soft eyes pleaded directly to her heart. Introducing him to Andrew couldn't be avoided. It would only raise questions with her fiancé if she didn't make introductions.

Her mother approached them in the entry. "Maggie, darling, how are you feeling? Your mother was saying you have a month left. Where's your husband?"

"Diane, good to see you. I'm feeling good. Trent couldn't come. He had to stay home because of an emergency at the ranch. Chad was in town for another reason, and I strong armed him into being my escort for the evening."

"I'm glad you could join us to help celebrate Chloe and Andrew's engagement." Her mother's attention focused to Chad.

"Mother, this is Chad Rogers. Chad, this is my mother, Diane." *Keep it short. Please, Mom, don't ask questions.* Her stomach tensed with unease.

"It's a pleasure to meet you, Mrs. Atwood." Chad shook her mother's hand with a delicate touch Chloe'd never seen before.

"A pleasure to meet you, Mr. Rogers. And how do you know my daughter?" Diane tilted her head ever so slightly with curiosity in her eyes.

Chloe's throat tightened. This was what she feared. She faced Maggie with wide eyes, pleading for help in escaping this conversation.

"We graduated from college together. I'm also business partners and friends with Maggie and Trent."

"I don't remember meeting when we visited Chloe on occasion during her college years."

"Oh, we never met because Chloe and I were involved in different activities on and off campus."

Damn, he's good.

"Diane, have you begun planning the wedding?"

Chloe smiled thankfully at Maggie for the change of discussion.

"Yes, planning is underway. Maybe we can get together for lunch while you're visiting."

"Mother, if you'll excuse us."

"Of course. I'll have the staff prepare the champagne for the toast." Her mother disappeared through the crowd to the back of the house.

Chloe maneuvered past guests toward the last place she'd seen Andrew. The place she heard painful words.

As the threesome neared the study, men's laughter burst from the room. Chloe entered through the open doorway and cleared her throat to make her presence known. "Father, the staff is preparing the champagne for the toast. Andrew, there's someone I'd like to introduce you to."

"I'm a lucky man." Andrew stepped to her side, taking her hand in his. "Is there a friend I haven't met yet? I'm going to need more groomsmen for your large bridal party."

"You've met everyone in the bridal party," Chloe said with a forced laugh. The four inches of heel, added to her five-eight height, put her within an inch of meeting Andrew eye-to-eye.

"Maggie Carlisle, look at you. You've gained a little weight but still gorgeous as ever." Andrew chuckled, releasing his hold on Chloe's hand. He embraced Maggie. "How are you feeling?"

"Great, thank you. And I go by Randall now." Maggie flashed her simple intertwined gold and silver wedding band with Chad standing by her side.

"This must be your husband I've heard so much about. Hi Trent, I'm Chloe's fiancé, Andrew Lockhart."

"This isn't Trent, Andrew." Chloe stated. "This is Chad Rogers, a friend of mine and the Randall's."

"A friend, huh?" Andrew glanced at her with a raised eyebrow and a 'we'll-talk-about-this-later' look. "Sorry about that, Chad. It's nice to meet you." He shook Chad's hand. "Welcome to Texas."

Chloe watched as the two men sized each other. Andrew stood a several inches taller than Chad. When Andrew pulled back his shoulders his chest puffed out, making for interesting behavior on his part. She'd never seen him act in such a manner. Was he jealous or threatened by Chad?

"Thank you. It's been a few years since Chloe and I last talked. Congratulations on your engagement. She's an exceptional lady."

A lopsided smirk formed on Andrew's long oval face, and a short condescending laugh escaped from his mouth. "Indeed she is." He slid his arm around her waist, lowered his face to hers and delivered a forceful kiss on her lips. Chloe ended the kiss as he pulled her into a tight embrace.

What the hell?

A slight twist at her waist and he released her. Her older brother stepped from the study. *Thank God.* "Michael," she grabbed him by the hand. "I'd like to introduce you to Maggie's escort and my friend. Michael, this is Chad Rogers. Chad, this is my brother, Michael."

The two men exchanged quick pleasantries before Michael embraced Maggie.

"I'm missing all the fun over here." Her younger sister sidled up to her.

"Nicole, this is Chad Rogers. Chad, this is my younger sister, Nicole."

As Nicole and Chad shook hands, her father Robert's strong deep voice bellowed, "Attention, everyone. Would my beautiful daughter and future son-in-law please come to the stairs?"

She followed behind Andrew who stepped aside to let her stand at her father's side. A server held a tray of champagne flutes, and she waited for Andrew to hand her one. *What the hell? Thanks for ignoring me.* With a delicate hand, she took a flute by the stem. If she held the glass any other way, her anger would more than likely shatter the glass.

"Does everyone have a glass? Good," he said with a deep chuckle and a warm congenial smile. "Chloe and Andrew have known each other for over twenty years. I've watched as these two grew into a beautiful couple. Her mother and I couldn't be more pleased to welcome Andrew into our family and gain another son. Please raise your glasses for my beautiful daughter Chloe and her fiancé Andrew Lockhart as we celebrate the beginnings of what will be the wonderful union of two lives. Congratulations." Robert raised his glass followed by everyone around them and with a salute of "Cheers," everyone took a sip.

Andrew, on the other hand, drank half his glass with a gulp. Her parents hugged them with congratulations, and they continued to mingle with the guests. With no plans to finish her glass of champagne, Chloe carried it around with her to prevent anyone giving her a fresh flute. She would put the rim to her lips and tip the glass, giving the appearance of taking a sip. A trick her mother taught her early in life.

Chloe gave conversations as much attention as she could while concern for Chad's presence occupied her mind. A casual glance around the room would bring relief with his absence, but worry about whom he was speaking with and what about. She prayed he wouldn't mention their past history together. He had done well so far.

"Excuse me, little sister," Michael strode to them, "but it's time for me to steal away my best friend for a celebratory cigar. We'll be in the study."

Steph's hands snatched Chloe's as soon as the men disappeared. "Has Andrew met Chad?" she asked with a tense edge to her voice. "I thought he said he wasn't coming?"

"Yes, Andrew's met him. Chad's here because Trent couldn't make it. Trent wanted Maggie to have someone here in case something was to happen to her or the baby. Of course, they picked Chad. I'm not happy but managing. I'm assuming you haven't seen Maggie."

"No," Steph squealed in delight. "Let's go find her. How big is she?"

"Due in four weeks." Chloe rolled her eyes at her friend's thoughtless question of Maggie's size. "She looks pregnant."

In what her mother called the parlor, Maggie sat on one of the only comfortable chairs left on the main floor of the house. When the two women neared, she stood, but Chloe motioned for her to sit back down. Chad was nowhere to be seen.

As if reading her mind, Maggie stated, "He went to the bathroom. Then he's fixing a plate of food and getting me a drink."

Steph fired questions at Maggie about Trent before moving on to the subject of pregnancy. Chloe's smile faded when Chad entered the room.

"Maggie, this was a mistake. I'll call for a cab back downtown." Chad turned to leave.

Chloe grasped his hand. Her stomach fluttered. "Don't go. You're a special friend to me, Chad. And you're here for Maggie."

"Fine." It was a simple word, giving in to her request. He removed his hand from hers. "Maggie, I'll be mingling among the guests when you're ready to leave."

Chloe followed Chad with her gaze as he retreated from the room.

Handsome. Solid. Confident. Funny.

She missed his humor and the fun they had together. With a shake of her head, her focus returned to the women. She made a decision over a year ago. A decision to move on. A decision to marry Andrew.

Chapter Eight

Chad held a plate of fancy hors d'oeuvres and sat at a table alone. Soft orchestral music drifted from the party canopy where the food and bar were served. The dim lighting throughout the tent and into the seating area calmed his demeanor. The back yard couldn't go without being noticed. He admired the large lot with its perfectly manicured bushes, which backed up to a woodsy area. Not to mention the garden with the various vivid colored flowers. Trent would've appreciated the flowers.

The evening proved difficult, seeing Chloe yet again, but he hadn't expected it to be so painful. When they first arrived, she'd stolen his breath. She was stunning. Damn near killed him.

Her hair was pulled up, exposing her back with nothing to cover her delicate neck and collarbone. And the slight shoulder he kissed the other night. The loose fitting dress couldn't hide the slight frame beneath the fabric from the weight she'd lost. Her ample breasts were accentuated by the cornflower blue beaded, high waistline. The dip in the center of the top emphasized the luscious curve which led to the valley between her ample breasts.

Damn, he had to get out of there. His body responded to thoughts he no longer had a right to. She belonged to someone else. How many times did he have to remind himself?

A hand clapped his shoulder. The newly met male voice close to his ear asked, "Who *are* you, Mr. Rogers? What do you mean to *my* fiancé?" The words were said with spite. Chad was in for a hurt of trouble if he wasn't careful about how he said things.

"As *your* fiancé stated, I'm a friend. We knew each other in college. I'm friends with the Randalls."

"What is it that you do for a living, Mr. Rogers?" Andrew stepped around to face him. Chad hated the guy for the condescending way he said his name, like the Mr. Rogers television show of his youth.

"What I do for a living is not of importance to you, Mr. Lockhart." He was proud of what he did for a living. But Chloe's lifestyle and those she associated with was different from his standard of living.

Andrew teetered. The man had had too much to drink.

"Hey, Andrew," a dark haired guy their age called. "You're wanted for a private toast."

Andrew acknowledged the man with a nod, stepped to Chad's side, leaned down and whispered, "Enjoy your short time here in Texas, Mr. Rogers." He strolled away with a contemptuous laugh.

Chad really disliked his last name growing up. Nowadays, on infrequent occasions when talking to assholes he loathed the name. And Mr. Andrew Lockhart was one of those assholes. He took a pull from his beer and swallowed. Bare feminine arms slid from his shoulder to his waist. He turned, and Stephanie kissed him on the lips. He pulled back from her and glanced around, thankful no one seemed to noticed. "What are you doing? I thought the other night you would've gotten the idea." He took her hands, lifting them away from his body.

"You look too delicious to let sit here alone. I thought you would've let go of her. You are, after all, at her engagement party." Her jab hurt, but she was right. "Let's go upstairs and liven things up." She made to slide between him and the table to sit on his lap, but he held her back, placing his hands on her hips.

"I'm not interested."

She maneuvered to stand behind him. While running a red nail along the curve of his earlobe, she leaned in whispering, "Then let's go back to your hotel room."

"I'm sorry to interrupt." Maggie cleared her throat as she stepped up beside them. "Stephanie, I didn't realize you two knew each other so well?" The question was filled with a sarcastic surprise.

Stephanie backed away from Chad the moment Maggie coughed. He would thank Maggie later for the timely interruption.

"I've had the pleasure of meeting Chad on two other occasions. I was hoping to have a different outcome this evening. But unfortunately, his heart still belongs to my future sister-in-law."

"Stephanie, don't do this." Maggie slid an arm around her waist. Her tone was calm and cool, like a piece of chocolate melting on your tongue. "You know their past and nothing more. Chad is here because of his mother, not because of Chloe. He will be returning to Florida, without Chloe." Maggie removed her arm. "Move on to someone else here at the party."

Stephanie leaned into his ear and whispered, "Sweet dreams, Darlin'."

As she sashayed away, Maggie asked, "Are you ready to leave?"

"More than ready. It's still early though. Are you feeling okay?" He was there after all to watch out for Maggie and the baby's well-being.

"I'm fine, Chad. I'm tired and ready for bed." Maggie positioned her hand on the baby bump. "This kid is wearing me out. Chloe told me to tell you good bye."

An awkward silence fell between them. He didn't want to leave this way. Yet he couldn't stay either. Chloe was engaged to another man because he wasn't man enough to face his own fears.

"Go find her. Say good bye, Chad." Her hand rested on his forearm. "I'll meet you by the front door."

"I...okay." They returned to the house, and Maggie left his side. Chad perused the attendees, hoping to find Chloe without Andrew by her side.

He strolled through the groups and found her talking to some older people. "Excuse me, Chloe," and the group pulled away from them.

"I told Maggie you didn't need to—"

"Yes, I did. For me. Chloe, I'm happy for you and hope he gives you everything you deserve. Most of all, happiness." He embraced her. Her head fell to his shoulder. His stomach tightened. Unfortunately, she wasn't wearing the familiar light floral scent he loved. This new fragrance was too heavy in the spice department. "Congratulations." She was frail. Too frail.

Her head lifted, and moist eyes gazed at him. "Thank you." She kissed his cheek and slipped away.

He turned. Andrew stood in the doorway of the room. His eyes bore a hole through Chad like a nail being driven through a piece of wood.

With a slight shake of his head, Chad left the house to join Maggie at the bottom of the front steps. Maggie's car was brought around, and they rode in silence until they were on the freeway.

"I don't like him, Maggie. He's not a nice guy."

"Andrew?" Maggie glanced away from the road for a second to look at him. "Andrew's a good guy, Chad. He's been friends with Chloe's brother since childhood. I told you, we've known him for years."

"I don't care what you say. Something's going on. Something more."

"You still have feelings for her. Either you need to let them go, or otherwise, act on those feelings. Did you ever tell Chloe how you felt?"

"We both knew how we felt about the other. It didn't work out." He turned his head away to the passenger window and lowered his voice. "She has her life, and I have mine."

"What's that supposed to mean?" Maggie twisted her head sharply giving him a stern look.

"Never mind." He couldn't wait to get back to the hotel and get out of the tux.

"Never mind? Chad, you need to tell her how you feel if you do indeed have feelings for her."

"Why? She's engaged to another man. A man she must love if she accepted his proposal." His voice cracked. He swallowed. "I'm sorry for raising my voice. I don't want to talk about this. I am concerned though about how thin she's gotten."

"She's lost a little weight. Nothing to worry about. She'll put it back on after the wedding."

"If you say so." But Chad knew better. His gut knew Andrew influenced the weight loss in one way or another.

Maggie pulled up to the hotel's entrance. "Call if you want to talk about it."

Chad opened the car door. "Thanks, but I don't need to talk about it." He slid from the seat and closed the door.

Tired, he ambled through the hotel lobby and slipped off his coat while waiting for the elevator. The doors opened, and he stepped in, loosening the tie. While undoing the first two buttons of his shirt, he caught his reflection in the mirrored elevator wall as it rose to the twentieth floor. Numbness settled upon his heart. Chloe was engaged to be married. The engagement shouldn't have surprised him since they hadn't had much contact in the last year. Chloe had been right about a long distance relationship not working. She'd returned once for a week's visit, but he'd never made it back to Texas.

The elevator doors opened, and he meandered down the hallway. At the door to his room, he slid the card through the security locking mechanism, pushed the handle down and stepped into his sixty-eight degree room. He stopped at the closet, hung up the tux coat and draped the bowtie around the neck of the hanger. Further in the room, he tossed his watch onto the desk.

Chad approached the window looking toward the downtown Dallas nightscape. Chloe and her engagement to Andrew created chaos in his head. He tried blocking her out throughout the evening, but heard enough to know she followed the money and the family. Andrew was a close family friend. His family was friends with her family. God, Chad wanted to throw up at it all.

Granted, he and Chloe had been good friends and their few weeks together two years ago proved they were more than friends. But he couldn't move back to Texas. Visiting, not a problem. Moving, a problem. Chloe getting married to another man, a problem.

Throughout the evening the soft dimples from her smile would appear. His heart melted. He missed that smile. He missed a lot. In general, he missed Chloe.

"Well, do something about it then," his reflection in the glass hollered at him.

"She's engaged. What can I do?" Chad spoke to an empty room, turning from the window. "Women." He sat on the sofa and took off the patent leather spit-shined penguin shoes.

Here he was at thirty years of age with no wife *or* girlfriend. *Loser.* He hadn't had one since he and Chloe hooked up two years ago. Had he fallen that hard for her?

"Of course you did, otherwise her engagement to another man wouldn't bother you so much." He couldn't believe he'd been so blind.

* * * *

Chloe and Andrew said goodbye to the last of their engagement party guests and Andrew's parents. A valet attendant brought Andrew's car to the front of the house.

"Thank you for the lovely party, Diane and Robert," Andrew said, taking her mother's hand in his before embracing her father.

"It's our pleasure." Her mother stepped beside Chloe, placing an arm around her. "We're so happy for you two. It's been long enough."

"Mother." Chloe twisted from her mother's arm with a frown.

"I couldn't agree more. It's nice to have this cat and mouse game over with," Andrew said, sliding his arm around Chloe's waist.

"Andrew, really?" Chloe couldn't believe this conversation. One, their relationship was being compared to cat and mice. Cats hunt and eat the mice. And secondly, long enough? She was thirty years old. Plenty of women nowadays waited to get married after their careers were solidified.

"What would you like me to say? The hummingbird found its nectar? I'm a man, not a delicate woman."

"We'll leave you two alone to say good night." Her father gently pulled his wife by the waist as they ambled from the room, leaving her with Andrew.

"I don't care for the way Chad looks at you. *Or* touches you." Andrew spoke in a low vehement voice that smelled of alcohol.

"You know Chad. He's a friend from college and of the Randall's." She prayed the nervousness didn't come through in her voice. She slid her arms around his waist. "He's just a friend."

"Well, he's a friend who has a lot more than friendship on his mind. Stay away from him."

"Andrew, he lives in Florida. He's here visiting his mother."

He stepped from her embrace and opened the door. "I'm telling you—stay away." Chloe followed him outside where he stopped on the landing. "Come home with me tonight."

"I'm staying here until tomorrow."

He pulled her into a tight embrace and slid a hand down, clutching her butt. "I like you at this height. Allows me to grab and hold on."

"Well, my feet are screaming. They don't like these four inch heels."

"I do." He pulled her tighter into his groin and aroused manhood. "Sure you won't *come* with me."

"Andrew." She put her hands on his chest, putting a slight space between them. "I told you I'm staying here."

"We could always go up to your room. I'll leave afterwards and sleep in your brother's room."

"No. I'll be home Sunday to spend time with Maggie. Her flight leaves Sunday night."

"I guess we'll wait then." His mouth dropped to hers, taking possession, while his hand fondled her backside, tempting her to go home with him.

With a break in the kiss, she said breathless, "No, Andrew."

"You're no fun." He released her, stepping carefully down the stairs, she assumed due to his arousal. At the bottom he opened the car door and turned. "I'll try and give you a heads up about tomorrow night."

"Okay." She knew that was coming from what she'd overheard earlier.

In his black Mercedes with the door closed, the window slid down. "Will you be wearing those heels?" he called to her.

"Only if you'll be there." She lifted the hem of her dress, showing a little leg and the heels.

"God, you're such a tease. I'll let you know." His dark tinted window closed, and he drove off.

Back inside the house, Chloe stood with her back against the door and glanced at the emptiness, recalling the events of the evening. Things she had heard and seen—and felt. She wasn't the only one. Andrew was well aware that something happened in the past with Chad.

Chapter Nine

Late Saturday afternoon, Chloe sat on the hairstylist's chair when her phone vibrated. *'Not going to make it tonight. When can I come over?'* A text message from Andrew.

She responded, *'Monday night? Maggie leaves Sunday.'*

Several minutes passed before his reply flashed on the screen. *'Jesus! You stirred me up last night so much that I had to take care of things on my own. Again.'*

Nope, she wasn't responding to that. She screamed inside her head with frustration.

Another message popped up. *'Watch what you eat tonight. Banquet food can be damaging to a waistline.'*

Was she making a mistake? This wasn't the man she fell in love with. Was he trying to prove something? Had Chad roused something within Andrew to make him selfish? Chad revived something in her. That was for certain.

She checked her work email for what she swore would be the last time today. As the stylist brushed, combed, pinned and curled her hair, she gasped at a new message in her inbox. The grant with her father's foundation had been denied. Her heart sank at the loss of potential for the women's shelter.

"You look sad, Darlin'. What's wrong?" her long-time stylist asked.

"Nothing. Bad news about work." Chloe smiled guardedly. "It'll be okay. Tonight will be good and fix things." She could only hope the Winlet Fundraiser would bring in the funds the shelter needed. It usually did well, but they had also lost a large donor. Hopefully, a replacement would be found.

"Good. You'll look stunningly fabulous this evening. Do you have a picture of your gown?"

Chloe exited her email and showed the picture of the dress.

"That is gorgeous! The green is breathtaking. You must show Marcus! He's doing your makeup, right?" The stylist held a section of her hair while speaking to her.

"Yes, of course he is." She giggled. "I'll make sure to show him."

The conversation continued on about the fundraising event. Where it was being held? Who was attending? And then it turned.

"Andrew will look so handsome on your arm this evening."

"He's not able to attend." Her voice turned sad, and quickly she stated, "He has another function to attend."

"Mmm-mm." The stylist shook her head. "That man never goes to your functions. What's his problem?"

Chloe remained quiet for a moment. "He's busy."

The stylist gave another shake of the head and didn't say any more. Chloe wondered how many others saw this side of Andrew. If her stylist recognized the man's lack of participation in her life, then there must be other friends and co-workers who saw his absence of involvement. Was this what her father was talking about at the engagement party? Discouraging her by not being there for her important events?

She left the salon wondering about Andrew and his motives. She felt beautiful with her hair and makeup done for tonight's special event which was for an exceptional cause—The Arms of Safety Women's Shelter. A smile blossomed on her face. She didn't need anyone to be there for her, by her side.

An image of Chad in his tux from the engagement party snuck into the corner of her thoughts. He was so handsome and poised. The brief moment he embraced her sent chills over her body. She blamed the goose flesh on the absence of coverage and cool air of the house. Admitting he could still affect her in such a way was wrong. A life with Andrew was her future. Not Chad.

The more she thought about Andrew not attending tonight's event the more she reflected on their past. Even in the beginning he never attended her functions. He was always around and available when it came to spending time with their families. She was keen on this quality in him. Although of late his sexual desires wore on her. At least they were a sexually active couple. She'd heard horror stories of the sex disappearing after marriage, but knew that would never be the case for Andrew.

* * * *

Chad stood in front of the well-lit bathroom mirror checking that the bow tie was straight. He looked forward to spending the evening with his mother, although unsure of what the night would bring. Fundraisers weren't on his bucket list, but the circumstances were different this time. This was for his mother. For a well needed cause that in the past helped assist his family.

The car service should've dropped his mother off at the hotel about thirty minutes ago. His sister had called to inform him what color his mother's dress was that morning. The hotel's concierge assisted him with getting a corsage for her. Angel also confirmed the neighbor would be at the house to help his mom get dressed.

Good to go, he grabbed his wallet, room key and corsage from the dresser and left the hotel. A group of women whistled at him as he crossed the street to The Adolphus hotel, where he arrived twenty some minutes earlier than the fifteen his mom had instructed. The Adolphus put his swanky hotel into a whole different category. This place was too prim and proper for his taste. He liked the sleek modern designs of his hotel, though the old world style of the Adolphus was exquisite. The floral carpet was a bit overwhelming, and there was ornately carved wood—everywhere. European royalty came to mind. The furniture lent a stiff appearance. He wondered how anyone would be able to relax in one of the chairs in the lobby. He had to give them credit though for the beautiful artwork he strolled past.

With a warm smile on his face, he took the stairs to the Grand Ballroom foyer where tables were set up for tonight's guests. People talked in groups. He assumed they discussed the evening, as fingers pointed to empty tables. Heads turned viewing the large area.

An older gentleman approached him. "Can I help direct you, Sir?"

"Yes, I'm meeting my mother here. Linda Morris."

"Ms. Morris is in the ballroom with Ms. Atwood."

What would it be like seeing Chloe again? Would she be angry or happy?

"You're more than welcome to go into the ballroom."

"I'd rather not intrude. I'll just walk around." He wasn't ready to face Chloe. Not yet.

"Your mother has done amazing things for the shelter. Her strength and perseverance are highly regarded by Ms. Atwood."

"Thank you." He wished he had his mother's strength.

A door opened, and his mom came through wearing a beautiful deep purple, floor length gown. Her pace quickened once she caught sight of him.

"Mom, you look gorgeous!"

"Stop. You're just saying that because I'm your mother." She carefully embraced him with her good right arm.

"No." He stepped back holding her hand. "You really are beautiful."

She blushed. "I see you've met Mr. Winlet. He and his wife are the generous couple who make this fundraiser happen every year. Mr. Winlet, this is my son Chad Rogers." The two gentlemen shook hands.

"Ah, you're the young lad who helped fill the vacancy in our auction."

"I can't take all the credit."

"Yes, I understand Mr. and Mrs. Randall are part of the item up for bid. It should bring a fair price."

"I hope so. Anything to help a worthy cause." Chad silently prayed Chloe wouldn't come through the ballroom doors.

"I'm glad you were able to be here with us and your mother tonight. If you'll excuse me. Please enjoy the evening."

"Thank you. I will." Alone with her, he opened the corsage box and carefully took out the flower. "This is for you."

"Oh, it's beautiful."

"Don't cry. You'll mess up Angel's hard work on your make-up." He chuckled to break the heaviness. "It's a wrist one. I knew I wouldn't be able to pin one on, so I asked for one to go on your wrist." He slid the flower on her left hand in the sling, which rested on her chest. "I believe these are orchids mixed with some other stuff. Trent would know."

"Yes, they're miniature orchids with some waxflower and eucalyptus. It smells wonderful, and I can't even get it up to my nose."

"I'm glad you like it. It's the perfect color with your dress." He glanced around the area. "Mom, I want a drink. Do they have a bar somewhere?"

"There'll be a cash bar in a short while. Otherwise, I believe there's the Rodeo Bar restaurant in the hotel you could try." Her fingers lightly touched his forearm. "Why do you need a drink?"

"It's okay, Mom. It's just to relax my nerves. I'll be back."

"Find me in the ballroom when you come back." Her free hand came to rest on his cheek. "Thank you for coming and for the beautiful corsage."

On the main floor he asked where The Rodeo Bar was located. Following the directions, he stepped to the bar, ordering a shot of Tequila and a beer. He tossed back the shot, followed by a swig of beer. It was time to face her. He left the bar for the ballroom. Chloe was in for a surprise. He didn't think he'd get another shot to talk to her. Not seeing her fiancé Andrew anywhere, this would be his best and maybe last opportunity.

Deliberately taking the stairs slowly, the Grand Ballroom foyer came into view. There she stood with his mother. Chloe wore a strapless, shiny, dark green gown. The lacey corset top looked like something Madonna would wear, but with taste. Her hair was pulled back at the nape of her neck.

She spoke, and her eyes widened. With a purposeful strut, she drew nearer to the stairs landing. Her eyes became mere slits.

"Why are you here? Last night wasn't enough?" Surprise and confusion filled her voice.

"I'm my mom's date." Tonight she didn't tower over him, but met him equally. *She must not be wearing extreme high heels.* Her mink almond eyes met his eyes. Her perfect little nose could touch his nose. Her luscious lips so close to his.

Her voice low, she placed her hands upon his chest, stopping any forward progress. "Ugh, I should've known this would happen."

The warmth of her hands burned as he recalled how they slid over his skin when she stayed with Maggie two years ago.

"She hated to miss the event. With the doctor's okay, she asked if I'd be her date."

She removed her hands, clasping them in front of her. "I just never thought—"

"I'd be here?"

"Yes." Her eyes fell from his gaze as her tone softened.

"You don't want me here?" With a finger he lifted her chin to look once more into her brown eyes. "Do you? I'm not leaving." Sadness consumed her eyes. He received no response. "Is there someplace we can go? I think we need to talk."

"Not now. Things are starting." Grabbing the stiff skirt, she turned and glancing back. "I'll talk to you later."

His mom approached beaming but turned serious. "What happened? Chloe doesn't look happy." Her face scrunched in confusion, glancing to Chloe's retreating figure.

He took a swig of the warming beer. "She's not happy I'm here. I told her I wasn't leaving."

"Oh." Her eyes widened. "I guess it's a good thing we're not seated at the same table as her then."

"You got that right." He tipped the bottle against his lips and swallowed.

"Be careful. You hurt her once." His mom's hand rested on his forearm. "We need to go mingle."

"Mom, you can't stop with 'you hurt her once'." He faced her. "What more do you know?"

"She confided in me briefly about someone she'd met in Florida. She thought he was *the one*. I had no idea it was you until we were talking in the hospital. You didn't want to talk any further about it."

"The one? *The one*?" He swallowed. His throat was suddenly dry. He finished the beer with a final hard gulp.

"Yes, Chad. She thought you two were going to get married, but when you never came to visit, well that's when—"

"Okay, I get the picture." This new info agitated him. Why didn't Chloe ever say anything? *Because you didn't talk to her. You didn't visit.*

Chad accompanied his mom during the social hour and was thankful for the beer earlier because he was unable to escape for another.

"Ladies and gentlemen," came over the speaker system in the Grand Ballroom. "Can I have your attention? The live auction will begin in five minutes. Please make sure to have your number paddles available and ready. We have a multitude of fabulous items for bid. Thank you." Guests gathered at their tables in the ballroom. Once the noise settled, the welcome speech and introductions were made.

At his mother's side for the last hour, he didn't get the chance to approach Chloe. Glances were exchanged a few times, but with the auction about to begin, Chad's odds lessened. He'd wait until the music and dancing after the auction, pulling her aside then. This would be his one and only time.

The auction began. Chad was aghast at the amounts being bid. A framed piece of artwork, a simple painting, went for over a thousand dollars. To him, the painting was worth no more than a couple hundred. How much would the Triple R raise with their offering?

Forty-five minutes into the auction, the auctioneer announced, "This next item is not listed because it's a last minute donation, replacing one that had to back out. Thank you to Chad Rogers and the owners of Rolling Rock Ranch, Trent and Maggie Randall, for this fantastic offering. The item for bid by the Triple R is a one-week's stay for two at the all-inclusive Pine Golf Resort and Spa in Lake Pine, Florida. Transportation to and from the spa to the Triple R, where you can take a variety of riding lessons at their new facilities and also ride on the various groomed riding trails on the ranch's property. All airfare and transportation are included. We'll start the bidding at three thousand. Can I get three thousand?"

As the description of the item was read, whispering spread throughout the room. The auctioneer began the bidding. The room went ablaze with bids. Chad was amazed. These people were crazy. The price climbed higher than the value Trent put on the package deal.

* * * *

Chloe couldn't believe Chad and Trent made such a generous donation. Yet the price the attendees were willing to pay surprised her more. When the bidding was done, the winning offer raised fifteen thousand for the shelter. The auctioneer moved on to the next item. She glanced to the neighboring table where Chad sat with Linda. His chair was empty.

She excused herself and exited into the foyer. She wanted to thank him, but what drove her to do it now? At that particular moment? Chad wasn't in the immediate area. She strolled further down the hall toward the restrooms and ballroom. Thinking he was in the restroom, she waited for him. Her stomach wavered. Was she there because she wanted to be alone with him? And why? Several minutes passed with no sign of him. The vein in her neck pulsated with the thought and excitement of being alone with him. She wasn't over Chad. Pushing the women's door with more force than necessary, the restroom door banged against the door stop.

Back in the hall she bent at the waist to smooth the taffeta skirt when two black feet stopped in front of her. Men's shoes. Slowly she straightened. Without four inch heels, her gaze met stunning blue eyes. Chad. Her heart drummed. Her breath quickened.

"We need to talk. Can you step away for a moment?" At first demanding, his voice softened to a plea.

"For a moment, yes." When she took Chad's hand in hers, memories came flooding back. Memories of her stay in White Sand Key, Florida. When their friendship turned into something more. When most of her time was spent with him instead of Maggie. At least she thought it was going to grow into more than just a few weeks lover's fest. "Let's sit over here. Away from the party."

"I don't want to sit. I want to hold you in my arms again."

She released his hand. Butterflies danced in her stomach. Butterflies of the good kind. Butterflies of the wrong kind. She shouldn't have these emotions and reactions with him. These are things she should experience with her fiancé. Damn it, why couldn't Andrew have escorted her to the fundraiser.

Maybe it's meant to be. Her innermost voice spoke. *Chad's here for a reason.*

"Chloe, there's no easy way for me to say this, but—" He drew near, and she allowed him to take both hands. "I love you. I made a mistake letting you go. Not coming to see you. But there are things I couldn't face here in Texas."

Yanking her hands free, she backed away. "You love me? How can you say this when I'm engaged to marry another man?" Her throat closed off. Breathing became difficult. She blinked rapidly several times.

"That's why I'm telling you now. I don't want to leave without you knowing that I made a mistake. That I love you. That I want another chance with you. With us." Slowly he approached her. "I haven't been with another woman since you. Coming here was the hardest thing for me and yet the best thing. I realized how much I've missed you, loved you and needed you in my life."

"Kiss me." She ordered before thinking rationally.

"What? Why?"

"Kiss me. I need you to kiss me." She stood before him. With gentle hands he touched her jaw, then slid them to the back of her head. Tender lips touched hers briefly. He'd barely finished with the kiss before he came back for another. The kiss was filled with desire. Passion. His hands wrapped around her waist. One hand held her tight while the other slid up her back. Her body warmed with his touch.

They held each other in a tight embrace. As the kiss deepened, her passion rose as his taut length throbbed against her leg. The warmth between her legs grew to a burning need and pulsated with want.

This couldn't happen. Chloe broke away. "I can't do this," her voice rasped between heavy breaths.

"You want me, just as much as I want you. Tell him the engagement's off."

"And what then? I'm not moving to Florida. I know you won't move here." She wasn't going down that road again. No games. Andrew was stable. He was here for her when Chad wasn't.

"What if I did move here?" He regained the ever so slight space she'd put between them.

"I'm not holding my breath. I won't break off my engagement." Gathering the skirt fabric, she turned and stalked through the corridor for the ballroom foyer.

"Chloe," his voice rose. "If I promised you I'd move home, would you break off your engagement and give me another chance?"

She stopped. "I don't know." She stood, staring at the floral carpet. Would she end it all for a man who once couldn't be at her side? Would she end it all to be with a man who made her feel alive?

His arms wrapped around her waist. A heavy breath whispered below her ear. "Say yes, and I'll call Trent tonight and tell him I quit. Say yes, and I'll move for you. Say yes, and make me the happiest man alive."

Chloe lifted her head. Andrew stood rigid at the end of the corridor in front of the ballroom.

Chapter Ten

Chloe stiffened in the embrace. Chad moved his head from her shoulder. *Shit!* Andrew.

Narrow eyes glowered with contempt as Andrew's mouth tightened into a stubborn line.

Chad removed his arms and stepped away from Chloe.

Four quick strides and Andrew stood in front of Chloe. He seized her upper arm with a strong grip. "Wait by the door." His voice was firm and frigid. Chloe's arm swung forward with enough force to propel her forward. His jaw clenched shut as the muscle twitched.

Chad's stomach roiled with anger. Memories of his father flashed into his mind. The strength of Andrew's grip on her arm was visible in the red fingerprint indents left behind. There would be bruises later.

"I don't know who the hell you think you are, *Mr. Rogers.*" Andrew spoke in grudging tones. "But keep your fucking hands off my fiancée." The tip of his shoe hit the tip of Chad's. Andrew looked down at him.

Chad didn't understand what good Chloe could possibly see in this ass. Adrenaline coursed through his veins. He wanted to act out against Andrew, but he needed to be a better man than this piece of shit.

"If your fiancée wants me to put my hands on her, I will. I don't like you or the way you treat Chloe, pushing her around. Or the effect you've had on her. She's too thin." Chad stood his ground and wouldn't let the asshole push him around. He'd been pushed his entire childhood.

"I treat her the way a woman needs to be treated. Her weight has nothing to do with me."

Chad glanced at Chloe whose mouth hung open with disbelief at Andrew's comment. The piece of shit had everything to do with Chloe's weight loss as he'd first suspected at last night's party.

At that moment, he wanted to shove Andrew and take Chloe out of the hotel. Away from the danger he saw in Andrew. But it wasn't meant to be. She stood there. Taking Andrew's crap—waiting for him to come to her.

"I don't know what you're doing here, but you need to leave." Andrew stabbed a finger into his chest.

"I'm not leaving." He stuck his finger into Andrew's chest, "Until I'm ready to leave."

Andrew flung Chad's hand away. "Don't touch me unless you want to mess with me." His icy tone could freeze alcohol.

"Is that another threat? Because I believe you touched me first. I'm not leaving and will protect the woman I love."

"Love?" Andrew's eyebrows shot up in surprise. "If you loved her, you would've been here, but you weren't, and I was." In a whisper he said, "That's right. I gave it to her over and over again. I rode her like a real cowboy, and now she rides me. Good night, *Mr. Rogers*." Andrew turned and joined Chloe at the door to the Grand Ballroom.

Chad's fists curled into tight balls. He wanted to swing out and deck the ass. The childhood Mr. Rogers' Neighborhood mockery of his name added to the fury. He needed to calm down. He couldn't let Andrew win. Fingers flexed in and out as he worked to compose himself. Andrew slid his arm around Chloe's waist, pulling her tightly into his chest. He said something to her before bending to deliver a kiss. A kiss Chloe didn't seem to want as she turned from Andrew.

If Chad returned to the ballroom, he would be sitting in close proximity to them. Hopefully his mother would understand if he remained at the back of the room. Advancing toward the foyer, he stopped at one of the high-top tables. He just declared his love to Chloe. Turned around and confessed his love for her to her fiancé. What the hell was he thinking? He wasn't thinking. That was the problem.

The door opened to the room, and his mother exited. "What went on out here?"

"Nothing. Why?" Chad held his tone, not wanting to lash out at his mother.

"By the look on Chloe and *Andrew's* faces, I'd say it *was* something. The tension is as thick as pea soup."

"I told her I loved her. Now she and Andrew know."

"What do you mean, *Andrew*?"

"I couldn't help it. He was being a big man—an asshole, and it slipped out. I won't let him hurt her." Chad held his tongue from stating, *like Dad hurt you.*

"He doesn't hurt her."

"Mom, if you saw the way he grabbed her arm and ordered her to go stand by the door..."

"Chad, not every man is like your father." She rested a hand on his arm. He relaxed his hand over hers. "Andrew's a good man and treats her like a lady."

"How do you know?" It came out snotty, and he cringed.

"She's told me about how he'll come by the office every once in a while and sends flowers. He loves her. I'm sorry, Chad."

"I don't know, Mom. Tonight I question her love for him and vice versa. But now she knows, and that's all I can do. We'd better go back inside. I'm staying in the back of the room."

"Probably a good idea."

Chad escorted her, going no further into the room. The auction portion of the evening neared the end as the auctioneer announced the final item up for bid.

* * * *

Chloe sat on a chair with Andrew sitting behind to the side. His left arm draped the back of her chair while his fingers danced across her skin. He delivered unwelcomed wet kisses on her bare neck, trailing to her right shoulder. His right hand rested on her thigh near her hip. On occasion he'd remove his hand to adjust the crotch of his pants. The fourth time he yanked at the crotch of his pants her head swung around. "Knock it off."

"I can't help it." He leaned into her ear whispering, "I want you. Let's go to the bathroom."

"You disgust me." She turned to face the front of the room when Linda returned to her seat. *Chad isn't with her. Did he leave?* He'd left her with a lot to ponder. Would he actually move to Texas for her? Could she, did she, want to give him another chance?

As if Linda knew what she was thinking, Linda tipped her head toward the back. Chad stood along the wall. He avoided Andrew. Or maybe he was avoiding her?

The auctioneer announced, "Would all bid winners go to the foyer to claim and pay for your items. The party's not over yet. We have various desserts over here," he swept his hand to the left of the room, "and the DJ will provide us with music for dancing. The cash bars are open again. Thank you, everyone, and have a wonderful evening."

"All right," the DJ announced in an over-enthusiastic voice, "Let's start with a slow one before picking up the beat." The Righteous Brothers, *Unchained Melody,* swooned through the speakers.

Andrew moved around the chair and grasped her hand. "I want you in *my* arms."

He yanked her from her seat.

A shoe caught in the skirt causing her to fall forward. "Andrew," Chloe scolded. "Give me a second." She lifted the dress, shaking the skirt, while checking for any rips. No damage done, she continued walking.

On the dance floor, he pulled her into a semi-secluded corner. His body pressed and ground against her. Without her four-inch heels, his hard-on hit her stomach. He bent to whisper in her ear. "You're not wearing the heels I like. That's okay. You can wear them with nothing else on Monday night." He ground his hips against her.

"I'm not wearing them because you weren't coming." She didn't care how cold her tone was with Andrew.

"I'll *come* later." His hardness poked her abdomen.

"You're revolting, Andrew." She wriggled in his arms. "Why do you talk like that? It doesn't turn me on. If anything, it turns me off." She turned her face away.

"Does *Mr. Rogers* turn you on?" Clutching her jaw with his hand, he used more force than necessary to turn her face to him. "You want that little blonde surfer kid?"

"Grow up, Andrew."

"Did you *fuck him* in the bathroom? Is that why you two were cozy in the hall?"

"No! I'm done with this conversation." She pressed hard on his chest and twisted at the waist. "Let go of me." Thankful for the loud music and the older generation's hard hearing, their conversation seemed to go unnoticed. Unfortunately though, when she twisted in his arms, they earned looks from those close by. She nodded with a curt smile.

"I'm not letting you go—ever." His tone escalated to a murderous falsetto, as his eyes narrowed with contempt.

"Don't threaten me, Andrew." Her voice may have been firm, but inside she quivered from his warning.

"It wasn't a threat, Darlin', but a statement." His voice was calm, but acid filled his tone like a leaking battery.

"I think you need to leave." She couldn't smell alcohol on his breath. For the first time, she questioned if he used drugs.

"I'm not leaving you here with *Mr. Rogers*."

"Stop saying his name like that."

"Like what?" The ironic smile on his face needed to be wiped off.

"You know like what. He doesn't wear a cardigan or host a children's show. He's more of a man than you."

He sneered. "I'm not leaving you here with *him*. I'm much more of a man than he ever could or will be."

The right arm wrapped around her waist pulled her tighter to his chest before loosening the hold for a moment. He spun her around quick and hard, drawing her back against his firmness. One arm across her chest and the other went across her hips. He forced her to bend at the waist as he gyrated against her.

Enough!

With all her strength, she deftly threw her body into an upright position. Her head hit Andrew in the throat. He released his hold. She turned, and he held his neck while bent at the waist. "Go home Andrew. I won't put up with this type of behavior. Not from you or anyone else." She left him hunched on the dance floor with the patrons viewing the whole thing as she exited the ballroom.

* * * *

Chad never took his gaze from Chloe and her fiancé. Tonight he witnessed what her future would be like if she went through with this wedding. Controlling. Verbal abuse. Leading to full on physical abuse.

Chloe exited from the far end doors of the ballroom. Chad followed. She disappeared into the women's restroom.

Without a care of who was in there, he stepped through the door. "Chloe?"

A woman standing at the mirror blinked with surprise. Her eyebrows raised, and a hand covered the 'oh' made by her mouth.

"Go away, Chad. I want to be alone." Chloe sniffled through a stall door.

The woman left them alone in the bathroom.

"I won't leave until I know you're okay. Did he hurt you?"

"No." More snuffling. "He just says and does dumb things."

"Will you come out of the stall? We're alone."

"I need you to leave."

Ouch!

"Before I leave I need to see you."

"Haven't you said and done enough tonight?"

Double ouch!

"I wanted you to know how I feel about you...about us." He stood a short distance from the main bathroom entrance.

"There *is* no *us*," she yelled, opening the stall door. "What don't you understand? I'm engaged to another man."

"That kiss we shared tonight…that wasn't a simple kiss, Chloe. You know as well as me that you still have feelings for me." He stepped closer. "And I still have them for you." Another step and he gathered her into his arms. "Tell me what you want, and I'll do it."

When she pushed against him, he released her. Chloe's beautiful brown eyes were dark and rimmed in red from crying, but no tears fell now. Her body straightened as she threw her shoulders back. Her hands fisted in front of her. With a steely gaze she said, "I want you to leave."

"Before I leave..." He narrowed the distance between them, sliding an arm around her waist. He slipped a hand on the back of her neck. He delivered a delicate kiss on her lips. As his lips began to depart, her mouth took fiery ownership of his. She still wanted him.

He couldn't offer her the plush life she lived—but plenty of love.

It was he who broke the seal—reacting to what he couldn't have. He walked to the door, clutched the handle, turned and looked one last time at the woman he loved. "I love you, Chloe."

Her silence was the final slap in the face. His heart ached. He needed to leave this place. The door closed behind him. He needed to leave the state. But he still had to talk to his mom and face the other demon of his past—his father.

* * * *

Chloe remained in the bathroom until she figured Chad left, and it was safe to exit. She couldn't and wouldn't return to the ballroom, yet couldn't leave. She *didn't* want to see Andrew again tonight. In a few short steps, she turned the handle to the other large room on the floor. With its clicking release, the heavy door gave way.

She entered a dimly lit room, leaning against the door. Smaller than the Grand Ballroom, it was set up for a meeting, with the tables situated in classroom formation. She approached the nearest table and sat on a chair.

No idea about how much time had passed, she startled when the door clicked and opened.

"Chloe?"

Linda.

"I'm ahead to the left. Sitting down." Chloe wiped under her eyes, hoping to fix any smeared makeup from crying.

"Are you okay? Chad left, asking me to check on you." Linda approached and sat next to her. "When I didn't find you in the bathroom or hall...Well, here I am. I saw what happened with Andrew." Her voice held a sympathetic sadness.

"I'll be fine. Is Andrew still here?" She lifted her head to face Linda, not wanting her to hold on to the sympathy.

"As far as I know he's gone. He left the ballroom and hasn't returned." With a pause she continued. "It took him several minutes to move from the dance floor to a chair." There was a smirk on Linda's face. Chloe's mood lightened. "Do you want to talk about *anything*?"

"Now you know Chad was the one I thought..." She couldn't finish. It hurt too much.

"Yes. I also know he loves you, and *you* now know how he feels. I know you love Andrew, and well, are engaged to marry him."

"Damn it! Why did he have to come here? Things were normal. I had forgotten about him, found someone who cared about me and moved on with my life...without him. Now he's back, screwing with my mind." Her voice jumped several octaves and cracked as tears promised to fall. "At least I thought I was over him. Now I'm questioning my engagement in favor of a man who couldn't commit to me. Who now says he'll do whatever to be with me. What am I going to do?" Tears flowed down her cheeks. Chloe swiped them angrily away with the tissues snatched from the bathroom.

"This is something you'll have to sort out for yourself, Chloe. You'll need to search your heart for what you want. You need to do what's right for you. Not what's right for a man—any man. That includes my son. Do you want to talk about what happened with Andrew?"

"He's changed." She lowered her voice, unsure how much she should tell. After all, Linda was Chad's mother.

"And you don't like the change, right?"

Chloe nodded.

"Do you love him?"

Chloe didn't answer. She no longer knew what her feelings were for Andrew.

"You have a lot to work through, Chloe." Linda stood. "I'll tell Chad you're fine and won't say anything else." Stepping away she asked, "Do you want me to verify Andrew has left?"

"No. I'm sure he's gone. None too happy though." She chuckled at the thought of him unhappy but quickly cringed with the consequence she'd face the next time she saw him.

"Okay. If anyone should ask where you are, I'll let them know you weren't feeling well and went to the bathroom."

"Thank you." The door opened, and Chloe added, "For everything."

"You're welcome."

Sitting in the darkness, Chloe realized there was a lot to consider and figure out. She had another day to spend with Maggie before she left. Then she'd focus on her feelings and life. Returning to the ballroom, she was thankful no one asked about what happened earlier.

* * * *

In his hotel room, Chad stripped out of the tux and took a cool shower. Mental mind games held a battle over Chloe in his head.

You should have never said anything to her.

I couldn't ignore her.

You should have never confessed your love to her.

I couldn't live my life without her knowing of my love.

You should have never kissed her.

I didn't force myself on her, and she responded in return—again.

The showerhead sprayed water on his neck and rolled down his back.

Lifting his head, he turned from the spray and lathered the soap before rubbing the bar over his skin. He rinsed and dried off. As he looked in the mirror the battle continued.

You can't offer her what Andrew can. You can't give her the finer things in life that she wants and deserves. She's a lady, and you're a tramp.

I can give her unconditional love.

You left your relationship with her because you couldn't go where she was...to the one place that haunts you. Can you avoid becoming like your father and what you see in Andrew?

I've already beaten the odds with the life I've led and by being here now.

He tossed the towel on the tiled floor, pulled on boxer briefs, turned off the lights and crawled into the oversized bed. The night's sleep was light as he tossed and turned. Thinking and dreaming of Chloe.

When he awoke and glimpsed the clock it read ten forty-five. He needed to relax before going to his mom's. He rolled over in search of the TV remote and the room service menu.

An early lunch ordered, he checked for messages on his cell phone. There were two. Trent hoped all went well with the auction. The other was Maggie wanting him to call. Hitting the call button, it took one ring.

"Hey, Chad," Maggie's bubbly voice answered. "How was last night?"

"Interesting." He couldn't match her mood but forced as much normalcy into his voice as possible.

"Interesting? Do you care to elaborate?"

"I told Chloe I loved her."

"And?" Her chipper tone changed to concerned friend.

"Let's just say I felt things again between us. She asked me to leave, and I did. But not before Andrew arrived." His blood pumped faster, remembering the way her fiancé handled her. "He caught me holding her and manhandled her. I wouldn't be surprised if she's bruised because of him."

"What did he do to her?" She didn't blow up angry, but was audibly upset.

"Why don't you talk to her?" He changed the subject. "The riding went over big at the auction. It raised fifteen thousand dollars alone." She gasped. "You should have seen the women taking the paddles from their husbands, trying to get the highest bid. I couldn't get over what these people were willing to spend on some of the simplest of items." He laughed as did Maggie, and it felt good. "When does your flight leave?"

"Tonight. I'm having lunch with Chloe before going to the airport. Trust me, I'll be asking her about last night."

"Have a good flight. I'll be back Monday night. Trent's picking me up."

"Sounds good. Bye."

Chad ended the call and clicked on the TV. Ten minutes later the food arrived. He sat in bed until three before getting ready to leave for his mother's. Chloe wasn't far from his thoughts. He was concerned for her well-being and wanted to right the wrong. The wrong he had created by not making more of an effort—an effort to talk to her and be with her. The wrong he created by not telling her why—why he avoided Texas. The wrong he created letting her go—go with another man.

Chapter Eleven

More accustomed to driving his pickup, Chad slid onto the leather seat of the rental Mustang. He brought up the map on the GPS and checked the volume for the turn by turn driving instructions. Brad Paisley's voice belted through the speakers as he tuned in a country station. His body ached from a sleepless night filled with dreams of Chloe married to another man and having children with that man.

Chad pulled out from under the hotel canopy and headed west on Tom Landry Highway for Grand Prairie. He inhaled deeply and slowly released the air, flexing tense fingers gripping the steering wheel. This would be the first family gathering he'd been to in more than seven years. He and Ryan were off to a new start, but he wasn't sure what it would be like today.

Taking the exit to 161, he headed south. As he neared West Main Street, he followed the crazy traffic flow before exiting for the side streets taking him to his mom's townhouse.

He parked on the short concrete drive and gawked with disbelief at the beautiful home she owned. His family's life changed the day she packed him and his four siblings into the two-door Chevy Chevelle, leaving their home on the outskirts of Waco. With a fresh black eye, fat lip and growing bruises on her biceps his mom had left his dad passed out on the couch with empty bottles scattered on the floor.

Chad shifted on the seat at the remembered pain he experienced with her. The night before they ran, his father used his belt on Chad's backside. He was five years old and didn't know what he'd done wrong. Now, he knew it was a beating for no reason other than being born.

The townhome was in a nice, quiet area, well-maintained with mature trees. When the doorbell chimed, his mother opened the door. "We need to talk," he said immediately.

"Is Chloe okay?" After last night, she was the first thing that came to mind to discuss.

They stepped into the house, headed to the enclosed patio off the kitchen.

"She's fine. She was in another ballroom. Would you like something to drink? I have ice tea, water?"

"Ice tea would be fine." He sat on one of the floral padded chairs.

"Are you going to see Chloe again? Before you leave?" she asked from the kitchen.

"I don't know...I think so." His mom set his glass on the table and sat down.

"You should. Say goodbye on better terms than last night." A hand rested on his forearm. "Feelings linger for you."

"I know." He took a deep sip of the tea, glancing through the screen of the patio with a heavy heart. "I've kissed her. She returned the kiss. Mom, I love her. But I'm afraid of becoming Dad...And I don't like what I see in Andrew."

"Last night shed a new light on my opinion of Andrew." Silence fell over the room as they drank. "Go to her, and don't leave until she hears you out. Tell her why you're so concerned about her marriage to Andrew. She knows about your father's history, but does she know you have doubts about yourself?"

"No."

"Tell her. Open up to her. If you love her and want any chance at winning her back, you need to open up. Be honest." She patted his arm.

He glanced at her and smiled. "Thanks for the wise advice. I will." Averting his gaze, he slowly turned the glass back and forth in the palms of his hands.

"What else is bothering you?" Her hand slid down his arm to the hand turning the glass.

A deep breath. "Ryan told me to ask you about my father. He said he couldn't talk about it and to ask you. What don't I know about him?"

Her focus turned to stare through the screening.

"Mom?"

"Your father and I had problems prior to my pregnancy with you." Her voice remained monotone. "I sought solace in talking about my problems with someone else. Over several months' time, we grew closer while things got more heated between your father and me." She got up and stood quietly by the patio wall. Her face was hidden from his view.

He remained silent, unsure of what he might hear.

"The other man was married, too. Had a beautiful family." Her voice brightened with the last comment, but returned to the drone voice. "After your father and I had a fight one night, he passed out. I called my friend, and he picked me up as I walked down the street, away from the neighborhood." She sniffled and raised a hand to her face.

Entering the kitchen, Chad searched for a box of tissue. He returned and offered her the box. Was she about to tell him what he was thinking? His dad wasn't really his dad.

"I had an affair with him. Your father found out. A month later I discovered I was pregnant with you. Your father wouldn't do a paternity test or admit there was a chance that you weren't his child. He wouldn't face the humiliation it could bring to him and his family." She paused for a length of time, and he gave her the time she needed. "Your father may not be your real father."

Chad touched her hand, swallowing the lump in his throat. "What about the other man? What happened when he discovered you were pregnant?"

She rested her hand on top of his and squeezed. "He moved. I believe your father threatened him. If you'd like to get a paternity test done, I'd understand."

"Do you know where he moved to? Is he alive?" Angst spoke heavy in his voice.

"I don't have an answer to either question. I can give you a name, but Chad," She faced him with red rimmed eyes. "You would only need to test with your father to know."

"I can't believe you had an affair, got pregnant and don't know who my father is." With his anger, his voice heightened. "Do you have any regrets about the affair? Did you ever think maybe Dad wouldn't have been such an ass if...?"

His mother sat crying in the chair.

"Mom. Mom, I'm sorry." He lowered his voice, kneeling on the floor in front of her bent head. "I didn't mean... Ah, hell. I'm the one to blame for Dad's anger. He hated me for my simple existence. Now I know why."

"Chad," her hand held his jaw, tipping it up to face her. She smiled through tear-filled eyes. "I don't regret having the affair. You are the best thing God ever gave me. No matter who your father may be."

"But because of me, your life was a living hell."

"You did not make my life miserable. Your...my husband did."

He carefully embraced her.

The man thought to be his monster of a father may not be his father after all. If he wasn't, did he want to know who his real father was? One step at a time. He would do a paternity test first.

* * * *

Chloe stretched. Her face scrunched at the soreness in her arm. "What the...?" she questioned in a low voice. "Andrew. He gripped my arm so tight." She rolled to her side, hugging an extra pillow. Last night was an eye opening experience. "Then to say he didn't have anything to do with my weight loss. Ha!" Andrew was a different person than when they first dated. The engagement brought on his obsession about her weight. Since the shooting, he'd become more moody. Chad's presence didn't help matters.

Her top teeth drew her bottom lip in repeatedly at the memory of Chad's lips touching hers. Remembering the words he spoke—love and second chances. She bit a little too hard on the next tug. Would he move to Texas for her? She loved Andrew. Didn't she? Why question the possibilities with Chad?

After their talk in the smaller ballroom, she had made sure Linda's car arrived. Then she excused herself from the party and strolled the short distance home. Her mind had been a mess, and falling asleep hadn't come easy. She released the hold she had on the pillow, tossed the covers aside and peered at the clock. Ten thirty.

"Good morning." Maggie greeted her from the kitchen.

"Morning." Chloe selected her coffee choice, set a mug on the platform and waited for the machine to brew her single hot beverage.

"So what's going on with you and Chad?"

Her stomach knotted. She opened the refrigerator door to avoid facing her friend. "Nothing."

"Do you still have feelings for him?" Her friend remained gentle in her questioning.

"And if I said I did?" She stood at the open fridge, looking at nothing in particular, nervous to talk openly about Chad.

"If you're attracted to Chad and don't deal with those feelings, it'll consume you for the rest of your life."

She leaned into the fridge, resting her forehead against a shelf. The cool air eased the sweat beading on her scalp. She licked dry lips.

"Do you want to tell me about last night?"

Her head shot up. "You talked to Chad?" The cold air receded when she closed the refrigerator door.

"Yes. I can see the marks on your upper arm." Maggie spoke calm and softly. "What happened? Be honest about what's going on between you and Andrew."

Chloe retrieved her cup of java from the brewing machine. She turned, leaned against the counter for support and faced her friend. "Andrew showed up last night unexpectedly. Chad was there with his mother." She played the situation down in hopes to keep herself calm.

"What about the bruises? Chad said Andrew grabbed you."

"Yeah, but I deserved it. I was in Chad's arms when Andrew arrived. Andrew didn't like what he saw and grabbed me by the arm. It's nothing." She looked away. "I'm hungry, and nothing looks good in the refrigerator. Let me get dressed, and we'll go grab something to eat."

"That sounds good."

Changed, Chloe took Maggie to a café she frequented with friends a block from her apartment. The conversation steered clear of Chad or Andrew as they walked. "You'll like this place. It's casual but upscale. For dinner they have the white table cloth, candles but it's business casual dress. Comfortable."

"If you like the place, I'm sure I will. Being pregnant, I'll eat pretty much anywhere."

"Here we are." Chloe opened the glass wood-framed door. Maggie stepped inside, and she followed, approaching the hostess podium. "Two, please."

"Very nice," Maggie stated with a genuine smile.

Seated at a table for four, the hostess cleared the other two place settings. Her friend refrained from changing the topic back to her relationship issues while they decided on what to eat.

As soon as the waitress left the table with their orders, Maggie seized the opportunity. "Tell me about Chad." Her cloth napkin disappeared under the table.

"He told me he loved me. That he made the mistake of not making more of an effort in having a relationship with me. He apologized. I told him to kiss me." As a form of self-distraction, she set her napkin on her lap.

"Why?"

"I needed to see if he still had an effect on me. I pushed him away. Said I couldn't do this. He makes me melt when he touches and holds me. I feel loved and cared for." Chloe's gaze fell to the wood table while her hands played with the table linen. The words tumbled from her mouth. "He wants another chance. Asked me to call off the engagement. Told me he would call Trent and quit."

"Damn." Maggie stated, wide-eyed in surprise. "He didn't tell me that part. I knew he told you he loved you, but to quit working at the ranch?"

She glanced into her friend's green eyes. "Maggie, how can I trust him? There's so much he's kept from me that I don't know."

The hostess strolled by with an older couple. Chloe eyed them holding hands. They stopped two tables away by a booth. The man politely waited for his wife to sit. A warmth filled Chloe.

"You're questioning your engagement, so what about Andrew? What are your feelings?"

The warm sensation faded. "He's changed, Maggie." Her voice turned serious. "Something's going on, and I don't know what it is. Before you arrived at the engagement party, I overheard a conversation between him and my father. Andrew didn't want to be at the fundraiser—nothing new, and my father said something along the lines of discouraging me."

"What does that mean?" Maggie's eyebrows drew together in wonder.

"Andrew wants me to quit working. The shooting was the first time he mentioned finding a different job. Then I overheard the conversation, and the next thing I know, he's telling me to resign. Let him take care of me. I told him I'm not leaving, and he dropped the subject."

As the hostess walked by with a group of men, Maggie lowered her voice. "What about the bruising? Has he done this before? Acted out with force?"

"Never." Chloe's voice hitched. She took a drink of water. It was the truth, but opening up and revealing her feelings was difficult. It didn't matter that she was talking to her best friend. "I blame his behavior on Chad's presence."

The waitress approached with their food. Not needing anything else, she left them alone.

"If Chad was truly willing to open up to you, quit his job, God forbid, and be here for you, would you break off your engagement?"

"Yes."

Silence came between them. Chloe thought for a moment about what she said—and said without hesitation.

"What would you be willing to do for him, Chloe? Would you move to Florida for him?"

The wood grain in the table garnered her attention. "I can't answer that." A finger traced a grain line.

"Why not? It's a fair question."

"Because I don't know." Her head snapped up to confront Maggie dead on. "I'd be quitting my job like Andrew wants. Then what's the difference?" She stabbed a fork into the salad, stuffing the oversized bite into her mouth.

"Has Chad ever said you wouldn't be able to work if you moved to Florida?"

Chloe finished chewing prior to responding. "No, but I like my job here."

"But if you *love* Chad, you could get another job in Florida."

"Chad could get a job here, too." Another bite, she chewed with more force than necessary, catching the inside of her cheek with her teeth. She winced.

"Not as easily as you could."

Chloe swallowed and sipped sweet tea. "You sure are pro Chad. What gives?"

"I'm trying to help you sort out your feelings. I can see you're troubled."

"I helped you in Florida, now it's your turn to help me in Texas. Is that how this goes?" Frustrated, she pierced the lettuce in the bowl.

"I guess so." Maggie hunched her shoulders. "You and I have known Andrew almost our entire lives. Do you love him because of the man he is? Or do you love him because of the family's expectations?"

Chloe chewed, contemplating the new questions. Was she in love with Andrew because of her parents? Did Andrew's parents persuade him to pursue her?

"I don't know the answer. I never thought our families could be involved in bringing us together."

"What do you love most about Andrew?" For the first time, Maggie bit into her club sandwich.

"He's stable and here."

"Interesting." Maggie swallowed. "Okay, same question about Chad?"

"You're mean."

"How is that mean? Answer the question." She took another bite.

"I could list a ton of things for Chad. I miss each and every one of them." Chloe turned away from Maggie's gaze. It felt good to be open and honest with her about these two men, but it weighed heavily on her heart.

Maggie swallowed. "I think you have your answer as to what you need to do."

"You make it sound so easy, and it's not. How can I trust Chad?"

"It sounds like you've already trusted him by giving him your heart. Talk to him. Ask him the questions you want him to answer. The questions you haven't asked."

"When did you become so wise?" She smiled wryly at her best friend.

"I wouldn't say I'm wise, but I learned a lot during your visit. I trusted you when you pushed me to date Trent. Trusting Trent and our relationship and the night I stood up for myself on the balcony against Kevin helped me grow. I've only grown more since then." Maggie's eyes welled with tears.

"Don't start crying." Chloe's eyes moistened.

"I can't help it. It's the emotions of pregnancy. Plus, I want you to do what feels right—in your heart."

"I have a lot to think about." She took a bite of salad.

"Chloe, you were there for me when I needed you. I'm glad I'm here for you in your time of need." Maggie dug through her purse, pulling a tissue to dab her eyes. "Remember, I'm only a phone call away. Whenever you need me."

"Thank you." She reached across the table, and the two women held hands. They were sisters by a friendship molded through the years.

"Thank you for putting up with my persistent questions and answering them. Honestly. Listen, I'm going to leave after lunch for the airport. I need to return the car and get through check-in."

"I'm going to miss you, but can't wait to visit after the baby's born."

"Me, too. I'm ready to deliver and have my body back. Don't get me wrong. It's been wonderful, but nine months is a long time." Maggie rested a hand on her belly.

"It'll be worth it. Hey, who's going to handle the lessons while you're on leave?"

"Being that I handle all the lessons, the clients were notified months ago that they would be suspended for several weeks. They've all been understanding. Chad and I have worked it out that they can ride during their normal lesson times if they wished. He'd be there to assist them."

"You two work well together then." Her mood sobered.

"Chad's been a great support, business partner and friend. I'd hate to see him leave."

"I get the hint." Chloe sipped cold sweet tea.

The waitress set the bill on the table. Maggie snatched the folder. "My turn to treat."

"Thank you. But not just for lunch, for pushing me to answer the tough questions."

"You have a lot of difficulty ahead of you. Call me. Even if I'm in labor. That would be a great distraction from the pain."

They laughed and left for the apartment. Upon entering the building, the attendant at the front desk caught Chloe and handing her a small floral delivery. She handed the vase to Maggie and took the card. They were from Andrew as she guessed. A meek, *I'm sorry*. No, *love you*. Simply, *Andrew*.

Chapter Twelve

Chloe packed a bag once Maggie left for the airport late Sunday afternoon. Andrew had said he would visit tonight, but she wasn't ready to face him. She had to get away to think. A decision needed to be made.

The car loaded, she left the apartment building behind and headed for the only place she could think of—home. She quickly realized that would be a mistake and turned around at the next available opportunity. Andrew would look there first. Her parents would ask questions. She drove back downtown but didn't go back to the apartment. Steph's place was out of the question because she was Andrew's sister. She couldn't go to any of her other girlfriends' homes because they knew nothing about the situation like Steph or Maggie.

Ten minutes passed, and her stomach growled. Chloe looked at the clock on the dashboard of her car. Eight-thirty glowed in the darkness. Andrew's car wasn't in the spare stall as she pulled into her parking spot. A positive sign. She returned her belongings to the apartment before going to The Knoll for dinner and a drink.

In a back corner booth that she waited over twenty minutes for, she nursed her second vodka cranberry while eating a juicy burger and French fries. The burger was so delicious, loaded with mayo, bacon, cheese and the other toppings. She ate the whole bun—top and bottom. Andrew would scold her if he knew. Swallowing her bite, she tossed back a gulp of her drink. Up until this past week Andrew had dominated her eating habits, without her realizing it. A large bite of her burger followed with some fries, she decided right then and there her eating habits would change. Tonight she'd have dessert.

The waitress weaved through the crowd and neared the table. Chloe asked her for a beverage napkin. She located a pen from inside her purse and opened the napkin. On one half she wrote *Andrew* and *Chad* on the other. Then she began listing:

ANDREW: successful, money driven, loves success and wealth, wants me to quit working

CHAD: self-successful, happiness driven, loves life, supports my happiness

When she finished writing the items on each list, the pen fell from her hand. She thought she had it all with Andrew, but the list showed she didn't. She savored the final bite of the greasy grilled goodness of beef. But how would she and Chad work things out? Would he leave everything to come to Texas? Was that fair to either of them? She remembered the conversation with Maggie earlier. Maggie stated how it would be easier for Chloe to get a job in Florida versus Chad getting a job in Texas.

Her waitress approached. "Can I get you anything else tonight?"

Without hesitation, Chloe said, "That chocolate molten cake thing."

"Lava Mountain Crunch?"

"That's the one." She delivered an enthusiastic smile. "Actually, can I get that to go? Is it possible to get two forks, too?"

"I'll be back with your check and dessert. I'll see what I can do about the forks."

She finished off her drink as her legs bounced with nervous energy, wondering if he'd be at the hotel. *Text him first? Nah, where's the spontaneity in that.* It was a night of taking chances. Taking chances that would alter the course of their history.

* * * *

Chad entered his hotel room after an enjoyable dinner with his family. He and Ryan got along without incident, bonding a little more. The shock of what his mother revealed about his dad possibly not being his biological father remained close to the forefront of his mind during the evening.

Who his father was became a priority. His laptop open, his fingers typed *DNA testing* in the search bar. He clicked from one site to another from the search list. A reliable, accredited company from multiple sources told his heart it was the right company to work with. He bookmarked the website to his favorites. He tapped his cell phone several times to make a call. "Hey, Trent."

"How's your Mom?" Trent asked with concern.

Voices in the background softened. Chad guessed he was watching TV.

"Good. She's home. Did Maggie make it home okay?"

"That's great news. Maggie's flight arrived on time, and she crashed in bed as soon as she could. The baby tires her out."

"Yeah, we didn't stay as long as I thought we would at the engagement party. Listen, I need to stay longer. Will that be a problem?" He roamed the room and stopped to glance outside. Nothing exciting to see, he continued strolling around.

"It shouldn't be. I'll make sure to have someone there to help Maggie. Is everything okay?"

"I've learned some information and need to take care of some things."

"Care to elaborate?" Trent pushed as a friend with concern. He had the right to know why he needed more time away from the ranch.

"My dad may not be my biological father." He leaned against the window frame, resting his forehead against the pane. "I want to get a DNA test done. I'm doing some research to see what needs to be done to do that. I think I've found a company but have more reading to do."

"How much time do you need?" A creak sounded followed by the sound of running water.

"I don't know. Can I touch base with you tomorrow when I've checked further into things?"

"Sure. How are you doing?"

"Honestly? Shocked." He pushed away from the window, stepping to the small table.

"Well, check in with me tomorrow night and take care of yourself." A swallowing noise filtered through line. Trent had gone to the kitchen for a drink.

"I will." Chad sat on the chair. "Hey! If Maggie, for some reason goes into labor, call me ASAP. I'll catch the next flight to be there."

"Will do. Catch you later." The voices on Trent's end grew louder as they disconnected.

He stared at his laptop. Research would wait until tomorrow. On the night stand sat the hotel's paper pad and pen sat. Chad snatched them up and sat back at the table. The first thing he noted was to talk to the front desk about keeping his room for a longer period. The next item on his list was to send his laundry out for cleaning. He hadn't packed enough for an extended stay.

Curiosity got the better of him. He opened the bookmarked DNA website on his computer. There were multiple options for testing. Ones needed for legal purposes, which at this time he wasn't seeking anything legal. They had a prenatal test which meant someone pregnant, and he hadn't fathered any children. They even had one for veterinarian testing for pets. The one that caught his attention was the at home testing. One click and he learned he wouldn't need to involve his dad. They had a siblingship DNA test. For this test they would use his mom, a sibling and his DNA to see if his father's DNA matched that of his siblings. He clicked on the red order button, filled out the form and entered his credit card number. The kit would be sent to his mother's house. Tomorrow he'd talk to her and Ryan about helping him, by being a part of the testing process.

Ryan was the only one who knew anything about their mother and father. Chad planned on keeping it that way. As far as what he'd do if his dad wasn't his biological father, he didn't know. This required taking steps—One at a time.

His cell phone rang. *Chloe?* "Hi. What's up?" He asked with caution since their last conversation together at the fundraiser had not turned out like he wanted.

"I'm in the lobby. Can I see you?" Her slight hesitation dissipated as confidence filled her voice.

"Ah, sure. I'm in 2045. Are you okay?" He grew concerned for her safety because of Andrew.

"Yes. I'm on my way." Confidence changed to energetic.

What was he in for? Why was she there? What could she want?

He turned the laptop off, quickly fixed the bed, put his suitcase filled with dirty laundry into the closet and closed the doors. In the bathroom he hurriedly brushed his teeth. As he spit, there was a knock at his door.

Anxious, Chloe stood with twitchy legs in front of Chad's hotel door. The diamond on her finger glared at her. Quickly she pulled the ring from her finger and tossed it into her purse. She loved Chad and wanted to make things work between them. But was he willing to make more of an effort this time around? He had told her as much last night.

The door opened.

Nerves filled her gut with butterflies. Her heart pumped ferociously.

"Don't stand there. Come in."

Through the door and into the room, his scent filled her senses. She closed her eyes and inhaled deeply. Clean, plain, simple soap. When she turned around, he was there. His hand slid behind her back while the other caressed the side of her neck under her hair. His azure eyes darkened to indigo, sparking a fire in her heart.

A ringing sounded from inside her purse. She dropped it to the floor. The call wasn't important. This moment, right here and now, was all that mattered.

The bliss of his work-roughened palms on her skin skittered gooseflesh across her body. He splayed his fingers into the nape of her hair before gently grasping a fistful and claiming her lips with his own. Her arm swiftly maneuvered up his chest to the back of his neck and into his hair. All the while in her other hand, the one wrapped around his back, she held the take out box containing the cake.

He drew away. "Does this mean—?"

She silenced him with a kiss, reaching for the dresser to set down the container. The other hand deftly dragged the hem of his shirt up and over his head, tossing it to the floor. *To hell with talking first.* "Chad, I want you...now." Both hands free, she worked to take off his pants, while he pulled off her top. Arms intertwined, they finished removing their own clothing.

Her eager heart raced as she stood before him in her lace panties and bra. He removed his underwear and shorts in one tug, standing ready for action. Roughened hands were like friction on her hips as tender kisses trailed along her collarbone. She quivered as he continued up her neck to her waiting lips. While they maneuvered onto the bed, she was keenly aware of his penis pushing at her panties. He guided her to lie flat on her back.

Her cell phone played the text tone assigned to Andrew. She smiled in pleasure because the man who loved her would soon be making love to her, and it wouldn't be Andrew.

Chad's hands yanked down the bed covering, with both of them using their feet to push it off the end.

She pulled at her panties. The lace kept a barrier between her and what she wanted—Chad. His hands finished the job and started another. She inhaled as fingers slowly penetrated. In and then out. Deeper with each touch. Her stomach quivered with his kisses. As he thrust his fingers deeper into her, his tongue tasted and teased. Her head pushed farther into the bed.

How long had it been since a man pleasured her instead of fulfilling his own desire? Not since the last time she was with Chad in Florida.

He continued to please until she couldn't take anymore. "Chad, now," she said breathy, while she fondled his shoulders to get his attention.

He planted a succulent kiss on her thigh. A wave of pleasure zinged to her core. His kisses continued to tickle her skin up to her collarbone where he stopped. Her back arched as he brought their bodies to become one.

Neither of them moved for a moment. They stared at each other with reverence. Chad's eyes were moist with tears sitting on the rims of his eyelids as her own eyes clouded. The pleasurable feeling of being one again was pure ecstasy.

He kissed her firmly. With a passion. With wanting.

"You...are the love...of my life." He drew his hips back and slowly slid within her between each phrase.

"I love you, Chad." She had to say his name. He had to know she knew this wasn't a mistake. He had to know she wanted him—now and forever.

He continued to slowly make love until she wanted more. "Roll over," she ordered huskily.

When he did as asked, she straddled him, slowly slid down his slick erection and arched her back. His thumb rubbed her clit, making her arch further and him thrusting deeper within her. Her moan matched his in depth. She leaned forward. He swiftly licked her nipple, and when he suckled the breast she thought she might melt from the fire of pleasure.

She nipped his ear, sat upright straddled over him and rode him until she came screaming. He clutched her hips, pumping between her slick folds. As his body shuttered with release, so did she. Two orgasms so close together was a new experience. One not to be forgotten anytime soon.

Chapter Thirteen

Chloe made the right decision as Chad held her in an embrace. Chad not only declared his love but cared about her well-being. By the list made last night at The Knoll, the one thing that stood out was Andrew's self-centeredness. Now came the hardest part—telling Andrew and her parents there would be no wedding. The engagement was over. Her mood sobered with the thought.

"Good morning." Chad said with a smile in his voice.

He wore a satiated grin as she faced him. "Good morning."

"We need to talk." Chad's serious tone wiped away her happiness.

"We do." She rolled, putting them into the spoon position.

"Don't turn from me." His tone was gentle. "I want us to look at each other. We have a lot to talk about."

He spoke the truth. She propped against the headboard. "I need to know if you meant what you said at the fundraiser. Would you move here if I wanted you to?"

"If that's what it takes, yes. I don't want to leave the ranch but will if that's what I need to do to be with you." He rested across her thighs. "You need to know why I never came to see you. You know much of the story because of my mother...but you don't know how badly my father scarred me emotionally." Sadness filled his voice as he sat up facing her. "I was afraid to commit to you and our relationship. I worry that I'll become like my father."

"But you never raised a hand to me. You've never been anything but kind and loving." She scooted to sit closer, placing a soft kiss on his shoulder. Her heart ached with hurt for him. "Why didn't you tell me?"

"I banished my past from my life, the reason for leaving the state of Texas and not returning. As to never raising a hand to you, we weren't together in an environment that would lend me any length of time to go that far."

"So at the fundraiser Andrew didn't piss you off? You didn't want to deck him?"

"You have no idea how badly I wanted to reach out with my fist." His face flushed with indignation.

"See, you're above your father. If you were going to be like him, you would've hit Andrew. You probably would've been more aggressive with me." With a nervous laugh she added, "I'm surprised you didn't grab me by the arm, taking me from the fundraiser. Away from Andrew."

"I wanted to." He stated it matter of factly.

"So what stopped you?" Her throat constricted.

He spoke softly. "You told me to leave."

Her chin dipped in shame.

"We're here now...together." With a light touch, his finger lifted her head up. "After you left Florida, I thought about buying you a ring and asking you to...but I was too afraid. I still have concerns because of my childhood. I saw so much abuse."

"But you weren't around it all your life. Your mother took you away from the danger."

"I know. That gives me hope. My brother Ryan and I are mending our relationship. Growing up, he wasn't compassionate toward me. I've resented him since childhood. I don't know if we'll ever get back the brotherly love you should have with your sibling, but we're on the road to becoming friends."

"That's good. He seems like a good guy. Then again, I only met him twice." Maggie had been right about the need for her and Chad to talk.

"Yesterday at my mom's, I learned my father may not be my biological father."

Chloe's mouth fell open with a gasp.

"My father forbid any testing while she was pregnant or after I was born. She doesn't know where the other man lives now. She didn't say, but I'm assuming he knew about her pregnancy. He moved his family shortly after she learned about her condition. She said my father confronted the guy and probably threatened him."

"So what are you going to do?" She grasped both of his hands.

"I ordered a DNA test kit last night. It will be done without involving my father. I'm staying in Texas a little longer until the samples are collected." He squeezed her hands and held a little tighter. "I need a sample from my mom, Ryan and myself. My other siblings don't know anything about this. For some reason my dad decided he had a right to tell Ryan about the situation. Ryan talks to him. I guess he watches out for him. You know, to stay on the straight and narrow."

"I talked to Maggie. Or should I say Maggie grilled me." She smiled because their conversation proved to be a good thing. "She brought up some to-the-point factors which led me here last night. I'm breaking my engagement to Andrew."

"Do you want me nearby when you tell him?" The concern in his voice couldn't be missed.

"No, you need to be as far away as possible. He's not going to take it well, as I don't think any man would, but if you're around...I'm guessing it would get ugly."

"When are you going to talk to him?"

"I don't know." She let go of his hands and rested back on the bed. "I need to talk to my parents first. For sure by the end of the week. Chad, I'm going to need time and space ending things with him. He's been part of my life since childhood, and for the last year he's been an even bigger part. I hope you understand."

"I do. This past week, seeing you with him, was the hardest thing ever. I hated him. I hated myself even more." He knelt beside her. "Chloe, you are the best thing to come into my life." Cupping her face, he kissed her lightly on the lips. "I was a fool to let you go. A fool for not bucking up and facing my fear of coming home to Texas."

"Have you met with your dad?"

"In light of this new information, I'm going to wait until I know whether or not he's my father for sure. We'll go from there."

"One step at a time."

Chad chuckled. "I've been telling myself that all week. We have a lot more to figure out about where we go from here, but shouldn't you be getting ready to go into work?"

"I guess I'm going to be late today." She pushed him back and straddled him, gliding her perky nipples up his chest. "I want you one more time before I have to leave."

He thrust his hips, pushing his erection deep to claim her body. It was his for the taking. Like the spider and the fly, Chad captured her heart in his beautiful web.

* * * *

"Why are you ringing the doorbell?" Linda asked, opening her front door. "I knew you were coming. You can come in any time."

"You taught me too well, Mom." He stepped through the doorway and gently hugged her, mindful of her shoulder in the sling. "How are you feeling?"

"Good. I can't wait to get back to work though. This sitting around is driving me crazy."

"I'm a bit restless, too." They entered the kitchen.

"Can I get you something to drink?"

"Your sweet tea would be great." He sat waiting for her.

She poured the tea and joined him on the patio.

"Mom, I ordered a DNA kit to be delivered here. I hope that's okay." He sipped the cool tea.

"Of course. So how does the test work?"

Ice clinked against the glass as he set it down on the table. "I'm not sure exactly. But I'm going to need DNA samples from family. I was hoping you and Ryan would be willing to give samples."

"You know I will, and I don't see why Ryan wouldn't help." She slowly rested back against the chair, careful of the wound site. She appeared more relaxed with her shoulder and arm.

"I'd ask Angel, but with Ryan being the only one to know about this, well, he was the first sibling I thought of."

"Have you asked him?"

"Not yet." His mind swirled at everything that happened within the last several days. With what he learned yesterday about his father and Chloe showing up at the hotel, he couldn't focus on anything else.

She picked up the cordless phone and dialed. "Well, no time like the present."

"Thanks." Chad sipped tea while looking through the screened window. The nervous energy wiggled his foot side to side. He turned at her voice.

"I'm fine. I'm sitting here with your brother—Chad." She involuntarily smiled at him. "Good, but we need you to do something for him—He's going to need a DNA sample from you for a test.—Yes. When the test kit arrives, will you help him?" His mom patted his hand. "That's what I thought. I'll give you a call when we know more. Stay safe.—I'll tell him, and I love you, too. Bye, Ryan."

"That sounded like he doesn't have an issue with it."

"No problem at all. He's glad you're going to find out. He said to say hi to you."

Chad stood and sauntered to the screened wall. "Chloe came to my hotel room last night." He stared out to the small green back yard. "She's breaking off her engagement to Andrew."

"What?" Linda exclaimed. She touched his forearm.

Chad jumped, startled by his mother's stealthness. "She told me she wanted us to work things out. I told her I'd quit working at the ranch and move to Texas if that's what it took, but that I'd prefer not to." In a moment of silence, the ceiling fan whirred above them. He worried about what kind of job he could find in Texas that he loved, yet be able to support Chloe's lifestyle. He faced his mom. "We didn't get the chance to talk through the details of what we're going to do, but *everything* is out in the open. There aren't any more secrets."

"Oh, Chad," she wrapped her arm around his waist, "I'm so happy for you two. I hope you can make it work."

"We will. If I need a place to—"

"You know you are more than welcome to stay with me." Her arm slid away, and she sat back down. "Are you two planning on getting married?"

Chad joined her at the table. "I don't know. She's breaking an engagement, so I'm sure she doesn't care to commit and announce another one." He took a gulp of tea.

"Will you tell me if you're going to ask her?"

"You'll be one of the first to know." He held his mom's hand as he changed the topic to her shoulder recovery and therapy.

* * * *

Chloe sat in her car parked on her parent's driveway. She had called from the office Monday afternoon to arrange some time to talk with her parents, and her mother invited her to dinner Tuesday evening. Taking a deep breath, she stepped from her car and entered the house. This would be easier than telling Andrew.

"Hello?" she called entering the house.

"In the kitchen," yelled her mother.

She took a few calming breaths, strolling to the back of the house to the kitchen. "Hi, Mom." She greeted her with a smile and a kiss to the cheek. "Dad home?"

"Not yet. Don't worry, he'll be here. He called to let me know he was sitting in traffic. He was in a lovely mood." She exaggerated as she rambled on, dashing spices into a bowl. "I don't understand why he insists on going into the office every day when he could work from home."

"It smells good. What are we having?"

"Barbequed ribs, a potato dish, corn, salad and coleslaw. I'm so glad you called. We need to discuss your wedding. How did dress shopping go with Maggie? Did you find your dress?"

Chloe's stomach knotted. Her heart beat kicked up a notch. "Shopping was interesting. I didn't know what I wanted, but my assistant was fabulous and helped me narrow it down." Not able to trust her legs to keep her upright, she sat at the marbled counter top on the high backed bar stool.

"Well, when do I get to see the dresses you're contemplating?" She opened the oven door and placed the pan of potatoes inside.

"I'm not sure." She didn't want to talk about anything wedding related. "Maggie looks so good for being in her final month."

"She was radiant at your party. Being pregnant definitely agrees with her. And that young man who escorted her, what a handsome gentleman." She drew a hand to her chest in a dramatic fashion.

"Mom, he's the same age I am."

"Well, you're young, too. What was his name?" She picked up a spatula, waving it around as though she could conjure up his name.

"Chad."

"That's right. And you went to college together, and he works with Maggie?"

"Yes. His mother runs the shelter. She's the one who was shot." She hoped to switch the topic away from Chad, steering clear of revealing things without her father present.

"Oh, no," her mother gasped, touching Chloe's hand in an empathetic gesture. "I'm relieved it wasn't you who got shot."

"Thanks, Mom." Her eyes rolled in disgust at her mother's lack of compassion. "Linda, Chad's mom, is okay by the way."

"There is no need to act like a snotty teenager."

"Sorry. I didn't mean to. I'm a little stressed. I'm going to go sit outside for bit." Her legs stable, she stood.

"Can I fix you a drink?"

"Only if you'll have one with me, and come relax on the patio." Chloe strolled outside to sit on a chaise. The evening sun sat below the tree line, delivering some relief from the heat. The grass in the back yard was trampled from the engagement party guests. She sighed at the thought of telling her parents the news.

"I made us Mojitos." Her mother handed her the drink before sitting at the patio table. "You seem to be a little on edge. Is everything okay?"

Chloe took a long slow sip of her drink. "I'll be fine after drinking this. It's just been stressful with the shooting at the shelter and the past weekend full of events."

"How was the fundraiser?"

"*Very* successful, considering a big donation for the auction fell through. But Chad, Trent and Maggie put together an awesome package that raised an amazing amount." The Mojito hit the spot as she swallowed.

"That was generous of them."

"Here are my two lovely ladies," her father said, opening the patio door.

Her mother immediately stood, greeting her father with a kiss. "I'll be right back with your drink, Dear. Dinner should be ready in fifteen minutes."

"So," her father took the chair her mother left. "I hear you need to talk to us. Andrew's not here, so I'm guessing you're not announcing you're pregnant."

"Dad! No! I don't want kids yet." *At least not with Andrew.* "How's work? The shelter didn't get the grant. I read the email on Saturday."

"I'm sorry. I would've voted for you if I could've."

"Thank you, Dad. If we don't apply, we can't get the grant monies. There are others out there. I was just telling Mom about the fundraiser and how well we did. The money raised will help the women and children who need the safety the shelter offers."

"Safety? I thought there was a shooting there not too long ago? Maybe you should think about a new line of work. Or don't work at all. Andrew can support the two of you once you're married."

She gawked in disbelief. Adrenaline coursed through her veins as she wanted to raise her voice. This was no longer an issue. Her jaw clenched tight. Andrew wasn't a part of her life.

"I need to use the bathroom before dinner." Chloe snatched her drink from the table, making it slosh within its confines. She stalked into the house. There her mother, Susie Homemaker, prepared their meal— the picture of who her father thought she should become. *No way in hell!*

Chapter Fourteen

Chloe sat at the kitchen table closest to her mother who sat at one end and her father at the other. They finished their meal as she finished her second mojito. "I asked to speak to you both because I have made an important decision regarding my future."

"You're quitting your job," her father interjected with a grin.

"I'm breaking my engagement to Andrew. The wedding is off." Solid, yet quickly, she spoke.

"Like hell it is!" Her father pushed his chair back and stood defiant. "You will marry Andrew, and if we need to make it a fast wedding, then so be it."

"Robert," her mother's voice was stern. "Sit down, and lower your voice." She faced Chloe. "What is this all about? Why are you calling off the wedding?" Although the caring mother side was asking the questions, there was a conceited tone to her voice.

"I don't love him." Chloe stated firmly, changing to a softer tone. "My heart belongs to someone else. Did you push Andrew to call me after I returned from visiting Maggie? Did you bribe him, Dad?"

"I mentioned something about calling you." Her mother's voice was low.

Her head jerk in disbelief from her father to her mother, who stared into her plate, hands under the table, sitting rigid.

"No, someone's pushed him." She spoke tersely. "I didn't go out with him until several months later."

Her mother's meek voice spoke. "I did. You were so unhappy, and you two live close to each other. I wanted to see you happy again." Diane lifted her gaze with tears in her eyes. "And you are happy."

A phone rang, and her father answered his cell. "Give me some good news." Stepping from the table, he strolled into the family room. "Damnit, find out where the money's going. Call Lockhart and get whatever reports you need from him." His voice drifted as he stormed away further into the house.

The women sat quietly at the table.

"Mom, I can't marry Andrew. I'm *not* marrying him." Chloe kept her voice low.

"What happened? Something had to happen to cause you to end this suddenly. Now, just like that, you're calling it off?"

Dinner gathered at the base of her throat. She swallowed hard. This was her mother. She should be able to tell her everything.

"Talk to me. Has Andrew done something?"

"I can't deal with you and Andrew right now." Her father huffed, entering the room. "Diane, deal with your daughter," he barked before disappearing.

"I've never seen Dad this angry about work. What's going on?" Concern for her father flooded Chloe.

"I don't know, and you're not getting off the subject of your impending wedding. Why are you calling it off?"

Chloe went to the wine refrigerator and pulled a bottle of Chardonnay.

"You're not answering me." She heard the irritation in her mother's voice, but Chloe remained silent.

The wine open, she poured two glasses, setting a glass in front of her mother and the other on the table. She pulled her sleeve up as she sat, revealing the bruises on her forearm. "These are from Andrew. They're not the first."

Her mother didn't say anything but stared at Chloe's arm. She slid the sleeve down. Took a sip of wine. "Mom, he's gotten possessive. Sunday night he was at my place, but I didn't go home. I didn't want to go home to him. He showed up Saturday night at the fundraiser, and his behavior was disgusting. We argued, and in the end, I hit him in the throat."

Chloe drank more of her wine while her mother remained quiet. "He was waiting for me when I came home late Monday morning." She swallowed the lump in her throat. "He asked for my cell and when I handed it to him, he grabbed me by the arm with force. Shoving the phone in my face, he yelled at me about not answering and responding to his text." Her vision blurred with tears. She swiped them away and took a sip of wine. Her mother's silence grated on her. "I can't marry someone who's becoming what the women at the shelter are seeking protection from."

Her mom's touch was soft on her hand. "He's not abusive, Chloe. He simply used too much force. He won't harm you. He'll be a good, loving husband." Her mother's tone was even and sounded almost programmed. The Stepford Wives came to mind.

"Are you not listening?" Chloe's voice cracked on a strained high note. "I'm not marrying him. It's over." She stood, slammed the remaining wine down, snatched her purse, stomped out of the house and got in her car.

She sat in the driveway several minutes, breathing heavily from the anger flowing through her body. "Well, that didn't go as planned. Far from what I expected."

Not comfortable with going back to her place, worried Andrew would be there, she located her phone inside her purse. Two voice messages and multiple text messages from Andrew. She read the text's and responded, *'Sorry. At my parents and left my phone in my purse.'* Next she listened to the voice messages. One was Chad wishing her a good evening with her parents. The other was from an upset Andrew. He wouldn't be available for the next several days because something had come up at work, but would see her Friday evening. Friday evening she would tell Andrew the engagement was over.

Relief washed over her like a downpour rushing through a gully.

* * * *

Wednesday afternoon Chad and his mother sat on the screened patio when the doorbell rang. "I'll get it." Opening the door, he saw the FedEx man strolling back to his truck after leaving a package on the doorstep. "Thanks," he hollered and waved to the guy.

In the kitchen he pulled his key out, cut the tape and opened the box. "Mom, the kit's here." He took the package to the patio, located and read the instructions.

"Well, what does it say?"

"Pretty plain and simple. We use the swabs included, swabbing the interior side of our cheek. Seal the swab in the included tube and mark the tube with the appropriate name. Then mail them back to the company." He glanced in the box, and the future stared back at him. But what would that future be? Only one way to find out. "Are you ready to do this?"

"If you're sure this is what you want, then yes, I'm ready." She touched his hand. "You need to know, no matter what the result is, I love you."

He was silent for a moment. "Who do you want to be my father?"

"It doesn't matter, Chad. God gave me you, and that's all that matters. Now let's take care of this, and call your brother." A tear streaked down her cheek, and he gently swiped it away.

They took their cheek samples, and then his mom called Ryan.

"He said he'd be by within the hour. It's close to dinner time. How 'bout I fix us something?" She got out of her chair and stood in the patio doorway.

"Nothing big. Can I use your computer?" He stood. "I need to book a flight home now that the testing will be finished."

"What about Chloe?"

They entered the house. "We'll talk more tonight. But I need to get back to work at the ranch. With Maggie getting toward the end of the pregnancy and all, I'll be picking up some more duties. Don't worry. I'm not letting go this time."

"Glad to hear that. My laptop's in the living room on the coffee table."

He sat on the couch, pulled the cell phone from his pocket, and while the laptop came to life, he waited for Chloe to answer. He tapped the keyboard, and the airlines reservation page popped up.

"Hi, I'm glad it's you," Chloe answered with happiness tinted with sadness.

"You okay?"

"I'm fine. Can I see you tonight?"

"Actually, that's what I was calling about. I'm booking my flight home as we speak. The DNA test arrived, and we're waiting on Ryan now."

"Will you leave tomorrow?" There was apprehension in her voice.

"Are you sure you're okay?" His knee bobbed in anxiety.

"I told my parents last night, and it didn't go the way I thought. I don't want to talk over the phone." She sniffled. "And now with you leaving...I'm worried."

"Don't worry. Will you stay the night?"

"You're questioning? Of course I'm staying with you. There's no other place I'd rather be."

"I'll call you when I get back to the hotel. Should be there in about three hours. Mom's making dinner. Can't pass up a free home cooked meal." He chuckled.

"I'll be waiting."

"I love you, Chloe."

"I love you." She couldn't hit END fast enough because he heard her cry.

Tonight he'd get to the bottom of why she was crying. Could she be reconsidering calling off the wedding? He shook his head and made his return flight reservations, forwarding the information to Trent. The plane would touch down in Florida at dinner time, which could be sticky for Trent. He could always take a cab back to the ranch.

The front door opened, and Ryan stepped in wearing a suit. "Hey, Chad."

"Are you working?"

"Just got off. Smells good. Mom in the kitchen?"

"Yup. Thanks for doing this." There was still a distance between them, but they were talking, and that was a big step.

"Hey, it'll be nice to have an answer. I'd want to know."

"Thanks. Let's join Mom." Chad walked side by side with his brother into the kitchen.

One step. Two step.

* * * *

Chloe knocked on the hotel door, and when Chad opened it, she ran into his arms and cried. Not what she wanted to do, but her parents' reaction was more than she could handle alone.

"Hey, don't cry. I'm here. Tell me what happened with your parents." He embraced her and spoke softly in her ear. "Let's sit. Unless you'd rather lie down?"

"Just hold me. Tell me you love me and that things are going to work between us." The worry had eaten at her all night and day.

She followed him to the bed where he fluffed the pillows. Gently, he guided her by the hand to join him.

"Chloe, I'll do whatever it takes. I've already told you. I love you, and I'm not letting you go anywhere but with me this time. Now, tell me what happened with your parents."

Chloe relayed last night's events while lying in Chad's arms. At one point, he went into the bathroom and got the tissue box for her. When she finished, they both remained silent in each other's arms.

"So you didn't tell them it was because of me that you're ending things?"

"No, and I think that's best for now." She propped on an elbow. "Are you okay with that?"

"Yes. They need to get a good handle on the fact that you're not marrying who they wanted you to. Eventually you'll be able to tell them. I'll wait until you're ready. I love you." One hand slid behind her neck while the other went around her waist, drawing her to him. He delivered a tender kiss, but she wanted all of him.

Her hand fumbled with his belt buckle. "Make love to me." The kiss was possessive this time. No tenderness with his lips, but his hands were another story, and her body warmed from wanting him. Her shirt flew across the room, and she straddled him, deftly pulling off his shirt. Fingernails trailed through chest hair to catch on his belt buckle. With both hands free, she was able to undo the cumbersome buckle. She finished the job of getting his jeans off, tossing them to land at the end of the bed.

The table turned when he flipped her on the mattress and slowly removed her pants. Seductively trailing kisses down her stomach and thighs, he slid her panties off. Her heart beat accelerated with each kiss, and when his tongue slid between the labia, she cried out a moan of desire. When his fingers joined his tongue in the foreplay, her back arched, and heavy breathing filled the room.

She grabbed his shoulders, trying to pull him up. She wanted him in her now. His fingers continue working their magic as he kissed his way to her neck. Reaching her ear lobe, the head of his throbbing cock slid in and out of her wet folds, teasing and pushing her to the edge of orgasm.

"Let it go, Chloe." The warm breath and softness of his voice in her ear was all it took. She clutched the bedding, and as she came, he pushed his hips into hers and brought them both the release they wanted.

As she cried, out of pleasure, he said, "I love you, Chloe."

She kissed him and returned the endearment. But this didn't solve the biggest problem in their relationship—distance.

Chapter Fifteen

Held in Chad's arms, lying under the covers, Chloe asked, "So how are we going to work this? You and me. Two different states. We've tried this, and it didn't work." Hiding her worry wouldn't do them any good.

"I'll need time to wrap things up in Florida with the ranch and the business." His demeanor was calm. She knew she made the right decision. "Depending on the timing, you can either come out for a visit to see the baby, or I'll come visit you."

"I'll come to you. It will be good to get away for a weekend or longer." She propped herself up on his chest.

"What about living arrangements once I move here? Do you want to stay in your apartment, or should we look at homes?"

"I want to find a place of our own," she stated quickly, excited at the idea of them owning their own home. "Maybe we could find something close to your mom and siblings." Her fingers wandered through his chest hair. She liked that he didn't follow the trend so many young men did of manscaping. A man, a real man, had hair on his body, excluding the back.

"Are you sure?" He snared her hand in his. "That takes you further away from your parents."

"Consider it a compromise for you moving home." She kissed his chest, while warmth filled her own. "What about a job? It could be tough getting a house on my income alone."

"I'll find something. With my business major and the riding business at the ranch well under way, that will look good on the resume.

Maybe Trent will let me remain as part owner. I can do some of the work online."

"In the interim we'll stay at my place. Unless my parents kick me out." Sadness and worry replaced the warmth of moments ago. She rested her head on his chest, listening to the steady beating of his heart. And Chad was steady. Chloe didn't feel that way when he first arrived, but he had changed. *They* had changed.

"They wouldn't, would they?" Concern, not panic, filled his voice.

"I do have a signed lease with them, but that could be broken if they really wanted me out. Or they could deny me a renewal in seven months when the contract expires. Hopefully we'd have a place of our own by then." She lifted her head wearing a gleeful smile.

"Depends. We need to get a loan approval, find a house and then close before then. Not to mention, I need to find a job."

"Let's not worry about it until the time comes." Feeling satisfied with where they were headed as a couple, she changed the subject to learn more about how things were going with Ryan and the others. "So, things must be going *well* if you're willing to come back." She rested against his chest.

"We had a good time talking over dinner and catching up. Ryan and I are taking slow steps every time we talk. It's good. We're both healing. The results of the DNA test are another step in the right direction."

"How are you feeling about the test? Do you want it to go one way or the other?" These were questions not only for Chad's sake but for their relationship. From now on they had to be honest and open with each other.

"Who do I want to be my father?" His voice pondered the question.

Lifting her head she nodded.

"I bounce back and forth when I think about it. It's so hard because if my dad isn't my dad, then I become an outsider to my family. Yet I don't have to claim the asshole as my father. If the other guy is my father, the question of whether or not to go looking for him comes up. And if I do find him, what do I say? Would he even want to know? If my dad is my father, then I can move forward, and well, do I want to confront him with the truth? Do I want *anything* to do with him? I've done all I can. It's time to sit and wait for the results. Then I'll go from there." His hand skated down her back, resting on her naked buttocks.

A wave of goose flesh covered her body from his light touch. She shivered. He held her closer to his warm body.

"Has Ryan brought your dad up in any of your conversations?"

"We talked a little about him tonight. He's living in a small apartment outside of Dallas and works on a factory line. It's not much, but he's kept clean, Ryan says."

"I know your sisters and other brother are married, but what about Ryan?"

"I thought he was, but when I was at the hospital, my sister Angel informed me that the wedding never happened." He paused. "Um, his fiancé called it off."

"Oh." The last bit explained his hesitation. She propped herself to stare upon him. "Does he know about me? I mean us? He knows who I am, but does he know about us being a couple?"

"No, I didn't bring it up, and he didn't ask about you."

"When you do talk about us—and me—please don't bring up my breaking the engagement with Andrew. It could bring up a sore spot with him." With an inward laugh, she thought of all people, she should be the one to speak on the subject. She was about to do the same thing. Although the demise of her engagement had plenty of merit.

"Okay, I won't. Not that I was planning on telling anyone anyways. Have you told Andrew yet?"

"No." Her gaze fell to his chest as guilt filled her own. She resumed fondling his chest hairs. "I thought I mentioned I wouldn't until the end of the week?"

Chad shook his head.

"He's busy with work stuff this week. Said he'd see me Friday. I'm telling him then."

His finger gently lifted her face.

She saw the question in his eyes. "Don't worry. I'm not going to stay with him. It's over between me and him."

"I'm not worried you won't end things. I'm worried about *you*. Will you be okay alone with him? Maybe you should be in a public place when you tell him."

133

"I'll be fine. But I'll take your suggestion into consideration." She kissed his chest.

Chad slid from under her and got out of bed.

"Where are you going?"

He approached the little refrigerator. When he turned around, his luscious mouth wore a devilish grin while holding a takeout container. "Someone left this the other night. I thought about eating it all by myself, but saved it instead. Would you care to have some delicious chocolate dessert?" He waved the container in a teasing manner.

"And then some." She winked, patting the bed for him to come and sit.

* * * *

Chad waited at the curb for Trent to pick him up at the airport. The flight was miserable due to leaving Chloe behind in Texas. Not to mention the task ahead of him. He didn't know whose task would be harder, his or Chloe's. The more he thought about it on the plane, the more he worried about Chloe telling Andrew. Maybe he should've stayed.

A honking horn jolted him back to reality. Trent parked along the curb. Opening the back door to the four door pickup, he tossed his bag in before hopping onto the front seat. "Thanks for picking me up."

"Not a problem." Trent carefully pulled into the flow of traffic. "So when do you get results back on the DNA test?"

"A couple weeks."

"Wow. So soon?"

"Yup. How's Maggie?" He tried changing the topic to brighten his melancholy state.

"Fine. Are you anxious to get the results back?"

"Don't know if anxious is the right word. I just want an answer so I can move forward. What did Maggie have to say about her time in Texas?" Chad didn't know how to approach the subject of leaving, so he tested the waters to see how much Trent knew about what happened.

"She told me you and Chloe had a couple of run-ins with each other. Said you two are screwed up. Mind explaining for me?"

"Chloe is breaking off her engagement, and I'm moving to Texas," he blurted.

"What?" Trent exclaimed glancing at him. "You can't be serious?"

"Dead serious."

"Ah, shit." Trent slammed the steering wheel with the palm of his hand. "Maggie's right. You two are screwed up."

Chad stared out the passenger window while Trent focused on driving. The only sound in the truck cab was Jason Aldean on the radio.

"It's not like I planned this to happen. It just did. You didn't help sending me to that penguin party."

"Penguin party?"

"The engagement party," he stated using his *you-dumbass-you-should-know* voice. Sometimes when he heard a woman use that tone, he thought of the Valley Girls in California because they'd throw in a few 'likes'.

Trent laughed. "Oh, I get you. The tuxes."

"It's not your fault. Even if you would've been there for the party, I still would've seen her at the hospital." His voice faltered at the memory of seeing his mother at the hospital. "It's as though fate stepped in, wanting us to reconnect. I'll stay as long as you need me to. I was hoping I could possibly stay a business partner, at least with Maggie and the riding business. I could handle the finances and manage the website from a distance. I want to remain active if I can."

"Hell yeah! I don't have time for taking over for you. Shit, Maggie will have her hands full with the baby *and* the business."

The relief that escaped his lips as an exhale didn't last long. "I still need to find a job to support me and Chloe. As much as I'd like to go to work on a ranch, the drive would be too long back and forth. Looks as though business suits are in my future."

Trent turned his way wearing the biggest shit eatin' grin. "You'll look purty in a polyester suit."

"You ass. Thanks. And they don't make polyester suits anymore. It's a blend of shit, I think."

"Wouldn't that smell?"

"What are you talking about?"

"A suit made with a blend of shit. I would think that would stink to high heaven."

Chad shook his head at Trent, and they broke into a rage of laughter.

Trent wiped his eyes. "Damn, that was funny."

"Sure was. Listen, let me tell Maggie the news. Hopefully Chloe won't beat me to it. I forgot to tell her not to say anything."

"She's all yours. I don't want to be anywhere around her when you do. Her emotions are all over the map. Mix that with her feistiness...damn, you're in for a hurt of trouble."

"Oh, thanks for the confidence. Do you mind if I swing by the house tonight after dinner?"

"Nope. I'll text you when we're finished. Then maybe I'll go to the stables. You know, check on something—to escape the wrath of Mama Maggie."

When the laughter died a slight somberness fell over Chad. He would miss his friendship with Trent. Sure they'd talk on the phone, but sometimes you needed to go and grab a beer at the local bar.

* * * *

The text arrived on Chad's phone around eight o'clock that Trent and Maggie were finished with dinner. As he strolled along the path in the cooling mid-August air, Chloe came to mind. Tomorrow night would be hard for her. He wished he'd stayed, but he needed to get back to the ranch. They had a business to run. Leaving the Triple R was going to be tough, but at least Trent was willing to let him stay on long distance.

Hopefully Maggie would take it as well as her husband had. It was a two-way street for her. She had wanted to see he and Chloe fix things, yet she didn't want him to leave. The fact that Andrew was a friend pulled her in a different direction.

He crossed the gravel road. Trent and Maggie sat poolside. "Evening," he offered with a cordial smile. "Maggie, can we talk?"

"Sure." She relaxed on a lounge chair the girls used for tanning.

"I'm going to check on the horses." Trent's words stumbled as he stood.

"What's going on? He knows something I don't know," she said as Trent strolled toward the stables.

Chad let out an audible sigh as he sat on the chair Trent evacuated.

"Is your mom okay?" Maggie moved to an upright position as quickly as her pregnant body would allow. "Did something happen to Chloe? Tell me whatever you have to say without my husband around."

"Relax. Everyone is fine. I'm moving back to Texas to be with Chloe." Chad watched for her reaction and was met with a blank stare. "Maggie, did you hear me?"

"You're leaving the ranch? What am I going to do?" She was calm. Almost too calm. She turned to face the stables, quiet again. "I need you—but Chloe gets you."

This wasn't the reaction he was expecting, considering what Trent had said on the ride from the airport. "You're handling this far better than I thought. Chloe is breaking off the engagement. She told her parents already and will be telling Andrew tomorrow night."

"How did it go with her parents?" She whipped her head to face him with great curiosity filling her green eyes.

"Not very well. Her father told her mother to handle the situation as he took a call. Her mother proceeded to tell her that she and Andrew would work things out. Chloe showed her mother the bruises on her arm, told her how he's changed, and her mother pushed it to the side as though it were nothing. They'll be in denial for a while."

"When are you leaving?" Her voice was monotone.

"Don't know. I'll stay as long as I'm needed and a replacement can be found." He stopped when her eyebrows furrowed. "Are you okay?"

"Fine. Just a contraction." Quickly she stated, "A Braxton Hicks contraction. Trust me, if it was the real thing, I wouldn't be this calm."

"Is that why you've been so calm through this whole conversation?"

She beamed. "Yes and no. I'm glad you two have figured it out that you belong together. I'm not happy that she's taking you away from me and the business."

"Oh, I'm staying on long distance. I'm going to be an active partner from Texas. I'll come back as often as I can. Maybe I'll eventually persuade my beautiful girlfriend to move here and live close to her best friend."

A giddy smile filled Maggie's face. "I'd love to have her here, but it is what it is. I'm not going to ask any questions about your relationship with Chloe. Just let me know what I can do to help."

"You can count on it. Thanks for taking this so well. I'm not leaving my business partner high and dry. I'll be around for as long as she lets me stay."

"Good news all around." She slowly sat up. "I'm getting chilled. Think I'll go in. If you wouldn't mind letting my husband know, I'd appreciate it."

"Will do. Good night, Maggie. And thanks again for understanding," he said as she waddled to the back entrance of the house.

* * * *

Chloe entered her apartment Friday evening. The cardboard box sat on the entryway floor. Andrew's belongings were packed inside. One small royal blue box sat on the marble kitchen ledge. The ring was his. No one had noticed the honking stone ring missing from her finger at work. All for the better though—for now. The questions would eventually come, and she'd be prepared.

She picked up Kung Pao Chicken on her way home. Setting the brown bag on the ledge, she placed her briefcase and purse on the floor behind the large couch. In her room, she changed into loungewear. She'd be comfortable for tonight's confrontation. That was exactly what she was expecting with Andrew—a confrontation.

Back in the kitchen, she prepared a plate of food, turned the news on and sat at the table. Although she was dressed comfortable, she was anything but. What to say to Andrew had occupied her mind all day. The anticipation of how he'd react also consumed her thoughts. She found little comfort eating her Chinese food.

Her phone chimed as she finished eating.

'On my way over. I've missed you. Wear something sexy for me.'

"We'll see how sexy he finds my loungewear." She couldn't respond, and he wouldn't question her lack of reply. She finished the final few bites of Kung Pao with satisfaction. Andrew would smell it and say something about her weight. To hell with him. She did another sweep of the apartment, making sure she hadn't missed any of Andrew's stuff. He didn't need an excuse to come back.

In the bedroom, she heard the key in the door. Her heart banged against her chest. Breathing became difficult. She sat on the edge of the bed, closed her eyes and took several deep calming breaths.

"Chloe," Andrew's raised voice called.

Her heart didn't slow its tempo, but breathing came a little easier. She stood straight and strolled into the living room.

Andrew turned. "You had Chinese? I told you no more." He stepped in front of her. "And *why* are you wearing that?" His lips snarled. Waves of disapproval rolled over her. "Don't bother changing. Just take it off." He slid off his tie. "You're better off naked for what I'm going to do to you." He wiggled his eyebrows with a seductive grin.

When his hands began unbuttoning his shirt, she raised her hand. "No, don't take off your shirt."

"Whatever you say, Darlin'. I'll give it to you any way you want it."

As he closed the slight gap, she sidestepped him and went to the other side of the kitchen counter.

"I don't feel like playing games, Chloe. I want to bury myself deep in you. *Now*." He raised his voice and then just as quickly, softened his tone. "So, come give me what I want."

"No—"

"No?" His temper flared. Within seconds he held her by the arms. "You've denied me any action for over a week, and I've been nothing but understanding."

Understanding? She scoffed to herself. *I don't think so.* She swallowed. Fear threatened to make her cower to his nastiness. But in that moment, she thought of the women in the shelter and Chad's mom. She wouldn't let him push her around.

"No," she yelled. "*You* have *not* been understanding. It's over between us." She yanked free from his grip and snatched the blue box. "It's over, Andrew. The wedding is off." Her hand holding the jewelry box slammed into his chest. "Take your ring and box of belongings, and get out of my life."

The small box fell to the floor.

He seized her biceps and pushed her into the edge of the counter. "You're *fucking* Mr. Rogers."

Her skin prickled as her nerve endings pinged at the acidic menacing tinge in his voice. His grip tightened on her arms. Could she get free from him if she tried?

"Your silence reveals the truth. I should've taken him out when I had the chance." He leaned against her, and his voice grew husky. "Give me what I want, and I'll leave you alone." He bent his head and kissed her possessively.

She deftly lifted her bent leg, and her knee connected with his groin. "Give me your garage access card and apartment key," she screamed as he dropped to the floor coughing.

He reached in his back pocket, pulled the card from his wallet and tossed it to the floor.

"Where are your keys?"

He coughed, reaching into his front pant pocket and threw them on the floor.

She snatched the keys from the floor. Locating the apartment key, she quickly maneuvered it around and off the ring. She tossed the keys to him, stormed to the front door, opened it and snapped, "Get your shit, and get out."

Slow to stand, the small blue box disappeared into his suit coat pocket. The muscle in his jaw twitched. He picked up the box and as best he could, strutted past her into the hall. He offered a coy smile. "I'm not giving up so easily. He'd better be prepared for a fight." He turned, strolling toward the elevators.

Quickly she closed the door and locked it.

She stood against the door, taking several calming breaths before shrugging her shoulders up and back. She tilted her head side to side before slowly rolling it around to attain a further calm. With her key back he couldn't get in her apartment. *He won't do anything crazy.* Their families have too much affluence in the surrounding communities. If he becomes a problem, she'd call the police.

Chapter Sixteen

Chad worked on putting his resume together when Blake Shelton's *Doin' What She Likes* interrupted his train of thought. It was Chloe's new assigned ringtone. "Hey," Chad answered, his body tingling like a teenage boy. "How are you? I miss you."

Met with silence, his gut twisted. The he heard the sniffles.

"Chloe, honey, I love you. Are you okay?"

"I'm fine. I wish you were here."

"I'm here, talking to you. I know that's not the same, and it's not what either of us wants, but I'm here." God, how he wanted to be there for her. To hold her and comfort her. "Have you told him?" He didn't need or want to say Andrew's name.

"He just left."

"He didn't hurt you, did he?"

"Yes...No...He just grabbed my arms tightly and yelled at me. I'm okay."

"What did he have to say?" There was more to this than what she was saying. Getting angry at Andrew would do nothing to help comfort Chloe.

"He said some nasty things about you and me and that you had a fight coming. He's not going to let me go that easily, he said."

"Chloe, does he have a key to your place?" He couldn't hide the grave concern from his voice.

"Not anymore. I managed to get it back from him." There was a sick disturbing short laugh. "I kicked him in the balls to get it though."

He cringed as an imaginary pain hit his testicles. "Ouch. I'm sure he deserved it."

"Yes." Her voice filled with an undeniable anger.

Her anger struck him, and he forcibly asked, "What was he doing to you?"

"Chad, I'm okay."

"What was he doing?" His voice rose in anger.

"I'm okay." She didn't want to tell him. "He held me tightly by the arms and tried to kiss me. He's gone, and I'm okay."

"I don't want you to be alone with him *anywhere*. Do you understand?" The worry got the better of him.

"Chad, calm down. I don't plan on seeing him again. Okay?"

"Be careful. Have you talked to your parents again since the first time you told them?"

"No." There was regret in her voice. "Maybe I'll go see them this weekend. I don't know. Maybe I'll just stay home and veg out."

"You do what you feel is right. No pressure from me. Have you talked to Maggie?"

"No. Why?" Her tone was a mix of excitement with a tinge of worry.

"I told her about us. She's happy but sad to see me leaving. I'll be staying involved with the riding business though."

"Well, that's good for everyone." Her voice softened. "I love you, Chad."

"I love you, too. I'll be there again as soon as possible."

"And I can't wait to have you here with me."

* * * *

On an overcast muggy Monday, Chad scooped a pile of manure and stepped to the stall gate, tossing the waste into the cart. The young woman from two weeks ago that he'd seen with the bruises was back. Her wrist was in some sort of a brace, her eyes were circled in an all too familiar ugly golden yellow, and she wore long sleeves that he'd bet hid more bruises. She quickly strutted past him and approached the stall where Maggie waited with the horse readied for the lesson.

Maggie had asked him to help her prepare the horse for the next lesson. It was unusual for them to do this prior to the rider's lesson, as learning how to properly bridle and saddle your horse was a part of the lesson. Now he thought he knew why. Maggie knew of the woman's situation and in a sense was protecting her from Chad.

Anger flooded through him. The horseshit in the stall took the brunt of his fury as he scooped the manure with more force than needed. A shovelful missed the cart, splatting against the wall.

"Damn it!" He scanned the barn to see if anyone heard him. Thankfully the women had left the area. "Something needs to be done about this." His jaw clenched tight.

He worked through the day, unable to get the young woman out of his mind. Eventually an idea came to him, but he'd have to talk to Maggie first. See what she thought. Then talk to Chloe.

The last rider of the day exited the barn. Chad approached the stall where Maggie waited for his help. "Can I ask you something?" He released the surcingle on the saddle.

Maggie maneuvered carefully around the backside of the horse with the bridle. "Of course."

"The woman earlier this morning, you know the one with the bad wrist and marked eyes?" He waited for an acknowledgement but didn't get one. "She's telling you they're accidents. Right?" He removed the saddle and came out of the stall to face Maggie. She wouldn't look at him which he took as confirmation. "You know her injuries aren't from falling. You know she's being abused."

"She's fragile, Chad. This is her escape. And I don't want to take that away from her by asking a bunch of questions and confronting her about the abuse."

He raised his hand to stop her from continuing. "I want to do something."

"Chad, there's—"

"I don't want to confront her and solve her problems. You're right about her being fragile. I can see it in her eyes how afraid she is of me. Me—being a man scares her. I want to do something for those who have taken the step to seek help and have gotten away from those who have abused them. You said the words yourself. This, the riding, is their escape."

"Chad, that's the most wonderful idea." The baby belly bopped his stomach as her arms reached to embrace him.

"The problem is I don't know how. What do we need to do to get a program running for these women and maybe their children who have been affected by this?"

"I know who would know how...and so do you." A mischievous smile slowly filled Maggie's face as she spoke.

"I'll approach her tonight with our thoughts. Let's finish here."

They both maneuvered into the stall. Chad finished removing the tack, and Maggie took to the mare with a currycomb.

* * * *

The weekend of staying at home and relaxing was the prescription Chloe had needed. Going back to work though was a bit of a struggle. She found it odd not wanting to go to the office but pushed it aside. At work, when the floral arrangement arrived before ten with an apology from Andrew, she immediately knew why she didn't want to come in today. The card was tossed in the trash, while the vase sat on a table in the corner.

A text message from Andrew binged and flashed across her phone at lunchtime. *'I'm sorry. I want to work this out. Let's talk.'*

She tapped the address book icon and deleted his information. Good-bye and good riddance. Steph's name fell below Andrew's. Chloe tapped the keyboard, *'Any plans for dinner? We have A LOT to talk about.'* and hit Send.

A response came two hours later. *'No plans. Where and what time?'*

'Seven and you pick the place.' Chloe hoped it would be close to home because she'd have a drink or two tonight. It wouldn't be easy telling her friend...and ex-fiancé's sister...the wedding was off. But she wanted to be the one to inform Steph, *not* Andrew.

'Two Guys and a Bar'

Three blocks from her building. *'Perfect. Walking distance.'* Plans in place for going out lifted her mood. Yet how would Steph take the news? Their friendship was stronger than Steph's sibling relationship.

The ride home wasn't pleasant due to a three-car accident that shut down the freeway, forcing her to take back roads. She barely had enough time to freshen up before meeting Steph.

Chloe entered the bar and glanced around in search of Steph. The dim lights at the entrance made it difficult to see. The neon lights around the main bar and the low hanging lights above the tables helped as she strolled around. The patrons talked loudly over the top forty pop/rock music blasting through the speaker system. Someone yelled her name. She spun around. Steph sat in a booth with her arm raised.

"I'm glad you called." Her friend embraced her. "You said we need to talk so I thought a booth would be best."

"Thanks." She scooted across the leather bench seat to sit in the middle. "Sorry you had to wait. There was an accident making me divert to the side streets."

"No problem. Hope you don't mind I got a drink."

Chloe shook her head, as she would've done the same thing.

"So what's going on?" Steph's eyes widened, intrigued.

"Let me get a drink first."

Steph waved down a waiter.

"Evenin'!" A hunky young man stepped to the table. "I'm Bobby. I'll be servin' you lovely ladies tonight. What can I bring you all?"

Bobby's tight black tee shirt left nothing hidden. Well-defined arms exposed from under the short sleeves and tight abs rippled under the blackness.

"I'd like a Miller, chips and salsa and buffalo bites to start with."

"I'll be back with the beer."

The nice backside of Mr. Bobby in his tight jeans had her raising an eye-brow as she faced Steph. "I think you need to get his number."

"Let's see how the night plays out. He's not bad. You must be hungry."

"Yes, and something to munch on since I didn't have dinner. And not bad? Are you looking at the same guy I am?" Chloe surveyed the crowd.

"Okay, your drink should be here shortly. Tell me." Steph reached both arms across the table as though in desperation.

There was no other way to tell her friend other than to just say it. "I'm not marrying Andrew."

She was met with Steph's laughter. "That's a good one." More laughter.

"I broke it off. Told him Friday night." She stated it with the best deadpan voice she could. "I don't love him."

The laughter stopped.

"You're serious."

"Yes. Dead serious." Chloe held her left hand to show she no longer wore the diamond ring. Brawn Bobby approached, and she moved her hand to her lap.

"Here's your beer with the chips and salsa. The rest will be out shortly."

"Can we get two shots of tequila," Steph asked, still in shock.

"Anything in particular?"

Steph muttered, "Top shelf. I want the best for this."

"You got it." Brawn Bobby maneuvered through the crowded high top tables toward the bar.

"I don't want tequila, Steph."

Steph's head gradually turned. A wide-eyed stare landed on Chloe.

"Steph, you're not saying anything?" Next to Maggie, Steph was her closest friend. She hoped for strong support from her. Someone to talk to.

She blinked a couple of times as her head slowly moved side-to-side.

"Well, now you know." Chloe took a swig of beer before dipping a chip into the salsa. "I told my parents Tuesday night. That didn't go as I planned. My father proceeded to tell my mother to handle it as he took a call. My mother is in denial. She is telling me to give it time."

Bobby approached with the two shot glasses. "This is Don Julio Real. The bartender says you ladies should appreciate the smooth flavor."

"And what might those flavors be, Bobby?" Chloe asked to spark a conversation in hopes of getting Steph a phone number.

"He said it has vanilla flavors with a subtle, oaky finish."

"Thank you."

Brawn Bobby left, and she raised her shot glass. Steph lifted hers. "To new beginnings." They tossed the amber liquid down and swallowed. "Wow! Not bad at all. Nice."

Steph set her glass down. "So Chad won."

Is that disappointment in her voice?

"Yes." She scooped salsa onto a chip and ate it.

"Tell me there's more to this. He's my brother. He's a good guy."

Her friend struggled with the news but understood because of her history with Chad. "There is." Chloe told her about the events that took place at the fundraiser, leading up to her decision to call off the wedding.

"I can't believe Andrew would behave like that. Get that physical. But if you say he did, then I believe you."

"Here's your buffalo bites. How was the tequila?"

"Nice and smooth," Chloe answered with a cordial smile.

"Can I have another shot, Bobby?" Steph leaned on the table toward him.

"Did you want another?" he energetically asked Chloe.

"Sure."

"I'll see you two in two." Brawn Bobby disappeared into the crowd.

"Steph, if people ask, tell them I changed my mind. Plain and simple. Okay?"

"Yeah, I don't want to explain things."

They munched on the chips and salsa until Bobby arrived with another round of Don Julio shots. "So why the top shelf tequila? There's a story behind this."

"We're celebrating her reconnection with an old boyfriend," Steph spat.

"Oh." Bobby sounded displeased. "What about you?"

"No permanent fixture in my life." She popped in a buffalo bite.

Someone yelled out Brawn Bobby's name four tables down. "Excuse me, ladies. I'll check back with you in a short while."

"I think he's interested." Chloe picked up her shot glass. "Here's to love." She tossed back the liquid.

Steph drank her shot. "When Chad showed up at the engagement party I could see it in your eyes. I tried to divert his attention from you, but he wasn't interested."

"You hit on Chad?" Chloe exclaimed, taking a long pull from her beer.

"A couple of times, but he didn't want me—he wanted you."

When Steph met Chad that first night at The Knoll, Chloe saw the signs then, and it bothered her. "How far did it get between you two?" Her eyebrows drew inward with concerned curiosity. "Be honest with me." She grabbed another buffalo bite.

"It doesn't matter—"

"No!" She choked down the bite. "It does matter, Steph. I have a right to know."

"Chloe, he loves you."

"Don't protect him or yourself." She paused a brief moment as her stomach knotted with a possible realization. "Oh, my, God! Did you sleep with him?"

"No. He kicked me out of the hotel room before anything happened."

"So things did get hot and heavy?" A queasy sensation filled her gut. She closed her eyes.

"Yes. But Chloe, he couldn't go through with it. We only kissed and did a little groping. He told me to leave and said he couldn't do it. I continued to seduce him, but he locked himself in the bathroom. So I left."

Her head had hung in disbelief shaking to and fro until she heard the last parts of what Steph told her. She looked to her friend. "He locked himself in the bathroom?" She took a long sip of beer.

"That's what I said. Listen Chloe, he loves you. Don't make a bigger deal out of this than what it is. You were engaged to my brother at the time. Chad was free to do whatever he wanted."

"Okay, I'm done talking about this. Let's talk about the salon. How's business?" Like a piston, her leg pumped up and down, working out the nervous energy from hearing this new information about her good friend and Chad.

As Steph filled her in about the salon's business, she finished eating the buffalo bites and her drink. Wondering about the time, Chloe dug in her purse, glancing at her phone. The screen lit up, showing it was well past ten along with several messages from Chad. The phone fell somewhere into the interior of the large purse. "I'm going to settle my bill. Do you mind if we leave?"

"No, I don't mind."

"Thanks."

They paid the bill, and Steph left her name and number with Brawn Bobby. Steph drove her home the few blocks, dropping her at the curb. She waited to call Chad until she was in her apartment.

"Chloe! Where have you been? Why didn't you answer any of my texts or calls? I've been so worried about you." Chad spewed as soon as he answered her call.

The kitchen stove light and a light in the corner of the living room dimly lit the dark apartment. She kept it that way as she plopped onto the leather sofa.

"Chad, breathe. I'm okay. I'm sorry. I was out with Steph, and my phone was in my purse. I couldn't hear it over the loud music and people. As soon as I saw your messages, I asked her if we could leave." She kicked off her shoes.

"I'm sorry." He spoke calmly. "What did she have to say?" his tone curious.

"I'll get to that later. I told her everything when I got to the bar."

"And?"

"She couldn't believe I called it off at first. She jumped on you being the reason right away, before I told her about her brother's behavior. She understands why and agrees that I shouldn't stay with him." She wanted to let go of the incident between Steph and Chad but couldn't. The inside of her head swirled. Resting her head back onto the cool leather, she closed her eyes. "Steph told me about the two of you."

A heavy release of breath came through the line.

"Chad, as upset as I am about this, it happened when I was with someone else."

He sniffled several times. She knew he was crying.

"You didn't sleep with her which is why I'm not angry at you. But why didn't you tell me?"

The line was quiet. "What was I supposed to say? And when should I have told you? Would you have believed me if I'd told you that I was making out with your friend but then kicked her out of my hotel room?

After I confessed my love to you? You wouldn't have believed me. You wouldn't believe it until after confronting Stephanie...I know you, Chloe...I know you so well, I'm willing to give everything up for you...My love for you is that strong."

It was her turn to cry. "You're right. I wouldn't have believed you. I more than likely would've been furious at you. I love you."

"I love you, too. I'm so sorry. I shouldn't have let my emotions carry things as far as they got with her. But I was so upset about you...us...that I acted like a fool. Please forgive me."

"I already do. Let's talk about something else. Did you hear on the DNA test?"

"Nothing on the test yet. Hey, I was trying to reach you because I need your help with something."

"Okay." Chloe listened as Chad spoke about the abused rider, the talk with Maggie and how they both thought of her to be the one to turn to for help. "Wow, that's ambitious. I want to be a part of making it happen. Let me do some research and pull some information together. I'll come for a visit, and the three of us can sit down and go over things."

"When can you be here?"

"I need time, Chad." She giggled at his eagerness. "I'll send you my flight info when I make arrangements."

"Okay. Have you heard from Andrew?" There was bitterness and anger in his voice.

"No." Chad didn't need to know about the flowers or text. If he showed up on her doorstep, then she'd tell him. "Stop worrying. I love you."

"I love you. Goodnight."

The call ended, she went to the kitchen to jot some quick notes about reaching out to the women's shelters in the surrounding areas of the ranch's location. If distance or mobility were an issue, what would the possibilities of taking the horses to those in need? Chad had thought of this wonderful opportunity, and he was asking *her* to be a part of it. Warmth filled her heart.

Chapter Seventeen

A knock sounded on Chloe's open office door.

"These arrived for you." The receptionist smiled, setting the arrangement on Chloe's desk.

"Thank you," she said as the administrator left the room. Rolling back her desk chair, she snatched the tine holding the card and tossed it in the trash. She set the vase next to the other one on the table, shaking her head in Andrew's stupidity.

Around noontime a bing sounded on her phone. No name but the all too familiar number that had been deleted yesterday from her phone book. A message from Andrew. She ignored the text.

The day passed slowly as did the drive home. She poured a glass of wine and fixed a light meal. It would take time to break the light eating habits Andrew had instilled upon her. Finished eating, she sat on the couch with her laptop, searching flights to Florida and booked her trip. She called Chad.

"Hey, how are you?" he asked concerned.

"I'm good. I'm flying in on Sunday," she stated excited. "I should land around five. Is that okay?"

"It's perfect. Call me when you land. Will you email me your flight info?"

"As soon as I get confirmation I will. I miss you and can't wait until Sunday. I love you." She smiled at the thought of being in his arms again. Not to mention being with her best friend.

"I love you."

Saying their goodbyes, her phone beeped, signaling an incoming message. She tapped the MESSAGES icon. Andrew. With a swipe of her finger, the message was gone.

* * * *

The end of the work week arrived, and the text messages from Andrew hadn't stop coming. Sometimes he'd leave a random voicemail. Floral arrangements arrived around the same time every morning that week. Each time the tine and card were thrown away unread. Chloe stopped keeping the arrangements in her office, placing them on various staff members' desks. The first question was asked yesterday afternoon, carrying over throughout the day.

"So many flowers. You must have done something to deserve them?"

"I noticed you're not wearing your engagement ring."

When she told co-workers she ended the engagement, thankfully no one pushed further as to why she broke things off with Andrew.

Tonight she was going to her parents for dinner. She hoped it would be better than the last time when she informed them the wedding was off. Feeling better about her decision and the upcoming trip to Florida, she doubted anyone could dampen her mood.

The drive to her parents was slow due to the rush hour traffic. She relaxed and enjoyed a leisurely ride. Two hours later she turned onto her childhood street. She wanted to offer her children the same kind of childhood she grew up having, with neighborhood kids to play with, making lifelong friendships and stability in the home. One home. No moving from here to there and there to here.

She rounded the curve and turned onto the driveway. Her brother and sister were there. Was this a blessing or a curse? Chloe parked behind Nicole.

When she entered, voices floated from the back kitchen area. "Hello." She strolled into the kitchen. "I finally made it. Traffic was terrible."

"I didn't have any problems." Nicole piped in. She worked and lived about five miles from their parents.

"Be quiet, Nicole. Maybe someday when you join the grown-up world and live further from Mommy and Daddy, you'll know what we're talking about."

"Thanks, Michael. But Nicole has a great job, and it's not as though she lives with her parents." Chloe wrapped an arm around her sister's shoulder. "She chose to stay closer to home, unlike you and me." She fingered a section of Nicole's short black hair. "When did you add the purple? I like it."

"Thanks. A couple weeks ago. Needed to add a little more edge to the cut."

"You achieved the look."

"It looks stupid if you ask me," Michael added to their conversation.

Both Chloe and Nicole yelled at him, "Well, no one asked you." They faced each other and burst out in laughter. It felt good to laugh and be with her siblings again.

"Michael, go see what your father's doing. Let him know your sister's here."

"Okay, Mom." He vacated his stool and left the room.

"What's for dinner?" Chloe asked, sitting next to her sister.

"Steak, baked potatoes, steamed veggies. Need I say more?" She sliced the vegetables while they talked.

"No. Sounds great. Is there a reason we're all here tonight?" Chloe's curiosity got the better of her. Her mother was up to something.

"Your father and I thought it would be nice before we get into full swing with the wedding planning."

"Mom!" Chloe threw her hands in the air. "There isn't going to be a wedding. Nicole, come with me." She pulled her gaped-mouth sister from her stool. Dragged her upstairs to what used to be her old room. "Close your mouth. You look stupid," Chloe said as she closed the door.

Nicole sat on the bed. "What was that about?"

"I broke off my engagement to Andrew over a week ago." She paced the room, angry at her mother.

"No way." Her sister's eyes widened. "This was—"

Chloe stood in front of Nicole. "Mom and Dad aren't accepting the news that it's over, I guess. I won't be marrying Andrew, so whatever you do, *don't* encourage her."

"What happened?" Her sister's immaturity showed with the enthusiasm behind the question.

"My heart belongs to another man." Chloe shuffled to a shelf displaying various pictures. "Plus, something's happened to change Andrew. I don't want to go into details."

"Who's the other guy?" At twenty-six years of age, Nicole managed to act like a teenage girl getting her friend to spill the details.

One of the framed pictures caught Chloe's attention. It was a picture of her, Maggie, Michael and Andrew dressed for prom. She flipped the frame face down with enough force to shake the shelving before answering Nicole. "You met him at the engagement party. He was with Maggie."

"Oh my God! Are you serious?" Nicole's voice pitched high with the squealing inquiry. "He's hot!"

Chloe's face warmed with embarrassment. "I think so, too." A picture of her and Maggie on graduation day sat next to the prom photo.

"He's *so* different from Andrew."

She laughed at her sister's insight when Nicole had only met Chad once. "Just a little."

"When are you moving?"

"He's moving here." Another picture showed her and Maggie at Maggie's first wedding.

"Why wouldn't you go live with him?" Her sister's enthusiasm dropped. "You could see Maggie and the baby."

"His family is here. I work with his mother."

"No way? How cool!" Nicole's excitement returned.

"Girls," their mother yelled. "Please come down to the kitchen."

"Remember what I said. Don't encourage her about the wedding if she brings it up." Chloe led the way to the kitchen.

"Hi, Dad." Chloe embraced her father and let go. "I love the smell of food cooking on the grill."

"I have three seven ounce filets for you women and two juicy New York Strips for your brother and me. When I see Andrew again, I won't tell him how well I'm feeding you."

"I can eat whatever I want. Andrew has no say about my life." She strode to the wine refrigerator, pulled out a bottle of merlot, opened, poured a large glass and took a long slow sip.

"He's not going to want a fat bride walking down the aisle." Her brother pushed her to the edge with the statement.

"Well, he won't have to worry about walking my so called fat ass down the aisle because *I'm...not...marrying him!*" Chloe stormed from the room to the yard, sitting at the edge of the woods.

The family let her sit alone. Her father popped in and out of the house to deal with the food on the grill. Ten minutes later, Michael sat beside her with a beer. "I'm sorry." It was a humble and sincere apology.

They didn't make eye contact but gave each other gentle shoulder bumps.

"You didn't know. I thought he would've said something to you." She sipped her wine.

"I meant about the fat remark. You're anything but. I think you're a bit *too* thin. As for Andrew, I haven't talked to him all week. Dad said he's been distracted at work and that when he asked to take next week off, he had no problem letting him take the time."

"Andrew's taking this harder than I thought."

"How so?" He took a swig of beer.

"This past week, every day, he's sent me a floral arrangement."

"Every day?" he asked surprised.

"Yup, and he's been texting and calling. I don't read or listen to the messages, so I haven't responded."

"Ouch." Michael's knee bopped against hers. "You should respond at least once. Give him closure." Putting an arm around her, he said, "I know I'd want to have that final good bye."

"Maybe you're right."

"I have to ask." He removed his arm and sipped from the beer bottle. "Why haven't you told Mom and Dad?"

With a short laughed, she said, "I did. Last week. They're in denial along with Andrew."

"So what are you going to do about it?"

"What can I do? As much as it angers me, I'm just going to have to keep reminding them there will be no wedding."

"Michael, Chloe, dinner's ready," their mother called from the porch.

He helped her up. "I don't know why you broke it off with Andrew, and I'm not going to ask why either."

"Thanks. I appreciate that and any help getting Mom and Dad to understand." They bumped shoulders one last time as they approached the deck.

Her dad talked about Andrew. He didn't bring Chloe into the topic, while remaining focused on the issue they had at the foundation regarding monies disappearing. Both Michael and Nicole helped avert their mother from continuing anything to do with the topic of a wedding. Her contribution to the conversation was about her upcoming trip to visit 'Maggie' and to see the new riding facilities. Her sister beamed hearing this news, knowing she and Chad were involved.

* * * *

Chloe rolled over and looked at her clock through squinted eyes. It was past nine in the morning. She had things to get done before leaving tomorrow for Florida. Laundry and packing were the two main items on her list. She stretched her arms and legs before twisting to the right and then to the left. Sitting on the edge of the bed, her arms reached up to the ceiling and when they came back down, she went to start her day.

In the late afternoon, while moving a load of laundry along, her cell phone rang. "Hi, Andrew." She kept it simple.

"I've been so worried about you. You haven't responded to any of my messages. Are you okay?" He sounded normal but off. Maybe the situation at work stressed him.

"Thank you for the flowers. They were all beautiful—"

"None of them were as beautiful as you are."

Can I vomit? "But they were unnecessary. It's over between us, Andrew." She leaned against the washing machine.

"It doesn't have to be. We can work this out."

"No, Andrew, we can't." She kept her voice calm. Yelling would do no good. There was a pause. "Then come get your belongings," he stated simply.

"Can I come by sometime next week?"

"If they're not gone by this weekend, I'll throw the stuff away." There's the Andrew she knew.

"I'll swing by tomorrow before noon. Okay? I'll call before leaving." She almost revealed her trip to Florida.

"I'll be waiting." He ended the call without further comment.

* * * *

Chloe was packed and ready for Florida. There were no delays for her flight. She texted Chad prior to leaving. *'Stopping at Andrew's before catching my flight. See you soon.'* Anything left at his place would survive the week in her trunk. She dialed the number she didn't think she'd ever forget.

"Are you on your way?" he asked enthusiastically.

"I'm leaving now."

"You still have your key, so let yourself in."

"I should be there in less than thirty minutes. Bye." Her purse on her shoulder, she took one last look around, making sure she didn't forget anything.

As she drove north out of central downtown, she kept reminding herself that his place was on her way to the airport. This would be a quick in and out. She pulled into the parking ramp and took her ticket, refusing to use Andrew's spare parking spot. The security gate arm lifted, allowing her through.

In the elevator, she pushed eighteen, stepped to the rail holding on for dear life. The doors closed, and the elevator jerked. Her eyes closed. She took a deep breath. What was it about being up so high that attracted people? Ugh, she hated elevators. The ride didn't bother her so much, but the jerk of the starting and stopping was another story. The doors opened, and she strolled toward Andrew's apartment for the last time.

"Andrew, I'm here." She scanned the tiled floor of the foyer for a box with her belongings, but there wasn't one. Further into the apartment, she looked in both directions along the short hallway. His bedroom door was partially closed, so she went to the left, entering the open kitchen, dining and living room. Papers covered the glass dining room table and were strewn about the coffee table. White powder coated a small area of the glass table by his laptop. *Powdered sugar?* "Andrew, where are you?"

"In my room."

"Are you descent?" She wasn't in the mood for any games with him. "Yes."

She padded down the hallway, opened the door and entered the master room. As she passed the exterior wall to the master bathroom, she lost her balance and screamed. Regaining her steadiness from being pushed, an arm forcefully wrapped around her neck and waist, while a body pushed into her back.

"No! Help! Andrew," she shrieked, drawing out each word. Unsuccessful in reaching upward, she tried twisting but failed. Whoever held her had a tight hold.

Chapter Eighteen

"Shut up. If you do what you're told, I won't hurt you. Nod if you understand." Andrew's voice was calm.

Chloe nodded, while her heart pounded against her chest as an overwhelming sickness filled her gut. Coming to Andrew's had been a mistake.

"Good." He moved his arm from her neck. Slid his hand to hers, pulling her arms behind her. "Let's go to the guest room."

They stepped into the hall heading towards the kitchen, then turned right into his guest bedroom. Long strips of fabric were tied to the bedframe. She stopped. He slammed into her back. "Andrew, please." Chloe pleaded softly, while her heart raced.

"I said be quiet," he said gruffly. "Now get on the bed. Wait. Unless you'd like to get into something a little more comfortable?"

She shook her head and moved to the bed. The lump in her throat was tough to swallow as her stomach worked to bring up her breakfast.

"Okay, just let me know if you change your mind." Andrew's pupils were dilated, and there was a suppressed excitement in his smile.

Her purse with her keys had dropped to the floor when he attacked. If she were to fight him, she'd have to make sure to strike him hard because she'd need time to get her purse before fleeing out the door.

"I can see your little mind is trying to figure a way out of this. Don't do anything you'll regret, and we'll be just fine. Get on the bed and tie up your feet. I'd do it, but that would give you an opportunity to take advantage of me. And not in the way I'd like." He rubbed his crotch, but he didn't have a hard-on.

Now that's a first.

Her hands shook, picking up the cotton fabric. She tied her right leg with one knot.

"Make another one and do the same for your left leg."

She finished doing as he asked.

Andrew walked to the far side of the bed. "Now lay back and give me your right arm. Be a good girl, and don't try anything." Holding a strip, he wrapped it around her wrist. There was lag allowing some freedom of movement. He came to the other side. "Your arm, Darlin'."

"Andrew, please. What do you want?" She'd say and do almost anything to get out of the situation she'd put herself in.

Silent, he finished tying her wrist the same as the other, with a little leeway, and crawled on the bed. He straddled her legs, leaning over her. "I had hoped to someday do this to you, but in my fantasy, you'd be naked and begging for me to have my way with you." His face inched closer. "This will have to do...for now." He kissed her with force.

She refused to return the kiss.

He reached around, grabbed the hair at the nape of her neck and her mouth opened from the pain.

She was in trouble. If she put up a fight, she might not survive.

The grip lessened. Andrew got off the bed and turned on the TV, upping the volume. He leaned into her ear. "No more yelling. If you do, it won't be good. I know how you like the home shows, so here you go." He stepped away.

"Andrew," she yelled to be heard over the TV.

He moved to stand within inches of her face, glowering.

"What do you want with me?"

"In due time. You relax, and I'll be back in a little while. Unless you misbehave." He left the room with the door open.

The remote out of her reach prevented her from turning down the volume and scream for help. A pain pierced her ears from the loudness. She tested the cotton fabric around her wrists, twisting to see if her fingers could touch the knots. No luck. She wasn't *that* flexible. There wasn't enough slack for her hands to reach her feet. Plus, she knew the ones on her ankles were tied tight because Andrew watched her knot the bindings. She relaxed back on the bed, slowly maneuvering her wrists with hopes of loosening her fastenings to slip a hand free.

Her mind wandered from getting free of the ties to glancing at the clock. She missed her flight to Florida. Chad would figure it out. He'd know when she didn't show up and couldn't reach her by phone. Things were going to work out. She'd be fine but wouldn't sit back and wait for him to come to her rescue. She would do what she could to escape before Chad got to her.

* * * *

Chad waited for his phone to ring, but Chloe's call never came. The flight arrived slightly past the scheduled time. At seven o'clock he called her cell phone. After several rings, voicemail clicked on. "Chloe, where are you? Call me back ASAP. I need to know you're okay. I love you." He dialed her home number and left the same message.

To be sure he hadn't gotten the wrong day of her arrival he read her itinerary again—Sunday, August 29. That was today. He located a number for the airlines and made the call. When the polite receptionist answered, he anxiously blurted, "My girlfriend's plane landed over an hour ago, and she hasn't called me to come get her. I'm wondering if you can tell me if she ever boarded the plane."

"Sir, I'm sorry, but we're unable to give you that information."

"Listen, I'm worried something has happened to her. I have her flight information right here. Please, I just need to know if she checked in." He pleaded, troubled for where she could be.

"Sir, I'm sorry, but as I said, we cannot divulge that information. If she's in danger or missing, you should call the local authorities."

"I understand. Thank you for your time." He paced the living room while hitting speed dial and waiting for an answer. "Maggie, have you heard from Chloe?"

"No. Why? Aren't you picking her up at the airport?"

His heart rate kicked up a notch. "The plane landed over an hour ago, and she hasn't called. There's no answer at either of her numbers. I'm worried, Maggie." He roamed from one room to another.

"There must be a reason why she hasn't called or answered. Let me try getting hold of her. Maybe I'll give Stephanie a try. Maybe they're out together, and Chloe can't hear her phone."

"Okay. Thanks. I'll wait to hear from you."

"Chad, relax." Maggie's voice remained calm and soothed him for a moment. "She's okay. We'll get in touch with her."

"Thanks. Call me back as soon as you know anything. And if you get hold of her, have her call me."

"Okay. Bye."

Chad continued walking through the house, thinking of who he could call. The only person who came to mind was his brother Ryan. He thought about his mom, but quickly dismissed the idea because he didn't want her to worry when she needed to focus on her own recovery. Ryan would be a last resort call.

As each minute ticked by, the tension crept into his shoulders and neck. He dropped to the floor. In position, he pushed up on his arms, slowly lowering his body to linger above the floor in a horizontal position. He repeated the pushups in hopes of easing the stiffness in his upper body. When the phone rang, he anxiously answered. "What did you find out?"

"She didn't answer her phones like you said. I tried Stephanie, but she hasn't talked to her since Thursday night. I also called Chloe's brother, Michael. The last time he saw her was Friday night."

"What about Andrew?" He spewed the name he hated.

"What about him?"

"Exactly. Do you have a number to reach him? She texted me she was going to his place before the airport."

"Yeah, I could try calling him." There was doubt in her voice that Andrew would know Chloe's whereabouts.

"Please do. It's one more person. One more person who could know something."

"Chad, she's okay."

"She's not okay." He raised his voice. "Something's happened, and I'm going to go find her." Tears streamed down his face.

"Chad, don't do this. Don't get all worked up over something that could be a simple problem."

"I'm sorry, Maggie, but I have to go. I'm leaving as soon as I can get a flight."

"Okay. I'll try Andrew and call you as soon as I've talked to him."

"Thanks." They hung up, and he searched for the earliest flight to Dallas. Chad was certain something happened to Chloe. The old adage said *go with your gut instinct*. His gut told him something was wrong.

* * * *

When Chloe turned to the clock on the nightstand, it neared eight o'clock Sunday evening. Sleeping passed time but didn't make the situation any better. She hadn't eaten since morning. Her tongue moved around her dry mouth, swallowing the little spit she could muster. The TV blared, and she was amazed that she'd slept. Naps weren't her thing. Then again, neither was being kidnapped by her ex-fiancé.

"Andrew?" she called, followed by a cough due to the dryness in her mouth.

Several minutes later he strolled through the door. He turned the TV down. "If you can be a good girl and not yell for help, I'll keep the volume low." He stood at the edge of the bed. "How was your nap, Darlin'?"

Her skin crawled at the way he drawled out the 'darlin'. "Fine," she choked out. "I need something to drink, and I haven't eaten since breakfast."

"Well, let me see what I can find for you. I'll be back." He leaned down and placed a kiss on her forehead before leaving the room.

He seemed to have mellowed from earlier. Maybe she should continue trying to talk her way out of this situation. His phone rang, and she could hear him talking.

"Maggie, what a surprise. Did you have the baby?—No, came by and picked up her belongings and left. Why do you ask?—Huh, no, I didn't know she was coming for a visit.—Of course I'll call if I see or hear from her.—Okay, take care and let me know when that baby arrives."

Shit! Now he knows I was going to Florida. What did Maggie say? Or better yet reveal? "Damn it," she said hoarse.

"You got that right." Andrew stormed into the room with his voice raised. "Where's your purse?"

"In your room. I dropped it when you grabbed me." Not able to yell at him irritated her. But in this case, a soft voice was best.

163

He left and returned to the room with her purse, holding her cell phone. "You've missed a few calls and have some voicemails. Let's see who they could be from." Andrew tapped the screen several times before she heard Chad's voice. "I knew you were fucking him." He forcefully hit the phone's screen and tossed it to the floor. His voice took on a menacing tone. "I told you, I am never letting you go." A wicked smile filled his face.

Chill bumps covered her arms. Her shoulders drew back with the sensation of something crawling up her spine. In that moment, she remembered the day of the shooting. The man had yelled at the women, "I told you you'd never get away from me."

"We will be getting married. You're going to call *Mr. Rogers*, and you're going to tell him that you're fine. That you changed your mind and that you want to marry me. That you *are* going to marry me. Is that understood?"

She nodded her head.

"Good. But first we're going to let him worry about you for a while. I need to take care of some things, too, before we make the call." He stepped away from the bed, and Chloe spoke his name.

"What, Darlin'?" His mood switch flipped instantly from angry to sweet.

"Can I get something to eat and drink?"

"Oh, yeah. The phone call from Maggie distracted me. I'll be back."

"I need to use the bathroom."

"Now?"

"Yes."

"Fine. This will be a good time to get you out of your clothes anyway." He brushed his crotch. Again, there was no bulge in the crotch of his pants. He untied her hands. "Undo your feet, and don't try anything."

Knots undone, she moved to sit on the edge of the bed. Lightheaded from not eating or drinking, she closed her eyes for a second.

"Take off your clothes."

Her eyes shot open at his demand, but she did as he asked before shuffling into the bathroom.

As she closed the door, he pushed it open. "Nope. I don't want you trying anything."

"I can't escape from in here." The bathroom an on-suite, an interior room within the apartment. Meaning—no windows.

"I don't know what's in the cabinets. I forgot to search them, but I will when you're done."

Finished using the bathroom, he yanked her in an embrace with a hand groping a butt cheek and the other arm around her waist. "Later you can scratch my itch that you've ignored for the last several weeks." His hand slid between her thighs. His fingers slid between her folds. "Mmm, warm."

She tried to push away, but he only held her tighter against him.

"Don't fight me." The fingers went deeper. "You want this as much as I do. You're wet for my touch."

"Andrew," she said breathy. "Don't...do...this."

"See, you're breathing heavy for me. We'll finish this later." His hands gripped her hips. "Oh, I have an idea. Maybe when I'm giving it to you, you can be telling *Mr. Rogers* that it's not happening with you two, while I scream out your name. What do you think?"

"Andrew, I don't want you. Please, let me go." A tear escaped and slid on her cheek. She was naked and afraid.

"You do want me. Until you understand that we are getting married, I'm not letting you go." His voice was calm and cold. He released her from his hold. "Get on the bed and tie up your feet." He stood at the base of the bed watching her. "Lie back." As she did, he crawled onto the bed, on top of her. "Hand please." He tied both hands and kissed her.

She allowed him to kiss her because of the earlier incident.

He moaned in pleasure before pulling away and getting off the bed. "I'll be back with some food and drink. You need to have energy." He covered her with a blanket.

"Thank you."

He winked going through the doorway.

She frantically wriggled her wrists to free herself but with no luck. Taking calming breaths to slow her heart rate and her nerves, she heard Andrew talking. She slowly twisted her hands in the cotton bindings. It appeared he had ripped a shirt apart to make the ties.

"I need some more but don't want to leave. Will you deliver?—Fine. Do you have anything mild to relax a person?—No, I don't want that. I want her to just relax, not be dead.—Cool. Same place, say in a hour.— Okay, but only for one drink. I can't be away for too long."

Oh my God, he's going to drug me! Several weeks ago at the fundraiser he must've been using drugs. Erratic behavior and mood swings added with dilated pupils and one could only jump to conclusions. The white stuff on the table hadn't been powdered sugar. It had to be cocaine. The conversation she overheard confirmed he was using something and wanted to give *her* something.

I have to get out of here!

She continued working the ties holding her down. The familiar tone signaling Chad was calling played somewhere from the floor. Closing her eyes, she prayed he'd be able to find her if she couldn't escape from Andrew. When she opened them, Andrew stood by the bed, and she screamed. "I'm sorry. You startled me."

"You looked so peaceful. Like an angel." He untied her left hand. "I have your dinner. Fruit, cheese, meat and crackers. I poured you a small glass of merlot as well as a glass of water."

"Thank you, but I don't care to drink. Can you untie my other hand? You know I'm right handed."

"No. There's less chance of you trying something with only your left hand to work with. You'll manage." He picked up the juice glass containing the small amount of wine and drank it on one gulp. "Your loss."

"Andrew, talk to me. What do you want from me? I can't remain tied up forever in your apartment."

"No, no you can't. But I have to trust that you won't leave me again. We belong together." He talked kindly. Then the switch flipped. His breath became heavy. His eyebrows drew together. "I didn't realize this until *Mr. Rogers* came to town. You flaunted yourself all over him, playing me as a fool. Your work for the shelter will come to an end. I hoped the failure in receiving the grant would've discouraged you. I want you to focus on us and what I need from you. Maybe I'll knock you up right away so kids can keep you occupied at home." His hand slid up her leg. "Maybe we'll start working on making a baby tonight."

Aghast at his thinking, and the possibility of that happening, she inhaled sharp. She'd missed taking her pill tonight. Her stomach turned. Breathing came faster and harder.

"I'm going to leave you to eat." He walked around the bed and checked the bindings for tightness before exiting the room.

As upset as her stomach was she had to eat what he provided, or she'd never have the strength to fight. First, she questioned the water for fear he may have put something in it. She drank it based on the fact that he had asked for something during his phone call, meaning he probably wasn't drugging her *yet*.

"Time for me to go," Andrew stated, entering the room twenty minutes later. "I'll take the tray and be right back to let you use the bathroom."

"I'm good." She didn't want to risk him touching her again.

He set the tray on the nightstand. "Well, in that case, your hand, Darlin'." He tied up her free hand. "You be good while I'm gone." Turning up the TV, a cartoon alligator smiled at her. "I can't have you yelling out for help and be heard." He delivered a firm kiss on her lips before closing the bedroom door. He must've figured it was an added sound barrier.

After several minutes passed, Chloe frantically worked to unbind herself.

Chapter Nineteen

Chad took the eight o'clock flight to Dallas, the last one out Sunday evening. He booked a room at the Pegasus, the same hotel he stayed in when he came to see his mother, as well as a rental car. Maggie had called Stephanie and Michael, and they agreed to help him any way they could. When he checked in at the hotel, it was nearing midnight. Too late to do anything, but he could call Chloe's cell phone again. The damn voicemail turned on. He cried at the sound of her voice. When the beep sounded, he hung up, not willing to leave another message. Relaxation would be tough to come by, so turning on the water he took a long hot shower.

Sleep eventually took his weary body into a world of darkness. He woke later than he wanted but welcomed the rest he'd gotten. Dressed with room service ordered, he dialed Chloe's brother Michael.

"Hello?" a male voice answered.

"Michael? This is Chad Rogers. Maggie—" He paced the room.

"I know who you are." He sounded irritated. "What can I do to help?"

"Have you heard from your sister?"

"No. As I told Maggie, last time we talked was Friday night. Are you the reason she called off the engagement?"

Chad paused his walking. This wasn't just Chloe's brother; this was also Andrew's good friend. "Yes. I'm very worried about her. Have you seen or talked to Andrew since Friday?" He stared out the hotel window, not really interested in what was on the other side of the glass.

"Why?" Michael got defensive. "He has nothing to do with this. And he sure as hell wouldn't hurt my sister."

"I never insinuated any of that. I just want to know if you've seen him." He deeply inhaled to remain as calm as possible. It wouldn't help to get angry.

"No," he snapped.

"Would you mind calling him? See if he's seen or heard from Chloe." He had to ask for help, or he'd never know. The pacing resumed.

"Yeah, sure. For my sister."

"You can get me at this number if you hear something. Thanks." As he pulled the phone away from his ear, he heard Michael's voice and put the cell to his ear.

"Do you love her?" Michael's tone softened.

His stopped at the foot of the bed. "Yes, I love her." The lids of his eyes closed as the pain in his chest grew. He sat down.

"I'll call you back." The line went dead.

Another deep breath then he dialed Stephanie and got her voicemail. He left a brief message, then called Maggie. "Have you heard anything?" he blurted as soon as the ringing stopped.

"No. I called her work. She hasn't shown up or called in."

Not able to sit still, the carpet was at his mercy. "I'm going to call my brother. He's a cop here. Maybe he can help me."

"I'll keep trying and let you know as soon as I hear something."

"Do you have Andrew's address?" The hate for Andrew boiled within him.

"Chad, you can't go over there and barge in."

The hate turned to anger. "Why not?" he exclaimed and raised his voice.

"Chad." Maggie scolded him like his mother would. "As much as I agree with your thought of action, there are laws to abide by. Chloe needs you to remain out of jail and calm."

"I'm worried for her. I'm one hundred percent certain Andrew's done something."

"Follow the rules, and let the law handle it. Call your brother. Ooh," she said with what sounded like pain.

"Maggie?"

She didn't answer, but he heard her breathing. "Um, I need to go, Chad. Bye." Her line cut out.

"Shit! She's going into labor, and I'm not there to take care of the riders. Damn it!" He made a few calls, getting barn coverage taken care of as well as someone to contact any riders Maggie may have had on the books for the remainder of the week.

The next call could be tough, but he needed Ryan's help.

"Rogers," Ryan answered casual but with authority.

"Ryan, its Chad."

"You have the results back?"

"Huh? Oh, no. No, I need your expertise." The DNA test was the last thing on his mind at the moment. Chloe was the only thing he was concerned about.

"Okay, what's up? My curiosity's peeked."

"You remember Chloe Atwood?" Chad ran a hand through his hair to rest at the nape of his neck.

"Yeah. Why?"

"She's my girlfriend, and she's gone missing."

"I'm listening."

"She was flying in to visit yesterday but never arrived. She texted me she was leaving her place and stopping at Andrew's before going to the airport. There's no answer on her cell or at home. She didn't show up or call in to work today. Ryan, she was engaged to this guy and broke off the engagement over a week ago. I saw marks on her arm and had run-ins with the guy."

"What do you mean *run-ins*?" The cop side of Ryan came out with the question.

"Nothing where your colleagues were involved, but he was very in your face with me. I saw how he acted around Chloe. I don't like him, Ryan. He's not good."

"Okay. Who's this guy?"

"Andrew...Andrew Lockhart. He works for Chloe's dad." Chad actually forgot the asshole's last name for a second.

"What have you done other than what you've told me? Who else have you talked to?"

"Maggie made some calls to Chloe's brother and a friend who also happens to be Andrew's sister. They saw and talked to her last on Friday and Thursday."

"What about Andrew? Has anyone called him?" It was on. Ryan was in full detective mode.

"Maggie called him last night, and he claims she came to his place before her flight and left. Chloe's brother was going to try reaching Andrew today for me."

"So you've talked to...what's her brother's name?"

"Michael, and yes, we talked not less than an hour ago." He had done the right thing by calling Ryan.

"Do you know where this guy lives?"

"No. Maggie wouldn't give me an address. Can you find out?" He strolled to the window.

"Yeah. Listen, you can't file a missing person's report yet, and I don't have enough information. I'll call you back later. Give me a little time."

"I'm in Dallas, Ryan. You only have a little time before I lose it. I love her and need to find her." The street below was filled with pedestrians. He wasn't high enough where they resembled ants.

"Just relax, brother. I'll help, but you need to take it easy. Don't do anything stupid."

"Fine. And Ryan, thanks."

"You're my brother. I'm here to help. I'll talk to you later."

While pacing the room, he wondered if anyone else had a key to Chloe's place. Maybe they could find a clue there as to what happened. Ready to dial Maggie, he remembered she hung up in pain. He tapped the buttons and hoped Stephanie would answer.

"Hello?" Her voice sounded so sweet.

"Stephanie, it's Chad."

"I'm sorry I forgot to call you. It's been crazy here." She was headed off on a tangent.

"Stephanie..." He steered her back on track, anxious for answers. "Have you heard from Chloe?"

"No. I told Mag—"

"I know." Patience worn, he snapped. "Do you have a key for Chloe's apartment?"

"No, but I can get one."

"How soon?"

"Well...I guess I could be there in thirty minutes."

"I'll meet you in the lobby." He disconnected, not wanting to give her the chance to drag the conversation longer. The trek wouldn't take but fifteen minutes from his hotel, but he couldn't sit in his room any longer.

When he exited the hotel, his strides were fast and filled with purpose. He slowed his pace when he realized how quickly he was moving. No need to arrive early. He didn't want to lurk around the lobby or outside the door for twenty minutes waiting for Stephanie.

As he stood in front of Chloe's building, he remembered their shared kiss after catching up over dinner. He strolled inside the lobby to wait for Stephanie. He would kiss Chloe again.

"Hi, Chad," Stephanie approached, all bubbly. "I'll be right back with a key." She approached the guard's desk and a couple minutes later came back. "Okay, let's go."

"How'd you—"

"Chloe has me listed as a person to have access to her apartment as are her parents. So why did you want to come here?"

They took the elevator to Chloe's floor.

"To look around and see if something happened at the apartment. I want to know if she was taken by force."

"Oh, yeah."

Was Stephanie playing stupid or was he simply irritated by the fact Chloe was missing?

"Well, here we are." Stephanie unlocked and opened the door.

"Don't touch anything." He stepped past her and entered the apartment's hall. His heart raced with adrenaline, wanting to find something, yet not wanting to. Something could lead them to her. Nothing would be a dead end.

The first bedroom was clean. The bathroom was clean. They stepped into the large kitchen, living room area—everything was clean. In her bedroom and bathroom, nothing was out of place.

"I've only been here once. Do you see anything out of place or wrong?" he asked frustrated. "It's too perfect to show us any sign of anything. Damn!"

"Nope, things are as if she left on her own."

His phone rang, and he answered in a huff. "Hello?"

"Aren't you pleasant?" It was Ryan. "Where are you?"

"Sorry. I'm at Chloe's place—"

"Damn it! I told you to stay at the hotel."

"I didn't break in. I'm here with her friend who has a key." His hand ran through his hair.

"Well?"

"There's nothing. No sign of a struggle. Everything is picture-perfect." As disappointment consumed him, fury filtered through the cracks.

"I want you to leave and come back to the hotel." Ryan remained calm.

"Wait, you're at the hotel?"

"Yes, so get back here."

"Why?" He and Stephanie stood at the edge of the kitchen.

"I have some info." There was nothing to read in his tone.

"Tell me what you know."

"Not on the phone." That wasn't positive sounding.

"Fine. I'll be there in fifteen." He hung up, grabbing Stephanie's arm. "Let's go. Nothing here for us. My brother has some info."

She locked the door. "Is your brother a cop or something?"

"Yes." Chad was curt. "I'm sorry," he said on the elevator. Frustration ate him from the inside out. "I'm just worried about her."

"I am, too, but she'll be okay. She puts up with my brother, so she's tough."

"What does that mean?" The doors opened, and he stood in the elevator, waiting for an answer.

She stepped onto the lobby's marble floor. "Nothing. He's my brother. I meant that in a smart-ass way." She returned the key, and they left for his hotel to meet Ryan.

He practically ran on the sidewalk, leaving Stephanie in his wake.

"Hey, slow down," she yelled after him. "It's hard to run in these heels." She lagged behind.

"I wasn't running." He stopped on the sidewalk. "You could take the stupid shoes off."

She gawked at him. "Humph." She darted in front of him. Her hips swung as she strutted. He caught up, matching her stride in no time.

"You should know, I don't like your brother and believe he's involved somehow."

"Sometimes he can be a little overbearing, but he's a good guy."

"Well, I hope I'm wrong." Chad opened the hotel doors.

Ryan paced the lobby wearing a suit. He was working.

"Nice place," Ryan stated, glancing around the urban décor.

"Yeah, whatever. It's a place to stay. Ryan, this is Stephanie. Stephanie, Ryan."

The two looked at one another. Shook hands and exchanged pleasantries.

"What do you know?" Chad almost burst at the seams wanting something. Anything to get to Chloe.

"Let's go sit over here." Ryan gestured to a small furniture grouping. "I found Chloe's car."

Chad kept his mouth shut, but his body wouldn't relax. He was wound tight like a coiled rattlesnake ready to strike its next victim.

"It's parked in the building ramp, in the location of the ex-fiancé's apartment. Nothing seemed out of place with the vehicle. I have a description of his car and the plate number, so I'm going to be on the lookout for him. I'm going to ask around with some of my street connections to see if they know him."

"Andrew doesn't do drugs." Stephanie blurted, looking to Ryan, appalled by the suggestion.

Ryan ignored her and simply stated, "I've learned that he's on vacation...at home."

"Stephanie, I want you to take me to his place. Now!" Chad demanded.

A hand yanked him to the sofa. "You're staying right here, Brother. Do you understand?" Ryan spoke in a low growl. "You let me and the department handle this. I'm investigating as time allows, since this officially isn't a missing person case—yet. I'll try to keep you informed as to what's happening. *You* do anything, and you could put her in danger. Do you understand?" Ryan accentuated each of the last three words.

"Yes." Put in his place, Chad was downtrodden. He wanted to be the one to find her.

"Stephanie," Ryan remained professional. "I need a number where I can reach you. We may need you to help us. Are you willing to help?"

"Of course," she said, bubbly with a flirtatious attitude.

Ryan pulled a notebook and pen from his inside chest pocket and handed them to her.

She wrote the info and gave the pad back to Ryan. "I'll do whatever you need to help find Chloe."

"Chad, lay low and try to relax. I'm working on it. Go visit Mom." He stood. "Ms. Lockhart, I'll be in touch." Ryan nodded and left them sitting in the hotel lobby.

"Is he married?"

"Really, Stephanie?" Her timing irritated him. Not a minute passed, and guilt got the better of him for being brusque toward her. "No, he's available as far as I know." He stood. "Listen, if you don't mind, I'd like to be alone."

"I should be getting back to work anyway. My employees are probably wondering where I am." She gave him a quick hug. "She's okay, Chad."

"I hope so. Thanks for your help and putting up with my crabby ass."

"You have a nice ass. It's not crabby in any way." She winked, turning for the exit.

"We'll talk soon." She waved over her shoulder as he headed for the elevator.

* * * *

Panic washed over Chloe as her eyes shot open. When did she fall asleep? The clock read past four in the morning. *Monday. Another day.* The bedroom door remained closed. The TV blared which didn't do much for her head. She needed to stretch the aches in her body. Not to mention use the bathroom.

"Andrew," she screamed as loud as possible, waiting several minutes without an answer. Yelling again, there was no sign of him. She worried that something happened to him last night.

She pulled on the cotton restraints. Pain shot up her arm. Lifting her hands, a bright red ring seared each wrist. Tears streamed down her cheeks. She had an opening, a chance to get out of there.

A primal scream escaped her lungs while she wrenched against the ties that bound her. Her hands yanked out with so much force that her body lurched forward. Stunned for a second at the reality that her hands were free, she quickly untied her legs. She used the bathroom before getting dressed. Locating her phone, she dialed Chad, but after one ring it died. Not wasting time, she grabbed her purse and ran for the front door.

Chloe opened the door. Andrew stood in the doorway.

Chapter Twenty

Andrew shoved Chloe back from the door with a stiff arm. The force made her fall hard onto the tiled floor. "Help," she screamed. Her heart raced, and she swallowed hard.

He moved swiftly inside and closed the door.

Large dilated pupils hid the brown iris of his eyes as he turned facing her. His breaths came fast like in the old cartoons as he lumbered toward her. Her feet scrambled under her. She willed her legs the strength to stand. His open hand struck her face. Her back hit the wall as she fell to the floor again.

Tears streamed down her face immediately at the stinging pain and disbelief of what he had done.

He gripped her arm, yanking her. "Get up! Get in the room, get undressed and on the bed." He pushed her toward the bedroom.

"Andrew," she cried, careful not to raise her voice. "Please don't do this. Let me go. I won't say anything to anyone about this."

"Strip. Now." He lowered his tone. "You'll run as quickly as possible to your *daddy* and the police. Not to mention, *Mr. Rogers.*"

She stood next to the bed, head throbbing and continued to plead. "I won't. If anyone asks, I'll tell them I was here to talk to you. That we had to work through some things."

"You couldn't lie if your life depended on it. Take off your clothes, or I'll be happy to do it for you."

When he stepped closer, she turned to take her top off.

"No, face me. I want to watch you undress." His voice took on a disgusting tone, while lecherousness formed on his face.

Not wanting to get slapped or worse, she came up with an idea and faced him. Slowly, she guided her top up her arms and over her head.

"Nice. You didn't bother with a bra."

"Andrew, if I comply and give you what you want, will you let me go?"

A short-lived maniacal laugh escaped as he pulled her in a tight embrace. "I get what I want whether you comply or not." He grabbed her hair by the nape of her neck and yanked back while taking possession of her mouth. He tasted of alcohol and cigar.

Chloe gave in, giving him what he wanted. Maybe if she played this right he'd listen and let her go. Or she'd escape.

He moaned, deepening the kiss, while releasing his hold on her hair. He withdrew his lips from hers. "That's more like it." He yanked his black silk knit shirt over his head, tossing it to the floor. "I want to finish undressing you. Get on the bed."

She did as asked and watched in disbelief. No raging hard-on. Normally he would be stiff at the thought of sex. She smirked.

"You like what you see."

Between her legs, he slid her pants down. "Mmm, you left the underwear off, too." Pants tossed to the floor, his hands slithered up her thighs.

Chloe's voice shook as she played along with the sex act. When he couldn't get stiff and was unable to perform, relief flooded through every nerve. Only to be replaced by fear.

"God damn it! We're going to do things a little differently. Get on your stomach and put both hands behind your back."

She couldn't help but sob. She wanted to go home. No, she wanted to go to Chad.

"Shut up," he yelled, punching her in the middle of her back.

The hit knocked the wind out of her. The binding around her wrist hurt the already raw skin from twisting to escape.

"Feet." His demanding voice scared her.

She didn't know which was worse, the angry Andrew or the sexual Andrew.

He yanked her to the end of the bed, so her feet were over the end of the mattress. Spreading her legs, he tightly tied each ankle to the bed post with the fabric. Escape was no longer an option. Her head turned to the side, she faced the covered window.

Andrew came into her view. He bent over, put his face an inch within hers and spoke softly in her ear. "You're not going anywhere now. And when I'm ready, you'll get your fill."

She closed her eyes to the meaning behind his words.

"I've got more money moves to make from daddy's company." He kissed her cheek, and soft steps receded with the door closing.

Hot tears flowed freely.

* * * *

Chad stood leaning on the fence post, lost in thought about Chloe. Staying downtown and not being able to do anything to find her drove him to get out of downtown. He had driven to the nearest horse facility to get closer to one of the things he loved—horses. There were horses in the distance, close to the stables. The ringing of his phone invaded his quiet space and jolted him.

With the possibility of it being Chloe, he answered immediately.

"Hey, Chad, Ryan."

"Did you find her?" His heart accelerated at the chance Ryan had her safe.

"No—"

"Then why are you calling me?"

"If you'd shut up and let me tell you," Ryan paused. "Okay then. I'm sending Stephanie over to Andrew's to scope things out. I've told her to observe as much as she can while there. See if he lets her into the apartment. My hunch is he won't because I believe Chloe is at his place."

"If you believe she's there then go get her."

"Chad, it's not that easy. We have laws to abide by. I'm doing more than I should as is. Are you staying out of trouble?"

Chad knew exactly what Ryan referred to. "Yes. I drove out to the country to get away. You have no idea how difficult this is." Tears welled in his eyes. "Not being able to go after her. Having to sit back and do nothing." The tears flowed down his cheeks.

"I do, Chad. I do know how difficult it is. We're going find her, and when we do, she's going to be okay. I can't promise *he'll* be okay after we get to him."

Chad chuckled, followed by a sniffle at his brother's attempt to lighten things. If only he could be the one to get his hands on Andrew when they arrested him. "I'm glad you're on my side...and that you're my brother."

"Continue to take it easy, and I'll be in touch."

They ended their conversation, and Chad slid his phone into his front jean pocket. Would Stephanie be observant enough to pick up any details as to whether or not Chloe was at Andrew's? He could only hope.

* * * *

Darkness surrounded Chloe. A blanket covered her naked body. Andrew had come back into the room. She had slept through his simple act of kindness if that's what you wanted to call it. She lifted her head and checked the time. It was well after six in the evening, and there were no sounds. She wondered if he'd left again.

"Andrew," she called out. A pain shot through her shoulders. It was the punch he'd delivered between her shoulder blades. She cringed at the throbbing. She breathed in, "Andrew!" The aching intensified. She relaxed as much as possible. He never came. She eventually drifted back to sleep, weak from lack of food and water.

Chloe woke to voices. A male and female. Slowly becoming more aware, she recognized Andrew talking to Steph. She opened her mouth to yell, only to be met by a dry parched mouth. "Steph," was nothing but a raspy whisper. She swallowed what felt like cotton. She prayed Steph would catch something wrong or out of the ordinary. Her heart beat strong against her ribs. The conversation was being held in the entry and couldn't be clearly heard. But the sound of the apartment door closing, shutting out any hope of a rescue from Steph, didn't go unnoticed.

The bedroom door opened. She feigned sleep. The door remained open for no more than a minute before closing. How did the women at the shelter survive? Hope slipped away slowly.

* * * *

180

Chad waited in his hotel room, pacing from one end to the other. He stopped to stare into the lighted night sky from the tenth floor window before repeating the pattern. The ringing of his phone stopped him dead in his tracks. "Hello."

"Chad, it's Stephanie. She's been there. I saw Chloe's purse lying in the hallway, but I didn't see her."

"What did Ryan say?" He returned to wearing a pattern in the room's carpeting.

"He asked me questions about Andrew, the apartment and anything else I noticed."

"And what did you tell him?"

"The apartment was a mess from what I could see. He wouldn't let me step beyond the entrance hall. The second bedroom door was closed, and that's normally open. And Andrew looked like hell."

"Ryan didn't say what he was going to do?"

"No. He thanked me and told me to go home. But I couldn't, so I'm at the bar having a drink."

"Have one for me." He thought about meeting her for drinks, but decided it was best to remain sober. There would've been no stopping at one drink tonight. "Thanks for helping, Stephanie."

"Call me if you hear anything?"

"I will. And you do the same. Goodnight." In the bathroom he started the shower, undressed and stepped under the hot spray. Not even the hottest water would strip away the anger and pain he felt in the last forty-eight hours. When the water ran cool, he shut it off and dried.

He checked his phone to find a message from Maggie. *"Call me. No matter what."* Boxer briefs on, he tapped her number and waited for an answer.

"Have you found Chloe? Tell me what's going on? We haven't heard from you." Maggie spoke fast and breathy.

"No. First tell me why you're calling me. Aren't you having the baby?"

"Yes." She was breathing as though in the middle of labor. "Sorry. Had a contraction. I'm at the hospital, in a delivery room and—"

Holy shit! He didn't know someone could scream so loud.

"The baby's coming. You need to find Chloe. I want her here." She panted, and there was another scream.

"Chad," Trent's voice came on the line. "Don't know what she was thinking, but we'll talk to you later." Dead air filled the phone line.

He briefly smiled at the joy he felt for Trent and Maggie. They'd be parents before the end of the day. When he thought about Chloe that joy quickly faded. He tapped her number, and the voicemail played. He swallowed, and let the tears fall. Her sweet cheerful voice talked to him. When he heard the beep, he choked the words, "I love you. I have always loved you. And I will always love you."

* * * *

The ringing of his phone woke Chad from a sound sleep. Groping the nightstand, he located it and answered with closed eyes.

"Did I wake you?" Trent asked.

"What time is it?" His head was foggy.

"Almost lunch time, your time." His mood was chipper.

"Oh."

"Hey, you okay?" Concern replaced happy.

"What the fuck do you think?" Chad was awake now, and sourness filled his tone.

"Whoa, sorry. I wanted you to know Maggie and the baby are fine. I thought you'd want to know."

Guilt punched him in the gut. "No, I'm sorry. Boy or girl?"

"Boy. Seven pounds nine ounces. Justin Connor Randall. Maggie was a trooper. She wouldn't let me take the phone away from her until after she talked to you. Stubborn woman."

"Congratulations, man. Make sure to give Maggie a hug and congrats, too."

"I will." After a brief pause, Trent added, "Listen, I'm not expecting you back until you can come back with Chloe. She hasn't said anything, but I know Maggie's worried. Keep us posted."

"Okay. Thanks for calling. I'm going to my mom's today. I've been ordered to sit back and let my brother and the officials take care of this."

"And you're following his rules? That's a new one." A chuckle escaped at Trent's dig.

182

"Shut up, dick. Most rules are bogus and should be broken. But this is one time I can't afford to break them."

"Does your brother have any leads?"

"I think so. I haven't heard anything since last night when I talked to Andrew's sister, Stephanie. She went to his place and saw Chloe's purse on the floor. Her car is parked in the ramp at Andrew's building." Sleepy, his mood was a somber one talking about the situation.

"What about Andrew's car? Is it still there?"

"As far as I know. My brother hasn't said anything to lead me to believe it's gone as if he took Chloe by car."

"Then she's got to be at his place. Why don't they go in and search the place?"

"They sent Stephanie to scope things out. My brother's working on it, I think." He scooted to a more upright position.

"You don't sound optimistic."

"I haven't talked to him since yesterday. I'm going off of what Stephanie told me. Listen, give Maggie a hug for me. I'll be in touch." They hung up. Chad ordered room service and dressed for the day.

* * * *

Chad arrived at his mom's after two and rang the doorbell.

"Chad, what are you doing here? Come in. I thought you went back to Florida?" The confusion registered in her voice as they entered the house. "Let's go to the patio." They walked through the kitchen. "Oh, a letter came for you." She stopped at the ledge, pulling an envelope from an organizer. "Here it is. Can I get you a drink?"

"Thanks. Water would be great." He read the envelope. "It's the results of the test."

"Well, are you going to open it?" She filled a glass for him.

"Let's sit down."

They sat at the table, and he stared at the closed letter. He never answered his mother's questions about why he was there, so should he bring it up first or open the letter? The letter won. He ripped it open and read the documents.

Minutes passed.

"Chad? What does it say?"

183

Chapter Twenty-One

"He's my father." Chad's mood was somber. He didn't know how to feel. Relief was out of the question because with either result there would be steps to take.

"He who, Chad?" his mother asked, curiously excited.

His voice flat, he answered. "Dad is my father." This step would be easier than if he had to go searching for the other man. Although, considering the deep ravine dividing them, this step would require building a bridge.

"What do you plan to do now that you know?"

"I'll tell Ryan since he knows about the past and the test, but I'm not saying anything to the rest of the family." A moment of silence and he said, "If Ryan wants to tell Dad, he can. Ryan says he's different now. I think I'll let Dad decide where we go from here. Right now, I can't say whether I'm happy or pissed that he's my father."

"As you got older, I never questioned whose child you were. In ways you're like your father, but in many others you're not. You have a heart of gold. Chloe is lucky to have you."

The mention of her name brought the current situation front and center. He broke down. His head fell to the table as he cried.

"Chad, what's wrong?" Worry filled his mother's voice as she touched his arm.

"I'm here because she never showed up in Florida, and no one can reach her. She's not at her place either."

"She's missing? Just disappeared?"

"Yes! Ryan found her car in Andrew's parking ramp, but Andrew claims she left after picking her stuff up from his place on her way to the airport. I know he's lying and has done something. Mom, I'm so worried." He went to the kitchen for a tissue.

"So Ryan's working on the case? That's good."

"She's been gone since sometime on Sunday. It's Tuesday." He sat back down.

"You need to let him do his job and have patience."

"I know, but my patience is wearing thin. We're talking about the woman I love."

"Listen to Ryan, and do as he asks, but remember you're not his only case, and it will take time."

"Time we don't have."

* * * *

Andrew brought Chloe a tray of food. It was the same she had eaten the last few times he fed her, meat, cheese, fruit, crackers and water. The water went untouched for fear it was contaminated with a drug. She'd heard him ask for something to knock her out and didn't trust Andrew any more. When she went to the bathroom, she would drink from the faucet.

After her lunch papers shuffled while Andrew talked on the phone, but she couldn't make out what was being said. He had mentioned transferring money from the foundation earlier. Her father had mentioned something about money missing.

He entered the room and picked up the TV remote. "I'm going out. I don't want to see you greet me at the door. You stay right here, and wait for me."

"Andrew, please. Please let me go. You can't keep me here forever." She kept her voice low, forcing herself not to whine. She prayed the nervousness remained hidden.

"I'm not going to keep you here forever. We're going away on a trip. Don't worry. I've made all the arrangements." He bent over, and she let him kiss her.

A tear slid down her cheek.

With the back of his finger, he wiped her face gently, whispering, "I know. It's going to be so special, just the two of us." He turned the volume up on the TV. An evil craftiness consumed his eyes as he closed the door behind him.

Her wrists were so raw she gave up on escape. Maybe her chance would come when he took her out of the apartment.

* * * *

Chloe woke when the door opened. Andrew turned the TV down and left the room, but came back in with a medium sized suitcase.

"I packed a few items for our trip. We can go shopping when we reach our destination. Although I think you'll find a swimsuit or nothing will be all you need."

"Will you tell me where we're going?"

"South America."

She feigned a smile. "When do we leave?"

"Anxious, are you? Well, no worries. We'll leave soon enough." He kissed her and left.

If they went to South America, she would need her passport. Did he know where hers was located? Did it matter? He would've searched until he found it.

"Oh, I'm making us a special dinner for tonight." Andrew popped his head in the bedroom then disappeared.

Tuesday evening, Andrew re-emerged, opened the suitcase and pulled out a robe. Tossing it on the end of the bed, he untied her feet and stood at the edge of the bed by her hands.

"I'm going to let you join me at the dining room table tonight. *But* you need to be a good girl and not try anything." His hand trailed along her jaw. He gripped her chin tightly, turning her face him. "Do you understand?"

Through his constricting hold she murmured a yes.

"Good." His hand skated from her chin, over her collarbone, down her arm where he untied her hands. "I'll give you a minute to freshen up before joining me in the dining room."

In the bathroom she used the toilet, then faced her unattractive reflection in the mirror. Black and blue marks covered her face from where he'd struck her to the floor. Her face was thin, and her hair a tangled mess.

186

There were deep indented red rings around her swollen wrists. She turned the faucet on to wash her hands. She worked the soap into lather on her fingers then gently washed the open wounds. The burning sensation brought tears to her eyes, the pain unbearable, but she worried about infection. She blotted her hands with a towel and left the bathroom. She pulled the silk robe up her arms, over her shoulders and wrapped it tightly around her waist.

As she entered the dining area, Andrew said from the kitchen ledge, "Please have a seat. Dinner is almost finished."

The large glass table was set with china and candles. Any signs of the previous paperwork had been moved to the coffee table and couch in the living room. A bottle of red wine sat open on the table with two filled glasses.

She moved to sit in the chair at the end of the table closest to the hall. Closest to the door. Closest to escape.

Andrew quickly said, "No, you sit on the side. I want you to have the view."

She sat on the chair against the wall and looked out the octagon floor-to-ceiling living room windows. The twinkle of city lights illuminated the skyline as darkness fell. She always marveled at his apartment view. It was better than hers.

Andrew approached with two salad bowls and sat next to her. "This is going to be wonderful. Just you and me. Let's eat."

"Thank you." Chloe took a bite. The salad was a packaged variety but tasted delicious compared to the food over the last several days.

"Slow down. We're in no hurry. We have all night."

She couldn't help inhaling the salad. Not trusting Andrew with the possibility of drugging the water or wine, she took a small sip of her water.

"Would you like to take a shower tonight?" His hand came to rest on her thigh. "We could shower in mine...like old times."

The silky fabric slid as his hand slowly moved up her leg. She clenched her thighs together as she crossed her legs. His hand fell, and she grabbed the robe to cover her leg.

"Don't lead me on. When I kissed you, you kissed me back."

"I'm not leading you on, Andrew."

"So then, we'll finish dinner and go shower." He picked up their salad plates, his unfinished, and turned to the kitchen. A gun was tucked into the back of his pants.

No escaping tonight.

"I remembered how you like fettuccini alfredo and made you some." Andrew returned with two bowls. One filled full, while the other held about a cup and a half.

The smaller serving was placed in front of her. "Thank you." *Still managing my figure.*

He went to the kitchen and returned with a basket which held a small loaf of bread. "May I?" he asked, holding a serrated knife over the bread.

She nodded. He cut a small section, placing the bread on her plate. "Thank you."

"You're welcome." His hand caressed her jaw with a knowing smile. "A toast," he said, picking up his wine glass, waiting for her to do the same. "To the journey that awaits us."

While he tossed the wine back, she pretended to sip from the glass. "Andrew, tell me where we're going. I'm so excited to be going to South America." She played him.

"Brazil."

"Will we be ocean side?" She continued to act enthusiastic while taking a forkful of pasta.

"You could say that. I don't want to say anymore because it's a surprise." He shoveled a bite of fettuccini into his mouth, slopping sauce on the table and his face. When his cell phone rang, he excused himself from the table and moved to the farthest edge of the living room. "Hey Michael, What's up?—Sorry man, but tonight's not going to work.—No, I really can't. I've got a lot of paperwork to get through.—No vacation for me. I just had to get out of the office environment. Hey, have you heard from your sister?—I've tried calling her. I really miss her." He turned and winked. "Well, I'm sorry I can't join you tonight. Let's try to get together this weekend.—Later." He tossed the phone on the couch and sauntered back to the table, wearing a pleasing grin on his face.

Her stomach knotted. No one knew where she was. Dinner was no longer appetizing, and she pushed the bowl away. "I'd like to return to my room. May I be excused?"

"No! You're going to sit here and finish this meal I prepared for you." He pushed her bowl in front of her. "Now eat."

"Andrew,—"

"Shut up and eat," he yelled before his hand connected with her face.

The force knocked her sideways in her chair. She grabbed onto the table edge for balance. Her eyes closed at the pain. It was the same side he hit before. When she opened her eyes, he reached for her. She grimaced as his fingers gripped her forearm, yanking her upright.

"Eat," he said through a clenched mouth.

She took a small bit and swallowed. It didn't stay down for long. Nauseous, she darted for the kitchen sink and threw up the little dinner she ate. Andrew stood beside her, holding the gun at his side.

"Jesus Christ! Rinse that down the drain, and go to the room."

This would keep him away from her, safe for another night. As she turned the water off there was a knock at the door.

Chapter Twenty-Two

"Get in your room, shut the door and be quiet." Andrew ordered in a hush, pushing her out of the kitchen toward the bedroom. "I'll be there in a minute," he yelled to whoever stood on the other side of the door.

Chloe went into the bathroom and sat on the toilet lid. This would give her an advantage to hear what was going on.

"Officers, what can I do for you?" Andrew answered the door.

He said officers.

"Can we talk to you about a missing person? We believe you know her." There was a pause. "Chloe Atwood."

"No, I—"

"Help!" She ran from the bathroom and opened the bedroom door.

Andrew hit the entryway's tile floor with two uniformed officers holding him. "You bitch!"

"Show us your hands and get on the ground," a man in a suit yelled while pointing a gun at her.

She lowered herself to the bedroom floor in the doorway.

Someone asked, "Are there any others in there?"

"No. Just me." Tears streamed down her cheeks, falling to the carpet. She couldn't see what was happening in the hall but heard scuffling.

A uniformed officer asked, "Are you Chloe Atwood?"

"Yes." She shivered.

"Don't move until I say."

Someone stepped over her, searching the room and bathroom and passed back over her stating, "Clear." She continued to hear him yell,

"Clear," several more times before the officer said, "Get up slowly, and sit on the bed, please."

"Chloe, are you okay?" Ryan entered the room. His eyes roamed over her body as he came to stand in front of her.

"I'm good now that you're here."

"Call for an ambulance and a backup squad to take Mr. Lockhart downtown," Ryan told the officer.

"I don't need an ambulance. I'm okay." Chloe sat shaking on the bed.

"You're not okay, but you will be. Chloe, I need to ask, did he rape you?"

She laughed. "No. He couldn't get it up."

Ryan snickered before turning serious again. "That's good that he didn't rape you. If he had, we would be taking a trip to the hospital for sure. Once the paramedics check you and give the okay, I'll take you to the station. We need to ask some questions, and then you'll be free to go."

"Can I call anyone?"

"When we're all done, yes. I know Chad is worried, but he can wait for a little while longer. You're safe now, and that's all that matters. Do you have clothes you can put on?"

"I have the clothes I wore here. I'm not sure what he put in the suitcase." She nodded to where the suitcase sat against the wall.

"We watched him go to your place. I'd like to leave the suitcase here for the search. Would there be any evidence on your clothing? I know he didn't rape you, but any blood on the clothes?"

"Not that I know of. I never bled except from my wrists. I think that's all on the ties and bedding." She shuttered at the thought of being raped by someone she knew.

"Okay. Go ahead and put on the clothing that you wore here. We'll have whoever picks you up bring a change of clothing and have you leave behind those for evidence. Sound good?"

"Thank you. And I won't want them back. You guys can burn them or whatever."

"Okay. I'll step out and let you dress. Please leave the robe and don't touch anything."

"I'm fine with you staying in the room to witness that I don't disturb anything." Chloe picked up the clothes Andrew had tossed on the floor. She turned her back to Ryan. With the robe on to cover her nakedness, she pulled the pants up easily enough. The top was a little more challenging.

"Ready? Let's go downstairs. The ambulance should be here any minute." They passed an officer. "Great job. Thanks."

"You, too. We'll see you downtown."

Andrew was nowhere to be seen. She appreciated his removal from the area. The shaking subsided, but the situation was still raw and real.

* * * *

Pre-dawn Wednesday morning, unable to sleep, Chad sat in the hotel room. It was time for him to act. He couldn't sit back any longer waiting for his brother do something. Dressed, he went to the hotel's business center to use the computer. Finding an address for Andrew Lockhart, he searched for a map of where to go. Andrew lived just north, outside of the downtown area. Twenty to thirty minutes tops to get there.

As he left the business center to retrieve his car, his phone rang. "Hello."

"Chad, Ryan—"

"Give me good news otherwise hang up," he snarled.

"Where are you?"

"In the hotel lobby. I'm leaving to get Chloe from Andrew's."

"Stop and sit down." He paused. "Are you sitting?"

"Yes." It was a lie, but his nerves wouldn't let him sit.

"We have Chloe. She's safe."

Chad stopped pacing a small area in the lobby and sat on the closest piece of furniture. "Is she okay? Where is she?" His heart raced in anticipation of seeing and holding her again.

"She's here at the station. She's bruised, has facial swelling, and her wrists are raw and swollen. She's okay. We've finished questioning her and have her statement. I told her you were here. She broke down crying, asking for you to come get her. You'll need to bring a change of clothes for her. Do you have anything?"

"No, but I'll find something. The asshole didn't..."

"No, and I can't tell you anything else. She's part of the investigation."

"You're an asshole, you know that."

"Thank you. I'll take that as a compliment."

"Fine. Thank you for finding her, Ryan." He raked a hand through his hair.

"You can come to the station as soon as you get some clothes. We're on North Lamar."

"I'll find it."

"I've got to go. Later." His line went dead.

Chad fell against the back of the chair and cried. Not wanting to garner looks or questions from the hotel staff or patrons, he rode the elevator to his floor. In his room he searched through his clothing. Nothing would fit Chloe's tiny frame. He scrolled through his phone, tapped the number and waited for an answer.

"Hello," Stephanie answered groggy with sleep.

"Stephanie, it's Chad. I need a huge favor. I need some clothes for Chloe—"

"Is she with you?"

"No, but she's at the police station. I need to go pick her up, but she needs a change of clothes. Nothing of mine will fit her. Can you pull together something?"

"I'll find the perfect outfit," her voice chirpy.

"No, not perfect…something simple. Sweats and a sweatshirt. Oh, and underwear, too. Can you bring them to me at the hotel?"

"Sure. Give me an hour."

"No, I need them now." This woman didn't get it.

"Okay. Meet me in twenty minutes at the curb. I'll drive."

"Thank you." He ended the call and with time on his hands called Trent.

"Morning, Chad. You're up and at 'em early when you could be sleeping. What's up?" Trent's voice held the early hour grovels.

"Baby keeping you up at night? You sound terrible." Chad tried to keep calm and low key, but his insides were buzzing.

"No, baby's a breeze. Working on this first cup of joe. So, has something happened?"

"She's safe. My brother wouldn't tell me much."

"Well, you aren't her husband—yet."

A smile warmed on his face. He closed his eyes. "I know. I'm waiting to be picked up to go get Chloe from the station. Listen, I'm not sure when—"

"Ah hell, Chad, you don't need to worry about when you get back right now. You got things covered since Maggie went into labor. The two of you had prepared everyone for when she did go on maternity leave. We're all good here."

"Hey, did Maggie go into labor because of this thing with Chloe? She wasn't due yet."

"Women go early all the time. Some go later than others. It could or couldn't have caused her to go into labor, but we'll never know the answer. Don't worry, man. Everything ran like clockwork. It was the most amazing, beautiful thing I've ever seen. Then to hold him in my arms...man, I can't wait for you to go through this."

"I think it'll be a while before that happens. I need to ask Chloe first. Will you let Maggie know the news?"

"Of course. I probably won't see her until lunch though. Glad to hear Chloe's okay."

"Thanks. I'll talk to you later." Too early to call his mom, he went to the lobby and anxiously waited for Stephanie.

After ten minutes passed, he stepped outside to finish waiting. A white Mercedes four door coupe pulled to the curb and honked. Stephanie sat behind the wheel wearing sweats and a form fitted tee shirt.

He opened the door, sliding onto a grey leather seat. "Thank you. He said they're at the office on North Lamar. You know where that is?"

"Yup. There's a bag behind my seat on the floor with her clothes. What happened?"

"I don't know. My brother wouldn't say anything because it's still under investigation. I'm hoping Chloe will talk to me and won't shut me out."

"She'll talk. She's always been a talker," Stephanie spoke with liveliness.

"She's been through an ordeal, but to what extent I don't know. She's going to need time to heal from this." Chad watched the city pass by his window.

"We should be there in a few more minutes."

* * * *

Chloe sat in a white room with no windows. Two black chairs sat on the other side of the simple small rectangular office table. Voices spoke through the open door, but she didn't bother listening to what was being said. The only voice she wanted to hear was Chad's while he held her in his arms.

Anger toward her parents filtered into her thoughts. Their attitude toward her for ending the engagement to Andrew was wrong. She told her mother about Andrew's change in behavior. Her mother denied the situation, not taking her seriously. Then there was her father who worked on Andrew's side to get her to quit her job. He told his wife to handle things about calling off the wedding rather than facing the situation.

She thought about her trip to Florida. Chad had an idea that Maggie supported and wanted to help them. The purpose behind going mirrored her current job. Her thoughts were interrupted.

"Chloe, Chad's here." Ryan spoke through the doorway.

Chad turned the corner, dropping a bag, as he reached for her. She ran the short distance into his open arms. He held her tightly.

"I can't breathe," she said breathlessly.

He released his hold, and his hands gently cupped her face. "I love you." Softly spoken, tears streamed from his eyes.

His tender lips touched hers with such delicacy, her insides turned to pudding. Her eyes flooded with tears. "I love you."

A throat cleared. Ryan stood looking at them. "The cameras are shut off. You can change in here. Place your clothing in this bag, and leave it on the table. We'll take care of it from there."

"I'll be right outside waiting," Chad said, giving her a peck on the cheek. "Stephanie got the clothes for you. Hope they fit." He closed the door.

She stripped the clothes from her body as quick as a pit crew working at the Dayton 500. She tossed the clothing worn from Andrew's into the brown bag. There *was* blood on the clothing. Steph's Victoria Secret bag contained black yoga pants, black thong underwear, a pink tank top and a loose fitting sweatshirt. Everything fit.

* * * *

While Chloe changed, Chad found his brother. "Hey. I went to Mom's yesterday, and the DNA results came. Dad...is my father. If you want to let him know, I'm okay with that."

"Do you want him to know?"

"For thirty-six years he's had to wonder. Okay, so maybe for a few years he didn't. I think he has a right to know."

"I'm not sure when I'll see him next. I'll play it by ear." Ryan leaned against a desk. "I'm glad it turned out we have the same dad." He delivered a genuine smile. "Stephanie seems like a nice person, considering her brother's crazy."

"Ah, yeah."

"How well do you know her?"

Chad swallowed at the not so past memory of their almost tryst. "Not too well. I've only met her a couple of times. We didn't talk much. She's a childhood friend of Chloe's."

The door opened. Chloe strolled into the hall.

"All set?" Chad asked, stepping away from Ryan.

"Yes, if Ryan says I can go." She went into Chad's waiting arms.

"Here's your purse. The only thing missing is your cell phone. If you leave the state, let me know. If you choose to get a new cell phone, please notify me. If we have any further questions we'll need to be able to reach you until the case is closed. I have Chad's number, too."

"Thank you for everything." Chloe extended her hand to Ryan.

"Just doing my job. Take care, and I'm sure we'll be seeing you more...both of you at family gatherings."

Chad embraced his brother. "Thank you. Stay safe, man." They firmly patted each other's backs before releasing the hold. "Stephanie's waiting for us. Let's get you home."

Chapter Twenty-Three

Steph raced from the car and delivered a hard hug.

"I'm okay. Thank you for helping Chad."

"I'm sorry about my brother. I don't know what happened." Steph backed from her arms.

"He's been using cocaine. Which explains why his behavior changed. If you don't mind, I really don't want to talk about this. Just take us back to my apartment."

Chloe and Chad climbed into the back seat of Steph's car.

The ride was quiet. When they arrived at Chloe's building, Steph dropped them at the curb. Chad stayed in the car for a minute longer before joining her on the sidewalk.

"What was that all about?" Chloe asked when he finally joined her.

"There's a mutual interest between her and my brother. I was just letting her know Ryan's interested."

"Oh." She waved to Steph, who drove away from the curb in the six o'clock morning traffic.

They entered the building foyer. She waved to the guard as they headed to the elevator. The long sleeves of the sweat jacket covered her wrist bandages. In the elevator, she went into Chad's open arms again.

"Will you stay with me?" Her body shook.

He held her tighter. "Of course. Should I check out of the hotel and stay here?"

"Please."

"I have the rental car to take care of, too."

"You can park it in the garage. Or you can return it. I have my car we can drive."

The elevator doors opened, and they strolled to her front door. Chloe entered the apartment, stopping in the hall before entering the kitchen. Leaning against the wall, she slid to the floor crying.

"Hey, it's okay. You're okay. I'm here." Chad gathered her in his arms. He carried her to the bedroom.

She crawled into bed. Beside her, he pulled her into his chest, stroking her hair. She cried herself to sleep. She was safe.

"Do you feel better?" Chad asked when she blinked her eyes open later.

"A little." She stretched her lean body. "How long did I sleep?"

"*We* slept about six hours. I've been awake for about an hour."

"Thank you for being here."

"I wouldn't be anywhere else than with you. Would you like to hear some good news?" He asked with a broad smile.

"Yes."

"Maggie had the baby."

Excited, Chloe sat up on the bed.

"A baby boy named Justin Connor. He weighed in at seven pounds nine ounces. Trent said Maggie breezed through it all."

Tears filled her eyes, and for a change they were tears of happiness. "When? When was he born?"

"Tuesday."

"I should call her, but—"

"No buts, call her. She needs to hear your voice." He rolled to the nightstand to grab his cell, tapped the screen several times and handed her the phone.

"Chad, tell me you have some good news," Maggie answered with concern.

Her reply was a simple, "Congratulations, Mommy."

"Chloe? Are you okay?" Excitement mixed with panic resonated in Maggie's voice.

"I'm fine. I'm at home with Chad. I don't want to talk about it right now. Okay?" Chloe asked humbly while gazing into Chad's comforting blue eyes.

"Okay. I'm glad you're safe and with Chad."

"So how is it…being a mom? How's baby Justin? I want to know everything." Chloe lay back on the pillows. Chad patted her leg and left the room. Maggie caught her up on the birth and baby.

* * * *

An hour later, Chloe emerged from the bedroom with his phone. "Something smells wonderful."

"I hope you're hungry." Chad hugged her. "I dug through your bare cupboards and managed to find some pasta fixings." He strained the pasta. "I know it's early for dinner, but we never ate breakfast or lunch."

"I'm starving. Maggie's so blessed. It sounds as though it's going well for them."

"They're happy." Dishing pasta into a bowl, he ladled sauce on top of the noodles and set the bowl on the counter.

"Chad, I've made a decision."

"What kind of decision?" He did the same with another bowl and took them to the table. "I hope it still involves me being a part of your life."

"Very much so." She took his hands in hers. "I don't want you to move here." Her fingertip touched his opening lips to speak. "I don't want to live here anymore. I want to be with you. I want you to be where you're happiest…on the ranch."

"What about your job? You love your job."

"After what…I can't, Chad. I can't do it anymore." Her head fell against his chest.

Chad gently lifted her chin so she'd look at him. "You don't have to do anything you don't want to. I'll support you in anything you do."

"I need to call work and go talk to my boss tomorrow. I also need to face my parents and tell them I'm moving. Are you up to driving back to Florida?"

"With you? Yes, in a heartbeat. Let's eat before the pasta gets too cold." They sat down and ate quietly.

Chad was full of excitement like a child waiting to open his birthday gifts. And it wasn't even close to his birthday. A reality of what quality of life Chloe was used to sunk into his happiness.

"Chloe, I need to make sure you understand I live a modest life. I won't be able to give you what you have here. But I can promise you a life filled with plenty of love."

"This..." her arms spread out, "is my parents, not my life. As long as I have you in my life, I'm rich."

"I'd kiss you, but we're eating." She laughed with him. "There's something else. I got the DNA results. My dad is my dad."

"How does that make you feel?"

"I don't know. I haven't been able to process it all because I found out while I was...looking for...you." He closed his eyes, fighting the tears, and he won. The bowl of pasta was his focal point upon opening his eyes. "I'm glad to know and not have the question hanging over my head. It puts my mom's mind to rest. Ryan says he's glad we're full brothers and not half." He stuffed a large forkful of noodles in his mouth.

"What about your dad? Are you going to tell him?"

"I've told Ryan he can let him know. I'm not sure I'm ready to see him yet."

"You should. Make some peace with him. You've made progress with Ryan. Haven't you?"

He nodded while chewing.

"I'm not sure how soon I'll be able to leave. Use the time to see him."

"I'll think about it. Trent's got things covered at the ranch. There's no hurry going back."

"Tomorrow I'll be busy, so why don't you go see your mom. Give some thought about seeing your dad, too." She took the last bite from her bowl.

He nodded again. More steps to take. Steps to healing. Steps to the future.

* * * *

Thursday morning Chloe handed in her job resignation. They were understanding and authorized her immediate release. She arranged to meet her parents, brother and sister for a late lunch. It wasn't easy to get them all to understand the urgency, but her brother helped, knowing a little about the situation surrounding the gathering. Being in public would hopefully make for a lesser chance of her parents making a scene. That would be socially wrong in their eyes.

She chose the Italian restaurant where she had planned to have the rehearsal dinner. It was upscale enough for her parents, yet centrally located for everyone. Once seated at the table, she ordered a glass of merlot to help calm her nerves. The hostess approached with Michael in tow, and she stood, delivering a quick hug.

"How are you?" Michael asked, sitting next to her.

"I'm okay. Michael...you're not...using, are you?" She had to ask since he and Andrew were best friends and hung out.

"Using? Using what?" His face scrunched in confusion.

"Cocaine." She kept her voice low so the other patrons couldn't hear. "Because Andrew is, or maybe I should say was, using cocaine."

"No." His eyes widened, and his head shook in disbelief.

"I'll explain more when we're all together."

Her parents and sister approached. She stood to briefly hug everyone, but her father held her longer and tighter than the others.

"Thank you for doing this on short notice. I know you're busy, Dad, so I'll try and make this as quick as possible. In light of these past few days, I've made the decision to move to Florida."

The table burst with whats, whens and whys. The waitress cautiously approached to get drink orders. Chloe breathed a sigh of relief.

"Hi, my name is Trish. I'll be your server today. What can I get for you to drink?"

Her mother ordered a wine spritzer, her sister a sweet tea, Michael a beer and her father ordered a scotch. When the waitress left, Chloe raised her hands to halt the barrage of questions.

"I've already talked to my boss, and it's final. I'm done working for the shelter. I'll be leaving as soon as I'm packed, and Chad is ready to leave." Her hand flew up to cut them off as their mouths open to interject. "He has some family things to take care of here. I'm going to be okay. Andrew didn't hurt me enough to damage who I am, but enough that I'm going to move with someone I love and who loves me." Chloe grew quiet when the waitress approached with their drinks.

"Are you ready to order, or would you like a few more minutes?"

"We'll need some time, Trish. Thank you," her father said before looking sternly at Chloe. "Who is Chad?"

"You met him at the engagement party." The last two words were spoken with a bit of regret. Not because she regretted calling off the wedding, but because of the expense and time her parents had put into the event. "He works with Maggie and Trent. He's part owner of the Triple R. Anyway, I'm going to live with him on the ranch. He and Maggie have a great idea, and I'm going to help them get it off the ground." She picked up her menu. "Let's decide what we want and order before I tell you about the last several days."

"You can't be serious," her mother said. "Andrew can get counseling. You two should go to couples therapy."

"Mother, I'm not talking further about this." A decision made of what she wanted to order, she flagged the waitress.

"Ready to order?"

"Yes, Trish," Chloe stated. "I'd like the lobster stuffed ravioli with a Caesar side salad. Oh, and can I get two servings of the lasagna and garlic bread to go."

"I'll bring the lasagna and bread out with your meals. And for you, ma'am?" The server asked her mother and worked around the table for orders before leaving.

Her mother spoke immediately after their waitress left the table. "Chloe, I deserve to know what's going on. Why are you walking away from Andrew and the family?"

"So, you know how Michael told you I was missing? Well, for the past couple of days, Andrew held me captive in his apartment. He wasn't kind to me. I'm not sure what else the police have discovered, but I do know he was using cocaine."

"*How* did he keep *you* captive?" her mother asked in a disbelieving tone. She pursed her lips with her head tipped to her shoulder.

"With ties, *Mother*." Chloe yanked her sleeves up, exposing her bandages. "See," and she shoved them under her mother's nose. "He's not so innocent, *Mother*."

"Chloe." Michael gently took her hands, placing them under the table. "Mom, you have to see that Andrew isn't the man we thought him to be. The cocaine affected him in ways that he made some bad decisions."

"Dad, if you haven't started looking at him as a suspect about the disappearing monies, you may want to. He said some things, making me believe he's your thief. I also believe he had something to do with the shelter not getting the grant from the foundation, but that's a done deal. We don't always get what we apply for. There are too many groups in need of help."

"Why didn't you run away before he tied you up? Or scream for help?" her mother burst out.

"I *did, Mother.*"

"Mom, stop. You're upsetting Chloe." Michael came to her aide again.

"But I don't understand."

"*Mother*, he took me captive. I screamed. He hit me with a rock-solid open hand. I tried escaping and ended up with sores." She shoved her wrists at her mother again. "When I did manage to break free, he stood in the door when I opened it. He knocked me hard onto the tiled floor. I yelled for help again. He slapped the hell out of my face. Makeup is a wonderful cover artist." Chloe pushed back from the table, rattling the glasses. "I'm done, Mother. I'm done trying to talk to you." She stormed from the table, angry and hurt.

Her father snagged her arm before reaching the door to the ladies room. "Come sit with me." His big arm slid around her waist and guided her to a bench. "I'm sorry about what happened back there. You're mother's been a wreck since you told us about breaking the engagement to Andrew. She still believes you two will work things out. I've been so wrapped up in work that I didn't give anything much thought outside of my business life. As to what you said at the table about him being a suspect, he's the prime suspect. All I know, since it's still under investigation, is that they found evidence at his place when they found you. I'm just glad they found you when they did. I'd like to meet this Chad again. And thank him."

"Thank you, Dad. We'll swing by before we leave town. Which brings me to my lease. I'll need to—"

"I'll talk to the owner. I know him pretty well. I'm sure he'll let you slide."

"Oh, thank you." Chloe sighed in gratitude, hugging him.

"Let's go back. I'm sure our food is at the table."

* * * *

"Thanks for picking me up, Angel." Chad hopped into the bucket seat of the minivan.

"Not a problem. It will give us time to catch up. But first explain why you're here and then why you're returning your rental car but not catching a plane out of here." She maneuvered through the traffic.

"Where to begin? Chloe was coming to visit me and never showed up on Sunday. Never answering her cell phone or home phone when I called, I knew something wasn't right and caught the last flight here. Monday I called Ryan for help, but there wasn't much he could do because a missing persons report wasn't filed yet. He did do some checking though and found her car parked in her ex-fiancés building ramp. She had texted me that prior to her flight she was stopping at his place. My hunch was right, Angel." Chad observed they weren't heading into downtown but south. "Where are we going? I wanted to go back to the hotel."

"Mom's. I thought you'd like to go visit *and* show her the ring you bought for Chloe."

"What?" he exclaimed shocked. "How did you know?"

"I saw you dispose of the blue bag and put the box in your pocket. That pocket is bulging, by the way. You'll want to try and disguise it better before Chloe sees it. When are you going to ask her?"

"Don't know. When I think the time is right."

"So why buy it now?"

"It felt like the thing to do. Okay?"

"Okay." She raised her hands up in defeat and quickly placed them back on the steering wheel. "I'm sure there's more to this story about Chloe. Did you want to finish?"

"I don't know what happened really, as Chloe hasn't said much. Ryan's not talking either because it's an open case. Andrew had her tied up to the bed—"

"Oh, my God."

"Her wrists have sores because of it. Andrew's sister helped by going to his place and saw Chloe's purse on the floor. Tuesday night the cops went over, and that was the end of it. I picked her up from the police station in the early morning hours yesterday."

"Jesus, Chad. The guy sounds crazy. She was going to marry him? What the...?"

"I guess he's been using cocaine. Chloe mentioned that much. She seems too okay with everything. That's why I'm waiting to ask her to marry me."

"Get her to talk to someone, or this could eat at her."

"I'm hoping Ryan will tell me more about it, so I have a better understanding for Chloe's sake."

"I can say something to try and push him to tell you."

"I'll keep that in mind. There's something else I need to tell you, but it'll have to wait until we're at Mom's."

"What?" she exclaimed. "Tell me, and I promise I won't say anything when we get there."

"It's nothing too exciting. You'll have to wait."

Chapter Twenty-Four

Chad and Angel walked into their mother's house after ringing the doorbell. "Mom?" Angel called out.

"Out here." They found her on the patio. "What brings you two by? Chad, has Ryan been able to find Chloe?"

"I'm sorry I didn't call you. It was early yesterday morning when I got the call from Ryan. She's having lunch with her family right now and breaking the news to them. I'm not moving back. Chloe's moving to the ranch with me. She's already resigned from her job. That's the news I wanted to share, Angel. I told you it's nothing big."

"She's starting over." His mom placed a hand over his. "And with my son. I like that."

"He's got big plans. Show us," Angel said excited.

"Show us what, Chad?" his mom inquired.

He stood, reached in his pocket and pulled out the light blue box. His mom gasped. He opened the box and handed it to her. "Do you think she'll like it?"

"It's from Tiffany's. Of course she'll love it." Angel leaned over their mother's shoulder.

"Where it's from doesn't matter. What matters is that it's from you. From the heart." His mom spoke in a humble tone. "I think it's stunning. But...don't you think it's a bit too soon?" She handed the box back to him.

"I don't know when I'll ask her. I told Angel that it felt right to buy this now. I'll propose when I think it's the right time." He closed the box and slid it back in his front pocket.

"As much as we will miss her and the work she has done to help the shelter, I'm glad to see her moving on. So, tell me what happened."

"Mom, he took her hostage. Tied her to the bed and hit her a couple of times."

"He didn't—"

"No." He hated to talk about this. "Ryan told me. Chloe said he didn't. She won't talk about the ordeal with me. I understand why. I got uncomfortable just now when you were going to ask if he raped her. Not to mention angry at Andrew all over again."

"You two will need to talk to each other about this traumatic situation, more so for Chloe's sake."

"I know. I want to give her space and time before pushing her to open up and talk."

"Don't wait too long. I'm glad she's safe. I'm assuming Andrew's in jail?"

"As far as I know. I haven't talked to Ryan since yesterday morning."

"You need to find out if bail has been set. And if it has, what's the possibility he'll get out?"

"I'll see if Ryan knows. I hope he can't get out."

"If he does, I'm sure the judge will have bail conditions, restricting him from being anywhere close to Chloe."

"Doesn't mean he'll abide by them." It was time for a new topic. "How's your shoulder?"

"Good. Therapy is going well, but tough. It tires me out."

"Well, don't overdo it. You don't want to do more harm than good."

"I'm not. I go to the doctor for a check-up tomorrow and hope he tells me I can go back to work. This not doing anything is driving me crazy."

Chloe's ring tone played on his phone. "Hey, how's lunch?"

"I'm on my way home. Did you take care of what you needed to?"

"Yeah, but my sister Angel didn't take me back to your place. We made a surprise visit to my mom's."

"Oh, I bet she appreciated that. Tell her hi, and give her a hug for me."

"Will do. Angel and I will leave soon, so if I'm not there, know I'm on my way. Love you."

"Love you, too. Bye."

He glanced at the women sitting at the table. "I'm sorry, but I'd really like to be there when she gets home. Do you mind leaving?" He looked to Angel.

"No, this should work out perfect for me to be home then in time for the kids to be getting in from school."

He and Angel got up from their chairs and gave their mother a hug. "Bye, Mom," he said, exiting through the kitchen. "Chloe and I will stop by before we leave town."

"You'd better," she yelled back as he strolled through the living room to the front door.

* * * *

Chloe found the apartment empty. Chad wasn't back yet. A cold chill seeped through her, and she shivered. She didn't like the quiet. To remedy the situation, she turned on the radio. The lasagna and bread went into the fridge. When Chad arrived, she'd warm it up for dinner.

Standing at the marble counter, she glanced around the apartment. Her parents owned almost everything in the place. If she wanted to pack she would need her clothing and bathroom items. There were a few pictures, nick-knacks and some of the kitchen utensils that were hers. She hoped to get everything into her car to save on shipping expenses. Maybe tomorrow they could pick up some boxes and finish packing by the end of the day. Then over the weekend say goodbye to family.

She opened the drawer in front of her and pulled out things to take to Florida. When she was done with the drawer she moved to the next one and continued doing this with all the drawers and cabinets. The counter only held a few of her favorite utensils, pans and serving bowls.

While she worked on the last cupboard, Chad opened the door. "Chloe," he called strolling down the short hall.

"In the kitchen."

"What are you doing?"

"Starting the packing process." She stepped off the stool and wrapped her arms around his waist. "Taking out what I'll be packing for the ranch." Placing a quick kiss to his lips, she added, "For *our* home."

Chad slid his arms around her. "I—" He pecked her lips. "Love—" Another peck. "The sound—" And another. "Of that." This time the kiss was filled with warmth and passion.

She stepped back. "Ouch! What is that in your pocket?"

"Oh, nothing. I'll go put it away."

"Well, what is it that it has sharp corners?" She reached for his pocket, but he grabbed her hand, stopping her. "Chad? Don't keep secrets from me."

"No secrets? Then you need to talk to me. *We* need to talk about—"

"Not now." She turned from him, returning to search the last cupboard. He didn't say anything, and when she glanced over her shoulder, he was gone. With nothing in the cabinet to pack, she closed the door and stepped down. She folded the stepstool and returned it in the small pantry.

"What did you want for dinner?" Chad's calm voice asked.

"I hope you don't mind, but I got some lasagna and bread for dinner. I need to heat it up though. Are you hungry?"

"How long to heat it?"

"Half hour."

"Why don't we wait for an hour?" He approached her. "Let's sit and relax together." Her hand in his, they walked to the smaller sofa. "I called my brother and asked him about Andrew."

She sat next to him, snuggling into his chest. She curled her legs up, stuffing her feet in the sofa's cushioned corner.

Chad wrapped an arm around her and rested his hand on her hip. The other hand held hers, stroking her fingers. "Bail has been set for his release. He's been ordered not to be in the same vicinity as you if he gets out. We need to inform the guard desk that if they see him to call the police immediately. They need to know."

Her head shook. "I can't...I can't tell them about this."

"Chloe," he tipped her head toward him. "They don't need to know the underlying situation. They only need to know he is not to be in this building. If you want, I'll inform them."

"Yes, please." She moved her head and sat secure by his side.

The music played, filling the silence between them.

Several minutes passed before Chad spoke. "How do your wrists feel today?"

"Fine," she clipped.

"You told Ryan he didn't rape you."

She bolted upright. Her pulse raced, thudding her heart against her chest like a charging elephant. "He had no right to tell you that!" The tears spilled down her cheeks.

"I asked." He stood in front of her, but she couldn't look at him. "I had a right to know."

"Did he tell you about how he sexually touched me? How he kissed me, and I kissed him back? How he tried to have sex with me, and I was willing because I didn't want to get beaten and raped?" The anger raged from her mouth. She put her hands to his chest. "Did he tell you about all of that?" she yelled, pushing him back and stormed to her room, slamming the door closed.

* * * *

Chad caught his balance then let his body fall onto the sofa cushions. He'd hurt her by revealing he knew. It got her to open up though. But the wrong way. *Jackass.* He needed to do something. *Go in there and apologize or let her be alone and come out when she's ready?* He swore under his breath.

In a few quick steps, he held the closed door knob. *Knock or go in?* He rapped on the door. "Chloe? Can I come in?"

No response.

He turned the handle. To avoid any possible thrown objects he slowly entered. It would be his own fault if things flew in his direction. Thankfully, nothing did. She was laying on the bed, curled in the fetal position. He sat behind her but didn't touch her.

"I'm sorry. I was so worried about you. I didn't mean for you to...I wanted us to talk about it when you were ready. I don't know what to say."

"You're right. You had a right to know." She spoke softly sniffling. "Chad, the things he did were so disgusting. I feel so dirty." She sobbed.

"He had me lying naked on the bed all tied up, with my legs spread. And the way he looked at me. Oh..."

He lay next to her, draping an arm on her waist. She held it tight against her.

"When he kissed me the first time, I tried to fight him. He got angry, and I knew not to fight him from then on."

"Why didn't anything happen between the two of you?"

"He couldn't get an erection which was really strange. He was always at the ready."

"Well, I'm glad he wasn't this time." He propped up and leaned to look at her. "Chloe, I'm glad you went along with his games. It probably saved you from a lot more harm." He gently kissed her shoulder. "Would you like to rest for a while?"

"If you wouldn't mind."

"I'm going to talk to the guard on duty. I'll check on you when I get back."

"I love you." She squeezed his arm before releasing her hold.

"I love you." He kissed her cheek and scooted off the bed. He snatched a blanket from the back of a chair in the living room and covered her.

"Thank you."

He closed the door and left the apartment.

* * * *

Chloe woke to the smell of lasagna and bread. She sat on the edge of the bed, stretched and glanced at the clock. Chad had let her sleep over an hour. With a final stretch, she strolled into the living room.

The dining room table was set. Candles burned throughout the room. A bottle of wine sat on the table with two filled glasses. Chad had his back turned.

"Aren't you a romantic one?" She approached the counter where he stood.

"Agh!" He startled. "And aren't you a sneaky one? How was your nap?"

"Wonderful. Thank you for the nap and getting dinner ready."

He pulled the food from the oven and dished it onto the plates. "If you'd be so kind as to set this on the table, I'll get our bread. So, the guard on duty understood and said he'd inform the other guards."

"Did he ask questions?"

"Yes, but I was able to explain without giving details. It's okay."

"Thanks for taking care of that." She took a bite, and when she finished chewing said, "I want to go get boxes and pack tomorrow."

"Okay. This is the best lasagna." He stuffed in another bite.

"If we can, I'd like to get everything into my car and not have to ship anything. There isn't anything big going with us, so I think it will be doable." She took a sip of wine and savored the smooth berry and oak flavor as it slid down her throat. "I'd also like to leave on Sunday. After seeing our families, of course."

"My mom mentioned that we'd better stop by. I assured her we would. We should probably see her first, then go by your parents on the way out of town."

"Sounds like a plan." She raised her glass. "To our future—together."

* * * *

Chloe and Chad returned Friday afternoon from the store with flat boxes in a variety of sizes and a three pack of moving tape. She insisted on buying packing paper instead of Chad's method of using old newspaper.

"You start getting the boxes taped, and I'll start wrapping stuff in the paper." She put the pack of tape on the table before going into the kitchen with the packing paper.

"What size box do you want for the kitchen stuff?"

"Let's use the medium size for the kitchen and living room stuff. Take a couple small ones into my bathroom for that crap. It should all fit in one or two boxes. The large ones will be for clothes, so put them in my bedroom. I also have my suitcases we can use."

They worked through the afternoon and into the early evening without eating lunch. Eventually Chloe's stomach protested. "Let's go grab an early dinner at The Knoll."

"No need to twist my arm." Chad's cell rang. "Hello?—Did you call the police?" He ran to the front door, checking the locks.

Her stomach revolted. She swallowed hard. Her pulse picked up.

"Send them up immediately. Bye." Chad pocketed his phone. "Andrew's on his way up. Get in your bathroom!" He shoved her in the direction of her bedroom. "Lock the door, and lie in the tub. Don't open that door until you hear my voice or the cops. Do you understand?"

"Yes." Was her response even audible? She did as told. The beating of her heart was the only sound in the room. She swallowed and strained to hear a sound of something. A voice, sirens, or Chad's voice saying it was okay to come out. What seemed like hours passing she knew were only minutes.

There was pounding on a door. It wasn't the bathroom door. A man yelled her name.

Andrew.

She closed her eyes. Chills skittered across her skin.

More pounding. "I know you're in there! Open the damned door, Chloe!"

She curled into a ball, hugging herself.

There were a few more pounds. It was quiet. Then she heard several gunshots before a thud. *Who was shot?*

"Chlo—" Andrew started saying her name and then grunts and groans.

The voices were inaudible. Chad would attack Andrew if he got in the apartment. Swallowing again, she feared Andrew and his capabilities. Bile worked up her esophagus.

A gunshot rang through the air.

Chapter Twenty-Five

"Police! Hands in the air! Drop the weapon!"

Chloe got up on her knees and threw up down the drain.

"No! I'm not going without her!"

Andrew was insane.

"Drop the gun!"

Rapid gunshots popped in the air.

She threw up again and turned on the water to wash the nastiness away. As she turned the faucet off, the door handle jiggled.

"Police. Open the door, and step back."

She did as asked, but bolted for the tub's edge where the rest of breakfast slowly slid down the drain.

A cop stepped in the bathroom and handed her a towel. "Are you okay?"

"Never better." She grimaced, sitting next to the tub on the floor. "I heard gun shots."

"Are you Chloe Atwood?"

"Yes. Who's been shot?"

"There are two men. Can you tell me who they are?"

"One is my boyfriend, Chad Rogers. I'm guessing the other guy is my ex-fiancé, Andrew Lockhart."

"Please come with me." The officer offered his hand to assist her up from the floor.

They left the bathroom and slowly entered the living room.

"Chad!" She ran to him. He lay strapped onto a stretcher.

"Ma'am, we need to get him to the hospital."

"Go," a uniformed officer said.

She collapsed to the floor in tears.

"How's he?" a male voice asked.

Turning her head, Chloe slowly got on her knees. Through tear-filled eyes, she saw a bloody body lying just inside the entrance. She blinked slowly, once and then twice, before she stood. Her body wavered. An arm steadied her. She swallowed.

One step. Two step.

"Is he dead?" she asked in a whisper.

"Yes," the paramedic stated.

"Can you verify who this is?" an officer asked.

"That's...Andrew Lockhart." Light headed, her eyelids fluttered, and she fell.

* * * *

"Chloe, wake up."

Chloe's eyes flickered before focusing on the face with the soft voice. A woman sat on the edge of her bed. "Who are you?" She startled, scrambling to sit up.

"Take it easy. You passed out." She left the room, coming back with a chair from the dining table. She sat next to the bed. "I'm Detective Monica Vergas. I'm wondering if you can tell me what happened here." She opened a notebook and held a pen, ready to take notes.

"I don't really know. My boyfriend and I were packing my belongings when he got a call. I assumed it was from the guard desk because he told me to lock myself in the bathroom and not to come out until he or the police knocked on the door."

"And who is your boyfriend?"

"Chad Rogers."

"Did you hear anything from inside the bathroom?"

"Can I get some aspirin or something? My head hurts."

"I'll be right back." The woman left the room and asked someone to bring the items to them. Resuming her place on the chair, she asked again, "What could you hear?"

"Andrew yelling and pounding on the door." Due to the headache, she closed her eyes. "Then there were gunshots. Followed by a thud and then grunting and groaning. Then another gunshot before the police came yelling."

A uniformed officer handed her a glass of water and two pills. She swallowed the offered medication.

"Can you tell me what the officers said?"

"I heard them yelling to someone to put up their hands and drop the weapon. Andrew yelled, *"No, not without her."* The next thing I know, there were more gunshots and an officer at the door."

"Thank you, Chloe. I need you to go with an officer to the station and write a statement."

"Didn't I just give you my statement? I want to go to the hospital. I need to see Chad." She cried.

"I'll be right back." The detective returned several minutes later. "Chad was shot in the hip area and is in surgery now, so you wouldn't be able to see him. Go to the station with the officer, and when you're finished they'll take you to the hospital."

"Okay. I need shoes." Chloe got up, sliding sandals on her feet. "Let's go. Who's taking me?"

* * * *

Chloe strutted with purpose through the hospital's entrance. Ryan stood near the reception desk wearing street clothes. Her head swirled at the site of him because of the resemblance to Chad. She stopped to regain her balance.

Hands held her arms. "Are you okay?"

When she opened her eyes, Ryan stood in front of her. "I'm fine. How's Chad?"

"He's in recovery and doing fine. He's been asking about you."

"Where was he shot?" They strolled to the bank of elevators.

"It entered through his hip and exited out the back of his thigh. He'll be out of commission for a while."

"He's alive, and that's what matters." She lowered her voice to make it difficult for others around them to hear. "I would think it wrong for Andrew to have a gun after what happened. Wouldn't you guys have taken away the gun he had?"

A bank of doors opened, and they stepped in the elevator. Ryan pushed the button, and the doors closed.

"We did confiscate the weapons. Chloe, guns can be found and purchased illegally on the street. If you know the right people, and Andrew did, you can get what you want at a price."

"You said weapons. What else did he have?"

"Another gun and couple of knives." The doors opened. "This way," Ryan said, stepping into the hall.

She followed him, surprised to learn Andrew had more than the one weapon while holding her hostage. A shiver skittered up her back as though cold water trickled down her spine.

"Chad's medicated and looks a mess. But don't worry, he's okay. Here we are." He opened the slightly closed door for her to pass him and enter.

Swallowing, her eyes flooded the moment she saw him. Chad was still in the flat bed. Needles connected to tubes stuck out of his arms. She wiped her eyes, slowly approaching his bedside. If it weren't for the monitor's beeping, she'd have sworn he was dead.

From the other side of the bed, Linda came around, embracing Chloe. She murmured the words a mother says to comfort her children. "There, there. It's okay. He's fine. He's a strong boy. He'll be happy to see you. Are you okay?"

With a swipe of her hand the tears vanished. "I'm better now that I'm here...with him."

"We'll leave you two alone for a little while." Linda joined Ryan by the door.

She sat on the chair Linda had vacated, moving closer to the bedside, mindful of the cords on the floor. She slid a palm under his warm hand and placed the other on top. The tears continued flowing from her eyes. She rested her head on her arms and gazed at the man who put himself in harm's way for her.

"You were willing to do anything for me. You put yourself in danger and look what happened." She cried and closed her eyes. "I almost lost you after getting you back."

Fingers squeezed her hand. Her eyes fluttered open to see Chad gazing at her.

"I love you," he croaked.

"I love you." She stood, bending to deliver a quick soft kiss to his warm lips.

"What happened to—?"

"He's dead, and I don't want to talk about it. I have something more important to ask you. Chad, you have made me realize how much I love you and need you in my life. I'm hoping you feel the same way." His mouth opened to speak, and she shook her head. "No. Let me finish. I want to have your children. I want to spend the rest of my life with you as your wife. Chad, will you marry me?"

Epilogue

Inside a white canopied tent, Chloe prepared for her early November wedding day. Maggie, her Matron of Honor, sat on a chair next to her, the finishing touches being done on their hair. Steph assisted Maggie with her gray beaded gown. With her long blonde hair elegantly styled on top of her head, the gown's back was open, exposing a long smooth stretch of skin.

"Okay, it's the bride's turn. Are you ready, Chloe?" Steph asked, holding the long mermaid gown.

"I was ready the day I asked Chad to marry me." The ladies laughed, and the photographer snapped shots of the three women.

"I can't believe *you* asked him." Maggie stated, while sliding her feet into low-heeled silver shoes.

"I *love* that you went with a non-traditional gown. This is so gorgeous." Steph held the dress open as Chloe carefully stepped inside.

"This whole thing has been non-traditional, so why not the gown? After trying on dresses with Maggie, I decided those dresses weren't right. I saw this Jovanni gown and knew it was what I wanted. Finding something for Maggie, to coordinate, took a little time."

"Suck it in." Steph tugged the zipper up, and the gunmetal colored satin fabric grew taught against her body. "Perfect."

Chloe's hands ran over her hips, turning to face the full-length mirror. Tendrils of chestnut hair hung here and there, while the majority was pulled in a low bun of twisted and twirled sections. She swore her hair was covered in shellac because of the exorbitant amount of hairspray the stylist used to hold it in place.

"Don't start crying. You'll get us all started, and we won't be able to stop." Steph blotted under her eyes.

"The father of the bride is here and would like to see his daughter."

"Dad!" She turned to the door, wanting to run into his arms, but the dress wouldn't allow any long quick strides. Maybe slow ones, but even that was questionable. "Come in!" She waved her hands in front of her face, warding off the tears. "You look so handsome."

Her father gently embraced her. "You look stunning. You're going to blow the man away."

"Dad."

"Maggie, you're husband's going to want to haul you off—"

"Dad," she scolded, embarrassed to hear her father talk like that.

"Well, it's true. You are a gorgeous group of women. Now, I think it's time for us to have a few pictures taken."

"Already captured the moment, sir."

"Well then," her father held his elbow out for her to take. "It's time."

Chloe took a deep breath and exhaled, placing her hand through her father's arm. A bittersweet moment but she wouldn't let her own mother's absence ruin this special day. Her mother lived in denial and went off the deep end with Andrew's death.

As they exited the tent, the florist was waiting with her small bouquet. Maggie entered the arena. Strands of white lights mingled with greenery, and cloth hung from wood frames. Another deep breath. Chloe stepped onto the aisle runner, glanced at Chad, standing in his monkey suit at the other end, and smiled. Tear-filled eyes clouded her vision. Thank God for her father being at her side.

* * * *

Chad didn't care about anyone else in the arena at that moment. Chloe floated down the aisle toward him. He couldn't wait to kiss her as his wife. And it wouldn't be long. They had agreed to a short ceremony followed with a wing-ding of a reception party. He leaned on the cane for support and took one step toward her and Robert as they approached.

"Continue to take good care of my girl." Robert shook his hand before placing Chloe's hand in his. "You two have my blessing."

"Thank you, Sir." He smiled at Chloe. "You're beautiful," as tears slid from his eyes.

One step. Two step. They approached the pastor and their new life together.

THE END

About the Author

Born and raised in Minnesota, Jody remains close to home, living with her husband of more than twenty years as well as three children and a cat named Holly. Growing up, she enjoyed reading V.C. Andrews' Dollanganger series, S.E. Hinton and Stephen King to name a few.

She's traveled throughout the United States, to the Bahamas and Cancun, Mexico. Between watching soccer games, scrapbooking and being the COO of the Vitek household, she writes contemporary romances.

You can find Jody on Facebook: Jody Vitek Author, on Twitter: @JodyVitek and you can email her at: info@jodyvitek.com

Other Works by the author with Melange Books, LLC

Florida Heat
Rescue Me